The Season of Forever
Seasons of Love and War
Book 6

by

Brenda Ashworth Barry

Published by
Melange Books, LLC
White Bear Lake, MN 55110
www.melange-books.com

Cover Design by Caroline Andrus

Dedications

First, I'd like to thank Matthew for all his support.

Cindy Watson: thank you for being my reading partner, family and one of my best friends.

To my parents who are always there with love and support.

To Mona, my childhood and lifelong best friend.

To Becky and Jess, who fly with the angels and are greatly missed.

To all my children: A mother couldn't be any prouder and grateful for all your love and support. Frank and Kellie, thank you for all you do.

To my dear friends: You know who you are. Thank you for sharing, supporting and being my biggest fans.

My chatter box group: Thank you so much for the encouragement and support that you give me every day. Lisa you rock and are one of my dearest friends. You have helped me in so many ways.

To my Beta Readers. Terri, Cindy, Shannon and Lisa.
You guys all rock.

To Joyce. Thank you for being such an inspiration.

Lori D. Thank you for working with me for so many years.

To my fans and cousins. You are the best and your support means the world to me. Thank you for loving my Saga and staying on this journey with me. Terri you have been amazing and helpful.

My editor Barb, thank you so much and thank you to the proof readers.

Caroline: thank you for all these lovely covers.

Melange-Nancy: Thank you for making me and my saga a part of the Melange family and for enjoying my stories

Chapter One

Blake's eyes flew open to unholy pain, but he fought like hell to focus. Why were fireworks echoing around him and where was he? Wait, this was winter, so why in God's name was he lying on the ground outside? The sounds around him vanished as the memory assaulted him.

Christ all mighty, it wasn't fireworks it was gunshots. Blake raised his head and tried to move, but couldn't budge anything. Damn, the burning was excruciating. He groaned in agony, feeling as though his guts had been ripped out. Placing his trembling hand on his stomach, he asked, "What the hell?" Something warm and wet gathered on his fingers. "Holy shit." He glanced at the blood as it dripped down onto his shirt.

He cringed. "Damn, that's not good." When he tried to wipe it off on the asphalt, he tasted a metallic flavor in his mouth.

Did that mean he was bleeding internally? Was he dying?

He caught sight of his friend, Johnny, who was firing his gun at Arnold, Ginger's deranged husband, who kept darting behind the telephone pole. Johnny was yelling into the phone with his free hand. "Get someone here now. Two have been shot and are bleeding. One is my fiancée."

Good thing Blake had a long cord that allowed Johnny to bring the phone out on the front porch. He heard Johnny say, "*hurry,*" before he dropped it.

The pain ripped through him, and his breathing became labored. Oh Lord, he remembered something else, Ginger had been with him, but where the hell was she?

"I'm calling the police," someone yelled, more than likely his neighbor.

1

"I called the ambulance," Johnny yelled back.

Blake heard several loud cracks and saw Johnny shooting at Arnold. After a few seconds, he saw the asshole finally fall to the ground and start to wail, like the coward he was. Thank God, Johnny had finally brought him down, and it appeared he had got him in both legs.

"Make sure you get his rifle, Johnny," Blake said with a ragged voice and knew damn well Johnny would handle it, but it made him feel something besides completely useless since he couldn't move.

Johnny ran over and handcuffed the piece of shit. "You fucking scum!" He grabbed the rifle.

Blake was sure as hell relieved that Johnny had been a detective and was his bodyguard. He knew how to handle this. No doubt, he was big enough to kick Arnold's ass from here to China. He winced, trying to move again, but couldn't.

"Ginger," Blake hollered. He needed to get to her and see if she was okay, but nothing worked. "Ginger!" he called out two more times. Where the hell was she?

Johnny hurried next to Dana, his fiancée, who was like Blake's little sister. "Oh, sweetheart," he said, trying to soothe her as she cried.

Next, he rushed to Blake "You're okay, boss. Help is on the way."

They both shot a glare at Arnold when he yelled, "I'm going to kill that bitch. You can't stop me. Ginger, get out here, you slut!"

"Bastard," Johnny grumbled. "I got him in both legs, but I should have shot him in the head." He touched Blake's arm. "Can you move anything?"

"No." Blake tried again with a raspy voice. "Check on Dana, and make sure she's okay. We have to find Ginger, too."

A few minutes later, Johnny was holding what looked like Dana's sweater around her arm. It was bleeding, but it didn't look too bad.

Dana looked over and met Blake's eyes. "Johnny, go to Blake," she cried. "I'm fine. I can hold my sweater on my arm."

Johnny ran over, pulled off his jacket, and stuck it under Blake's head. "I can't move you, boss. The people on the phone told me to wait and let the paramedics do it."

"I can't feel my legs." Blake glanced up at him and saw sadness shadow his eyes. "If I die, make sure Ginger is taken care of."

"You're not going to die," Johnny said, but Blake knew by the look in his eyes that he didn't believe it.

"Just promise me!" Blake raised his voice. "Now, check on Ginger."

"I don't want to leave you and Dana."

"She's here, damn it."

He looked around. "Where is she? I didn't know she was here. I thought you were just delirious when you were calling for her."

Blake pointed at the car. "Oh shit, now I remember. I pushed her inside the car. I think she was shot in the head." He closed his eyes and felt tears burning. He hadn't been able to keep her safe as he'd promised. There was no way to hold back his emotions. He'd grown fond of the redheaded beauty. After everything that monster had put her through, she couldn't die. Her crazy asshole husband had beaten her so bad that he'd almost killed her.

Blake saw Johnny open the car door. "Ginger," he queried, and then leaned inside. "She's still breathing, boss, and her eyes fluttered. Ginger," Johnny said again. "It doesn't look like the bullet went in. It's just a graze, and I think it knocked her out. I'm pretty sure she's okay."

Blake heard sirens and tires squealing a second before they came to a halt. Once they stopped, paramedics flew in all different directions.

"Check for weapons and get this idiot in the back of the other ambulance," a police officer ordered. "I don't want him around the people he shot."

Chaos hustled all around, giving Blake no time to think. He could hear his pants being ripped off, but there was no sensation.

"You're going to be okay, Mr. Tanner. We're getting you to the hospital, and we will get you stable," one of the guys said.

The paramedics kept Blake immobilized. One of them kept reassuring him that he was fine.

Before he could speak, they had him on a gurney and were taking him away. He didn't know if Ginger would live or die and wished they would take her with him. Once he was inside the ambulance, he could smell the scent of antiseptic as they started cutting off his shirt. The next sensation was some type of needle being poked into his skin. He sure as hell felt that.

The same dark-haired guy kept talking to him, asking questions, but he couldn't seem to answer. Voices were trailing away. The steady rhythm of the heart monitors was the one thing he could make out. It pierced the silence of his mind.

Warm blankets were thrown over him, which helped to stop the ice running through his veins. He was fading in and out.

"You're okay. Do you hear me?" one of the guys said again, but Blake knew he was lying. He still couldn't feel his legs.

"My name is Doug, and I'm going to make sure you're taken care of." His eyes widened, and Blake didn't miss his glance at the heart monitor. "He's going into shock; grab me some more warm blankets." Doug pointed. "Let's hit it. We need to speed it up," he ordered. "Go … go."

Blake was only half conscious, but was aware when they pulled up to the hospital and took him out of the ambulance. He could feel the bumps and the sound of the wheels on the gurney as they rushed him toward the double doors.

With no warning, everything was going completely black. The last thing he remembered was someone yelling.

"Gunshot wound victim."

* * * *

Beth Ann glimpsed around the living room at all the people she loved. Most of the family had come to spend time with the newest member, Kaylie, her baby girl.

Lisa, Beth Ann's best friend, stood. "I need to call home and take a shower. Is that okay?"

"Sure." Beth Ann smiled and watched her exit the room. She had a feeling she was missing her husband and son.

Gram picked up a tissue, and dabbed her eyes. "I can't tell you how happy this makes me. You've given me a wonderful treasure, a great-granddaughter."

"She is a little beauty," Nicky said and handed Gram another tissue.

"I agree." Beth Ann's mom moved closer to the bassinet. "She's the most beautiful baby I've ever seen."

Stanley leaned over and touched the baby's head. "Will she be allowed to call me Grandpa?" He seemed embarrassed by the question.

"Of course," she and Kaylob said in unison.

Beth Ann added, "You *are* her grandpa."

Beth Ann got up off the couch and went next to her mom and stepfather. "We do have a unique family, and we want everyone to take part. A child can never have too much love."

Kaylob glanced around. "She won't be lacking, that's for sure. She has my birth mom and Grandma, plus my adopted parents, and of course, my wonderful sister." He smiled at Shawna.

"Hey, don't forget me," Frankie said. "I'm the best friend and now your brother-in-law."

Everyone laughed, and Beth Ann knew they were blessed to have so much love around.

Kaylob had only met his birth mother a few months back, and Shawna had been part of the package, a sister he never knew. She and Frankie had fallen in love and married. Now, they all lived on the same land, in two separate homes, and Shawna and Frankie were expecting.

The next fifteen minutes were spent with the family loving on the baby while Goldie stood watch. Kaylie was not even allowed to fuss. If she did, Goldie started pacing and whining.

Kaylob laughed. "You would think she was the mom." He paused. "Speaking of parents, mine should be here soon. Well, Jackie and Harold," he explained. "This part is hard to make clear, although you guys know, so that's nice." He looked around. "My birth mom and grandma will be here next week." He grinned at Shawna.

"Kaylie will be spoiled … and talk about toys." Shawna laughed. "You better build a toy room and make it extra large."

Beth Ann agreed with that. "A house full of toys and love. My birth dad said he's coming to meet his granddaughter next month when everything calms down."

Beth Ann was actually happy about that. It would be a bit uncomfortable with her dad and Stanley in the same house. They'd gotten along fine at the wedding, but that was short term.

When Beth Ann was eleven, her mom had divorced her dad, but even after all this time, his eyes still flashed pain whenever her mom's name was mentioned.

Her dad and Vera had been living together for at least two years, which made Beth Ann wonder if they would ever get married.

The phone rang, and Kaylob jumped up. "That might be my parents. They should be here anytime."

"Hello," Kaylob answered in a happy tone.

Beth Ann watched the smile vanish from his face and moved next to him. "What?" she whispered.

"Come again?" Kaylob asked with a frown on his face. "When?"

He reached for Beth Ann. "We'll be right there. Palm Springs emergency, got it. Thank you for calling, Johnny."

Kaylob hung up and took a deep breath. "Blake has been shot three times, and it's serious."

Beth Ann felt her heart sink. "What? Shot by whom?"

"I don't know yet. I need to go to the hospital." He glanced around at everyone.

Lisa had walked back in the room and must have overheard. "Should I go or stay with the baby?"

"Stay," Beth Ann said. "Please. I have to go."

Lisa nodded in understanding, and Beth Ann's mom spoke up. "Go, honey. All of us are here and will watch over the baby. We'll take care of Goldie."

"Thank you," Beth Ann said. She knew she needed to go. After all, he was one of their best friends and had been her fiancé at one time. She would always care for him.

Frankie stood. "I'm going. Shawna, you shouldn't go. It might be too stressful."

"No, I'm going with you." She sounded adamant. "Being pregnant doesn't mean I can't handle stress."

Frankie took her hand. "With two babies. Don't forget."

"Do you really think I could forget that?" A grin played with the corners of her mouth as she touched her stomach.

The entire family wished them well, and Gram said she'd be praying for Blake.

They were in the truck before Beth Ann could blink an eye, with Frankie and Shawna following behind them. She was glad they were coming.

Her mind drifted back to Blake. He had no living relatives, so there was nobody to call. Beth Ann swallowed the tears that lodged in her throat.

Kaylob reached over and clutched her hand. "He's going to be okay."

"He has to be, honey." She laid her head on his shoulder.

When they finally pulled up to the hospital, Kaylob drove to the front door and let Beth Ann out. "I'll go park and be right there. This place is crazy busy."

* * * *

Beth Ann darted through the automatic doors at the Palm Springs Hospital. It was much busier than their little community hospital in the Redlands. Thank God, Kaylie had been born there instead of here. The place had garbage bins overflowing and Styrofoam cups were laying all around, while babies were crying. Gloom seemed to roam the room.

Once she crossed over to the desk, the nurse glanced up at her. "What can I do for you?"

Beth Ann started to answer just as another nurse called out.

"Mr. and Mrs. Johnson." She saw a couple rise. The guy was turning green. The minute they arrived at the door, he upchucked and people scrambled to clean it up.

Beth Ann had to collect herself from all the craziness. "Blake Tanner. He's here." She swallowed as Kaylob arrived next to her.

"Are you family?" The lady pushed her glasses up on her nose and waited for an answer. Beth Ann started to speak before she noticed Shawna and Frankie were there too.

"Yes, we are the only family he has," Beth Ann said, and Kaylob nodded.

She looked at the monitor on her desk. "The two other ladies who were shot are back there too. Give me a minute and I'll see if you can go in to see Mr. Tanner."

"The other ladies?" Beth Ann was confused.

Before she could finish asking, Johnny came rushing out into the lobby. His eyes looked red and swollen. Beth Ann was sure he'd been crying.

The minute he got there, he took a breath. "It's really bad, guys.

7

Blake has been shot three times, once near his spine. They are going to do surgery now. He's barely conscious. Ginger is going to be okay, and so is Dana." His eyes appeared sad.

"Dana." Beth Ann felt her legs get weak.

"What the hell happened?" Kaylob asked, taking Beth Ann's arm to steady her.

Frankie stepped up. "I think I know who did this. I hadn't had a chance to tell you that we met with Blake and Ginger." Frankie rubbed his hand through his jet-black hair. "Her husband is a maniac, and she was badly beaten. Blake was taking care of her and keeping her hidden. I guess her husband found out where they were." His deep green eyes flickered with concern. "Also, Ginger was afraid of her husband's brother. He's the chief of the police over in Riverside, and I guess him and Arnold are tight. At least, that's what he threatened her with."

Johnny shook his head "It's a long story, but his brother wants no part of him. He told the officers when they showed up to talk to him that Arnold is his adopted brother and nothing but trouble. Arnold's parents are not even in the country and want nothing to do with him either. I guess he embezzled money from their company."

"How did Arnold find Ginger and Blake?" Frankie asked.

"They had stopped by the townhouse to get some of Blake's clothes when the shooting started. But right now, we need to go. They will be taking Blake into surgery right away, and we need to get you in so you can see him before he goes." He paused for a long minute. "The doctors said his odds aren't good."

The look on Johnny's face was one of despair. Although he was Blake's bodyguard and friend, he appeared meek and hopeless.

Beth Ann couldn't let it take over. "No, he's strong. He will make it."

Kaylob took her hand and nodded. "Yes, he will."

Beth Ann saw the doubt in her husband's eyes.

Johnny motioned toward the double doors. "They won't let all of us in."

"We'll wait out here." Frankie pointed to the worn-out chairs.

"What about Ginger?" Shawna asked. "Is she?"

Johnny shook his head. "She and Dana are okay, like I said." He sighed. "Dana was shot in the arm and Ginger's head was grazed, but it was nothing serious. We need to go."

"Wait," Frankie said. "Where's her husband?"

Johnny turned. "I think they were taking him to another hospital. I shot him in both legs. I hope he's going away for life." He snarled. "I wish I would have killed the bastard. Guys like him need to be recycled."

Frankie nodded. "No shit."

Frankie took Shawna by the elbow. Leading her across the room to a private area, he had her sit down. Shawna was so beautiful with her long, blonde hair and tanned legs. Beth Ann noticed that everyone in the waiting room seemed to stare at her. Being pregnant hadn't changed the fact that she looked like a model.

"Come on," Johnny said. "We better hurry."

The three of them turned, went through some double doors, then headed down the long hallway. The entire place swirled with tension as they passed through the emergency unit. Nurses in scrubs hurried from patient to patient. They had to walk around a lady with white hair who was being pushed by paramedics. Beth Ann could hear grunting. Somewhere, there was a baby screaming. The smell almost made her stomach turn. It was a combination of antiseptic and cleaning products, which made her cover her nose.

They arrived at another set of doors, and Johnny opened it up. "Only two at a time," he said in a low voice.

Kaylob waved toward the door. "Beth Ann, go in alone and talk to him. If anyone can make him want to live, it's you." He gave her a gentle smile. "I'll be there in a few minutes."

Beth Ann wiped the tears from her face and walked inside the room.

The nurse stopped and glanced up at her. "You have about five minutes. We are getting ready to take him."

Beth Ann rushed to the bed and took his lifeless hand. His eyes fluttered and she thought he was going to wake up. There were tubes and wires hooked up everywhere.

"Blake, it's me," Beth Ann said and swallowed hard. "I love you, and you're going to be fine. Do you hear me? You'll be as good as new." She could hear the faint sound of the heart monitor, and it seemed a bit too slow. Her throat clogged and tears filled her eyes.

There was no movement and his face was pale. His twin dimples didn't even seem to be there, and his blond hair was dull and lifeless. Another nurse came in the room, carrying bags of some type of saline solution.

Beth Ann stood there, holding his hand, praying that God would help him through this. A couple of minutes later, she heard the door open and Kaylob walked in. She saw him flinch when he examined Blake.

"Jesus," he said while he stood next to Beth Ann. She could see the pain in his soft blue eyes. After standing there for a short time, the door opened again and the rattling of the wheels from the gurney drew their attention.

The shorter nurse turned and said, "Sorry, but we're going to have to ask you to leave. We are getting Mr. Tanner ready for surgery, so say your goodbyes."

Beth Ann nodded and leaned down close to Blake's ear. "We're here and won't leave until you're out of surgery."

Kaylob bent over too. "You'll be fine, buddy." He touched Blake's shoulder and it seemed as though he moved.

Beth Ann's heart hammered against her ribs when Kaylob took her hand. Once they were out in the hallway, she glanced around. "Where did Johnny go?"

"He went to be with Dana. She was just waking up. She's okay, but her arm is going to be sore for a while. They had to remove a bullet."

"Oh God, this is awful," Beth Ann said.

The moment they turned to leave, a tall, gorgeous redhead came barging down the hall with a look of urgency and pain misting her eyes.

"I think that's Ginger," Kaylob whispered. "I saw Blake with her once, and she had a bridal shower at the restaurant. Mike handled it, but I remember seeing her."

"She's the one Blake said was being beaten up by her husband." Beth Ann remembered him talking about her. She also noticed the side of her temple was bandaged when she arrived at the door.

"Is Blake in there?" Her voice cracked.

Beth Ann nodded. "They made us leave because they are getting ready to take him into surgery."

"I have to see him," she said and pushed on the door.

Beth Ann and Kaylob stepped to the doorway and watched when the nurses tried to stop her, but her determination was stronger.

"Please let me see him, just for a few seconds," Ginger pleaded.

The nurses nodded, and Beth Ann sighed in relief.

"Blake," Ginger whispered. "I'm so sorry he did this to you. Please forgive me." She held on to his hand.

Blake blinked and glanced up as moisture gathered in his eyes.

Beth Ann placed her hand across her heart and chewed on her lip.

"I'm so glad you're okay, darlin," Blake said in a low, raspy voice. "I wasn't sure how badly you were hurt." He gave her a partial smile and brought her hand up to his lips.

After a few seconds, she reached up and touched the side of her head. "It was just a graze. I'm fine."

The short nurse cleared her throat. "It's time for us to take him."

Ginger leaned down and gave Blake a gentle kiss. There was no missing the look between them. Even the nurses smiled.

Blake looked over and saw Kaylob and Beth Ann. "Hey, I thought I heard your voices, where's the baby?"

"At home," Kaylob said and grinned at his friend. "You need to hurry and get this done, so you can meet her."

Blake nodded, and then turned his eyes toward Beth Ann. "You look good."

Beth Ann gave the best smile she could conjure up, but she could feel her lip trembling.

The nurses shooed them all away. Once they were out in the hallway, Ginger rubbed her hand across her head.

"This is all my fault." Her steel-blue eyes filled with sadness.

Even though Beth Ann's heart went out to her, she wondered why Blake was seeing a married lady. There was no missing the fading bruises on her neck. Beth Ann was all too familiar with what that looked like after being attacked by some thugs not too long ago.

"Ginger, why don't you come with us so we can talk?" Beth Ann asked, placing her hand gently on Ginger's arm.

"Are you sure you want to be around me? I caused all this."

"From what I heard, you're not at fault," Kaylob disagreed. "Come with us, and when you feel like it, you can tell us what happened."

11

They entered the waiting area, but it was still filled with chaos.

Shawna stood and crossed the room. "I'm so glad you're okay. I was worried when I heard the news." She embraced Ginger.

"I'm so happy you're here, Shawna." Ginger's voice was raw with emotion. "Blake has to pull through."

"He will, won't he, Beth Ann?" Shawna glanced at Beth Ann.

"He's always been a strong guy and a fighter, even when we were kids. He'll make it just fine." She tried to sound convincing.

After a while, they all took a seat and started the long wait. Beth Ann prayed silently that Blake would live through the operation and that there wouldn't be any permanent damage.

Beth Ann had not expected December to blow in with chaos swirling in all different directions, but now it seemed life was full of all kinds of twists and turns.

Johnny entered the emergency area and waved at them. "Hey guys, there is a waiting room on the third floor where they took Blake to have surgery. They said it has coffee and snacks up there. It's supposed to be more private and comfortable."

"That sounds much better," Kaylob said and took Beth Ann's hand.

They stepped off the elevator into a nicer area. It had two big, round tables in the center of the room and two coffee pots over on the counter. It also had nice couches and chairs. The coffee smelled wonderful after being in the emergency waiting area.

Johnny looked around. "I'm going to sit with Dana. I'll be back in a bit. She's on the second floor."

"I'd like to see her after Blake gets out of surgery," Beth Ann said.

"She'd like that." Johnny gave a small smile just before he turned to leave. The guy was a giant, dark-haired Italian with deep black and normally mischievous eyes. Right now, though, there was worry fixed across his handsome face. There was absolutely no doubt in Beth Ann's mind he loved Dana, and Blake was like his brother.

Dana had always been such a fantastic person. Beth Ann and Dana had become really close when she was engaged to Blake. Dana always made her feel welcome and worried about her when she was having all those visions. Poor Dana, she'd endured so much with all the drama between Beth Ann and Blake.

When Johnny asked Dana to marry him, Beth Ann was the first person she called. The engagement ring had belonged to his great-grandmother, and was beautiful. There was no doubt in Beth Ann's mind that Dana was a happy girl. The two of them were great together, even though Johnny was well over six feet and Dana maybe stood five feet. She was adorable, with her curly licorice hair and extra-large chestnut eyes. Beth Ann loved the way little freckles speckled her nose. However, with all this going on she wondered when they'd be able to plan their wedding or at least set a date.

Pulling herself back to the present moment, Beth Ann noticed that Ginger seemed to be more comfortable around Shawna. It was obvious that she wanted to say something. "Ginger, do you feel up to telling us what happened?"

"I'll start at the beginning." She sighed. "I met Blake the night of Shawna and Frankie's wedding party." She glanced at her trembling hands and had to set down the coffee cup. "We had a one-night stand." Crimson crept up to her cheeks. "I'd never done that before. I wanted and needed to feel good for one night before I married Arnold. I know that sounds awful."

Shawna moved next to her and took her hand; it seemed to anchor her. "It's okay, Ginger. I saw what he did to you. Blake told us when he ran into you the second time, there were bruises all over you. He also said that's when he gave you his address and phone number."

Shawna glanced between Kaylob and Beth Ann. "That monster she was married to said if she didn't do everything he wanted, he would kill her family, including her baby sister, not to mention that he wanted to murder Ginger."

Hurt flickered in Ginger's eyes. "I never should have dragged Blake into this, but when he saw the bruises, he pleaded with me to come with him right then. He said if I ever needed anything, a safe place, a shoulder to lean on, he would be there and his door would always be open."

Frankie cleared his throat. "I want to help put this guy away for life."

Beth Ann's heart broke. It was bad enough to be beaten by a stranger, but by the person who you're married to? That was beyond horrific.

Shawna stroked her hand. "Take your time and only talk if you can." Shawna glanced around, and everyone nodded.

Ginger continued. "When I showed up at Blake's door, he was so kind. He took me to a friend of his that was a doctor. I had so many things wrong with me after being beaten and tortured. The only reason I got away was because Arnold finally fell asleep." She inhaled and paused for a long moment. "Blake took me to a private place called The Colony House. Really secluded and not like any hotel I'd ever seen. He nursed me back to health," she whispered. "I've never met such a wonderful guy. He even bought me new clothes and we swam and, and …" Tears filled her eyes. "I need to use the restroom." She got up and almost ran out of the waiting room.

Chapter Two

"I'm going to go talk to her." Shawna stood. "She's been through so much."

Beth Ann understood. This was so tragic.

Kaylob held Beth Ann's hand, and Frankie shook his head.

"We saw her after the guy beat her." He looked away. "It was appalling. She was covered from head to toe in bruises, not to mention the guy used her hands as an ashtray. The good news is the doctor took pictures and her so-called husband will go away for a long time."

"What a piece of work." Kaylob shook his head. "I hope he gets life."

Beth Ann nodded in agreement, and then shifted in her seat. She was a little sore after just having a baby. "Were Ginger and Blake involved?"

Frankie shrugged. "Not sure, but he sure seems taken with her." He gave her a hint of a smile. "I've not seen him like that with anyone since …" He stopped and studied Kaylob.

"It's okay, Frankie. You can say it," Kaylob said. "I know he loved my wife. He and I have talked about it more than once."

"Okay, I've not seen him act like that with anyone since he was with Beth Ann. It was nice." He let out a sigh before he continued. "I think he's pretty crazy about her."

Beth Ann placed her hand on her heart. "He has to pull through. God wouldn't do that, let him find someone again and take him away." Beth Ann leaned her head on Kaylob's shoulder.

Kaylob wrapped his arm around her. "He's gonna make it, baby."

A few minutes later, Johnny walked in the room. "Dana is sleeping. The surgery to remove the bullet took a lot out of her. Plus, she's worried sick about Blake."

"He's got a strong will; he'll pull through," Kaylob said again.

Johnny's eyes dropped. "He couldn't move his legs, nor could he feel them. I guess it's because it's so near his spine."

Beth Ann felt her stomach turn just thinking about it. Right now, she'd focus on him making it out of surgery alive. After all, he had someone he loved, and she obviously loved him back.

"I need to go find a payphone." Beth Ann stood. "I want to check on the baby and Goldie."

Kaylob pointed to the chair. "You need to rest. Let me go do it." He kissed her forehead. "I'll be right back."

Time crawled by at a snail's pace. Shawna and Ginger got back after spending what seemed like forever in the bathroom, although things did seem better when they returned. Ginger had composed herself. She even offered a tiny smile and held out some breath mints.

Beth Ann and Kaylob took one and thanked her.

It was taking so long to find out anything. Beth Ann played with her fingernails and noticed a spot of polish that was peeling away on her thumb, so she started picking at it. Kaylob reached down and covered her hand with his.

"Please don't do that." He frowned.

"Okay, fine." She stopped because she knew it drove him crazy. She'd let him get away with being, Mr. bossy O'Brien this time.

Her nerves tightened just thinking about Blake, not to mention that her breasts were painful and she missed Kaylie. She peeked down at her blouse and gasped. "Oh no." Heat crawled up her face.

"What?" Kaylob asked.

"My top," she said, pointing downward with her chin.

His eyes got big when he scanned her shirt. "Want me to go pick up a blouse from home?" He pulled off his jacket and helped her to put it on.

Shawna shook her head. "That would take you so long. I have an old overnight bag in the trunk. Want me to go see what's in there?"

"Yes, please." Beth Ann sighed.

Frankie got up. "I'll go get it." He left in a hurry.

"It's feeding time. I hope she's doing okay with the bottles," she said, worrying out loud.

"She's doing fine," Kaylob explained. "Like I told you before, my parents said she's eating great. They are having a blast taking care of her."

Beth Ann let out a deep breath. "I'm just being a worrywart."

"Our mom and grandma will be here tomorrow." Shawna gave them both a soft smile. "Kaylie will never be put down."

"She's going to have so much love and a stable life, unlike mine." Beth Ann sighed. "Or at least before I moved to Novato and everything changed. I started a new life there."

Kaylob wrapped her in a warm hug. "Yes, she met me, tied me up, and had her way with me."

"Kaylob." Beth Ann smacked his arm, but she had to chuckle. He always knew how to ease the tension.

Kaylie would never have to live out of a car as Beth Ann had done, or wonder if she was adopted, like her daddy. That was still a sore subject with Kaylob, so she tried to never bring it up.

Ever since she and Kaylob were kids and lived in the small town of Novato, Beth Ann always wondered if he had been adopted. Mainly because he never looked anything like his parents. They were both short with dark hair and pale skin. On the other hand, Kaylob was tall with blond hair and a beautiful, masculine body, even at age fourteen. His skin had always been golden brown and he had china-blue eyes, just like his birth mom and Shawna. From the first moment she'd met Kaylob, he'd thrown her emotions into a tailspin. When she'd seen his mom and dad, her first thought was that he was adopted. But as a teen, she never expected it to be some big family secret.

He'd been furious with his adopted parents and birth mom for waiting so long to tell him, but he was thrilled to find out he had a sister.

It was going to be so great to raise their children together. Beth Ann couldn't wait to find out if Shawna and Frankie were having girls, boys, or a combination.

Frankie walked in and handed Shawna's overnight bag to Beth Ann. "Here you go."

"Thank you, Frankie," Beth Ann said.

Ginger was dozing on the couch, and Johnny was back down with Dana again. He couldn't seem to sit still and kept pacing, so he finally took off.

"Need any help changing?" Kaylob asked.

"No." She gave him a scolding look.

"You know you love it when I help you." He wiggled his eyebrows.

"I would like Shawna to come with me and for you to behave." She arched a brow.

"Darn." He raised his hands in surrender. "Okay, okay."

"I need to use the restroom and stretch my legs anyway." Shawna grinned. "You'll live, brother dearest," she teased, and then peered toward Ginger. "She must be worn out after everything."

Beth Ann nodded. "I think we should let her rest."

"I agree." Shawna took a spare sweater and covered Ginger's shoulders.

"If anyone shows up about Blake, come and get us." Beth Ann requested.

"Okay, will do," Kaylob said and touched his lips.

Beth Ann leaned down and gave him a soft kiss. "Be back after I dry off."

Once they arrived in the restroom, Beth Ann was pleased to see Shawna had some blouses and even a couple of bras that fit great.

Beth Ann stood in front of the mirror. "Thank you, Shawna. That's much better."

"You're welcome. Check this out." She held up two more blouses. "Just in case it happens again, we have these as back up." Her grin spread. "I guess I'll be going through this soon enough."

Beth Ann nodded.

The rest of the afternoon dragged by. It was taking too long. Beth Ann was beginning to wonder if they had forgotten to come and give updates. She was just thinking about saying something when a nurse walked in.

"Tanner family," she announced.

"Yes." They all stood, including Ginger.

"Blake is out of surgery, and he's in recovery. The doctor will come down in about thirty minutes." She glanced around. "He's been through a lot, and the next twenty-four hours are the most crucial."

"Is he going to make it?" Ginger's voice trembled.

"We don't know." Her face showed concern. "He's in critical condition. The doctor will be here soon. At least right now, he's alive and hanging on."

Johnny wiped his forehead. "Thank God he made it."

Beth Ann had to sit down. She was feeling a bit faint. Going through something like this was never easy, but after just having a baby, she felt worn out and emotionally beat.

The nurse cleared her throat. "We are having some sandwiches and other food brought up to you. It should be here in the next few minutes. Mr. Tanner insisted on his way to surgery that we make sure y'all were fed." She was obviously imitating his Texan accent. "He wasn't going to take no for an answer. So one of the nurses got the credit card from Johnny." She looked around and Johnny raised his hand.

"That would be me," Johnny said.

Beth Ann was glad about that. She was starving.

"Thank you," Kaylob said and sat down with Beth Ann. "Thank you too, Johnny, for taking care of it."

Everyone went to sit down except Johnny. "I promised to let Dana know as soon as we heard anything. I've got to go tell her."

"What about lunch first?" Kaylob asked.

"I'll have some when I get back. I want to be here when the doctor shows up, too. Thanks though. I'll hurry." He left the room.

Ginger was visibly shaken, so Shawna and Frankie sat next to her to give her comfort.

It didn't take long for a nurse and orderly to carry in trays of sandwiches, chips, and different kinds of pies.

Johnny walked back in the door. "Dana was thrilled, and I am ready for one of those sandwiches." He pointed.

The food was eaten in silence, but it was a good distraction while they waited for the news.

Beth Ann glanced up and saw a tall man with a receding hair line walk in. He seemed to recognize Ginger because he grinned when he saw her.

She hurried over to him. "Hi, Doctor Adams."

He reached out for her hand and his hazel eyes showed tenderness. "How are you, dear?"

"Scared for Blake." Her voice shuddered.

Everyone walked over and introduced themselves.

"Well …" The doctor glanced around. "I wish I had better news, but at least he made it off the table. We won't know much for a while yet. The surgeon stopped the bleeding and removed all the foreign objects that were lodged near his spine. At least, what they could find."

"What's the problem, then, Doc?" Kaylob asked.

"The blood loss weakened him, but it's the swelling to his spinal cord that is the biggest issue. We are giving him medication to take it down, but we really won't be able to tell for the next twenty-four hours. If he does recover, his chances of ever walking again are slim."

"Oh god," Ginger cried. "This can't be happening."

Shawna wrapped her arms around Ginger and asked the doctor. "Have you ever seen anyone walk after this kind of trauma?"

"Yes, I have." The doctor nodded. "But it's rare."

"Well, Blake is a rare kind of guy, so we will keep the faith." Beth Ann spoke up. "He *will* walk again."

Johnny grinned. "She's right about that, and he will do it."

"Good." The doctor gave them a slight smile. "We need to be positive, and even more so in front of him. I'm not the surgeon, but I'm his friend. I want to see him get through this and be back to his old self. He's a good man."

They all nodded in agreement.

It was true; Blake was a good man. Beth Ann thought about him and how much he loved to travel and hike. He had always loved life so much. If he couldn't walk again, what would that do to him?

Kaylob clutched Beth Ann's hand and cleared his throat. "How soon before we can see him?"

She could feel his nerves.

"I'm afraid I can only let one person in today, and my personal opinion is it should be Johnny or Ginger. No offense to any of you. But …"

Beth Ann raised her hand. "I think it should be Ginger. I saw how he responded to her."

"I agree," Johnny said.

With that, the doctor stuck his hand out to Ginger. "Are you ready?"

He turned to the others. "You can go home and get some rest." He glanced at Beth Ann and Shawna. "I think some sleep would be a good thing. I promise to keep Ginger and Johnny privy with updates, and they can let you know. If he makes it through the night, you should all be able to see him tomorrow."

Beth Ann felt bad about leaving, but she needed to get home to Kaylie. "Okay, Ginger, you'll call us if anything happens. Also, if you need a place to stay, we will make room for you."

"She has a place." Johnny interrupted. His eyes filled with unshed tears. "Blake told me to make sure she was taken care of, so I'm going to stay at the Colony house with her. Dana will be coming to stay there, too. We won't let her be alone. I promised Blake."

Ginger glanced around at everyone. "Thank you guys so much. I'll be calling you." She turned to Johnny. "You have their numbers, right?"

"Sure do," he said. Johnny held up his finger. "When you guys leave, you might want to go out another way. There are reporters out front. They surrounded me when I came in. I declined any comments."

"Of course," Beth Ann said. "He's still considered America's most eligible bachelor."

Beth Ann was all too familiar with how life was when she had started dating him after Kaylob was declared dead. He was not only voted America's most eligible bachelor, but he was also a millionaire and the paparazzi were always sneaking around.

"Let me show you." Johnny nodded toward the door.

"I'll come and see Dana tomorrow," Beth Ann said, and Kaylob agreed.

Frankie and Shawna left out the front way since the paparazzi didn't know anything about them.

Beth Ann was exhausted from childbirth and lack of sleep. All she wanted was to get home to be with her baby girl.

Once home, Shawna and Frankie went to their house to rest. They said they'd put the phone by their bed and had informed them the place was crawling with camera crews.

When Beth Ann and Kaylob entered their living room, everything was quiet. Just a few nightlights were left on. They knew his parents were sleeping in one of the guest rooms, but they had no idea which one.

"I'll just see them tomorrow," he whispered. "Right now, I want to go hold our baby girl." He smiled. "I missed her."

"Me too." They both tiptoed down the hallway.

Beth Ann couldn't believe her eyes when she opened the door. Harold was cradling Kaylie, rocking her back and forth while singing, *Hush, Little Baby*. The shock on Kaylob's face told Beth Ann that she wasn't the only one surprised.

Harold glanced up, and Beth Ann was sure he blushed. "Oh, I didn't hear you guys get home." He cleared his throat. "I was making sure she was okay."

Kaylob arched a brow. "Well, it sure looks like she's happy." He smiled at his dad.

Beth Ann crossed the room, then leaned down and kissed Kaylie's head. "I'm going to go take a shower." She smiled and touched Harold's cheek. "Thank you, Grandpa, for taking care of her." She kissed Kaylob and left the two men alone.

The shower felt warm and inviting as she stepped inside. Her thoughts went to Harold holding Kaylie. It was amazing seeing him cradling the baby. Kaylob had been extremely angry with his adopted dad, but now things seemed to be getting better. Harold apologized and had been working hard to make up for past mistakes. Beth Ann prayed that everything would go smoothly when Kaylob's birth mom and grandma got there tomorrow. Reading the letter from his birth dad who had passed away before Kaylob ever had the chance to meet him was hard. However, finding out the details surrounding his adoption from his birth mom had helped him to cope with everything. Beth Ann stepped out of the shower and was drying off when Kaylob walked in with their baby girl.

"Here's our little princess," he said. "I thought maybe you'd like to feed her before you go to bed."

"You were reading my mind once again, Mr. O'Brien." Beth Ann kissed his cheek as she took the baby. It felt so good to embrace her child. God, could any love be more intense.

The last thoughts Beth Ann had before she fell asleep were of Blake. She said a small prayer that he would make it through the night.

Chapter Three

"Ginger," a voice whispered. She had to be dreaming because it sounded like Blake. "Ginger." She woke up and saw the most handsome blue eyes staring right at her.

"Blake, oh my god, you're awake."

"Looks like it, darlin." He coughed and winced. "Can't keep a good cowboy down too long." His Texan drawl was thick.

Ginger stood and leaned over, touching his cheek. "I'm so sorry, Blake. I never should have dragged you into this. You're going to be fine, though. The doctor said early this morning that you were coming right along."

Blake gave her a half smile. One she knew well. "None of this is your fault. Tell me what happened to Dana and why you have a bandage on your forehead." He searched her face.

"Remember before you went into surgery, I explained. I was just grazed, but it knocked me out. Dana might be released tomorrow. They had to operate on her arm, but she's good."

"I think I might remember. What about Arnold? Is he still out there?" His eyebrows furrowed.

"Johnny shot him in both legs, and he's locked up. Frankie said he's going to help put him away for an extremely long time."

Blake touched his head. "Oh, right, I remember that now. Things are starting to come back in stages." Ginger saw the moment he tried to move his legs.

"My legs won't move. I don't feel anything." He frowned.

"They operated on you, and there was a lot of swelling. The doctors said they won't know anything for few days."

"I guess I can handle this for a short time, but I want to feel my legs

23

again."

Ginger sat back down. "I'm sorry." She felt tears building. What if he never walked again? This would be her fault.

"Ginger, please don't look like that. I don't want you feeling sorry for me." Blake gave her a pointed look.

"Shut up." She swiped at her eyes. "You felt sorry for me when I showed up with bruises all over my body."

"Well, you got me there."

Before she could make another comeback, Dr. Adams walked in the room.

"Good morning, Blake. I see you're awake." He glanced between Blake and Ginger.

"I am. Thank you, Greg."

"Don't thank me. You had one of the finest surgeons around." He glanced down at the chart. "He saved your life, and you are doing better than we ever imagined."

Ginger's insides trembled thinking of how close Blake came to death. All because of her crazy, soon-to-be ex-husband.

"Greg ..." Blake cleared his throat. "I want you to be honest with me. Will I ever walk again?"

The doctor pulled up a chair and sat down next to Ginger. He hesitated for a few seconds, which made her heart crawl up her throat.

"We don't know." He flipped through the pages on the clipboard. "We have hope, but the truth is that you might not."

There was no missing the pain that flashed in Blake's eyes. "I might not ever walk again," he repeated, seeming to try to take it all in. Ginger watched the color drain from his face.

The doctor stood. "Blake, the most important thing is like your friend, Beth Ann, said. She has faith that you will walk again. She said you've always beaten the odds."

Ginger grinned. "Yes, she did say that."

"Is she here?" Blake asked. "I want to see her."

Ginger stood next to the doctor. "I'm going to go call now and give her an update. She wanted me to let her know the minute you woke up."

Blake nodded, and Ginger's legs felt like rubber bands. The empty look in his eyes broke her heart. He might just end up hating her. She wouldn't blame him. After all, he wouldn't be in this situation if it weren't for her.

Once she had called Beth Ann, she took her time going back to the room. She went into the restroom, washed her face, and changed. Thank goodness for Johnny. He'd picked up some of her clothes and brought her an overnight bag. One of the shirts he packed was one her mom had bought years ago. Just the two of them had gone shopping and had a great day. Her mother was always more relaxed when her dad wasn't around.

Maybe she should try calling her parents again. She'd only spoken to them once to tell them what had happened and why she was staying with a friend. They wanted her to go home to Arnold, and her dad had lectured her about giving up on her marriage too soon.

How could he say that? She'd told him Arnold had beaten her and lied to them about where she was. It was as if he didn't want to hear it. Her mom had cried, but her dad had started to raise his voice, so she hung up. There was no way she was going to let anyone talk to her like that again. She was finished.

Look at what she'd done to keep her family safe—she'd married the maniac. The truth was it was also to please her parents. There was no way she was going to lie to herself anymore. Pleasing her parents had always been important to her. Wonder what they'd think if they knew he'd tried to kill her and had shot two others? Maybe for the first time in her life, she should focus on pleasing herself. Would that be so wrong?

Now that he was locked up, it was time to find herself again. It was important to figure out what she wanted out of life. Not what Arnold or her father demanded of her. No more.

She walked in the room and Beth Ann was already there, holding Blake's hand. There was a bond between the two of them. She could feel it. Blake seemed to deeply love her.

"Hi Ginger," Beth Ann greeted her.

"Hi Beth Ann, I'm sorry for interrupting. I didn't know you were here. I'll step out and let you two talk."

Blake nodded. "Thank you, Ginger."

She walked out of the room and tried not to listen, but she couldn't help herself.

Beth Ann was talking. "I have every faith that you will walk again."
"Why?" Blake sounded sad.
"Why?" Beth Ann repeated. "Why not?"
"Because maybe I'm being punished," Blake answered.
"For what?"
"For all the people I've hurt in my life." He paused and added. "Look how I treated you when you broke off our engagement."
"I broke it off because Kaylob was found. You were hurt. I didn't handle things very well. I would have married you if he hadn't been found. You are a good, kind man, Blake Tanner, and I've known you since we were kids. I know a lot about you. So don't try to hand me that crap about being punished."
"You're a bossy little redhead. Some things never change." He chuckled.
"You will walk again, and you know what else?"
"No, but I would bet you're going to tell me."
"Yes, you have found someone you care about. I can see it in your eyes. As much as I wanted to set you up with Melissa, I was wrong. You have something special with Ginger, and I can see it."
Ginger knew this was something she didn't want to hear, so she took off. Once she rounded the corner at the end of the hall, she stepped up to a large window and gazed off into the distance, drinking in the sights of the sky. The dark, menacing clouds assured rain. She glanced outside at the people rushing to their cars. It was as though they were trying to outrun the raindrops that had just started to fall. She noticed an old lady, who appeared to be homeless, digging through a garbage can. Watching the woman made a knot form in her throat.
"How sad," she whispered as the lady put her findings in an old grocery cart. After a few minutes, the older woman strolled around the other side of the building. Ginger watched until she was out of sight.
Once again, she thought about Blake. No matter how she looked at this whole situation, she had brought this on him. What would his life look like if he never walked again? How would he feel every time he looked at her? There was no doubt he'd hate her and the bottom line was, like she had already said, she couldn't blame him.
Probably the best thing she could do was leave, maybe to another

state so he'd never have to see her again. However, she wouldn't do that until he was well. Once he was feeling better, she'd just write him a note or tell him to his face.

At least she should wait until physical therapy started.

Thinking about physical therapy brought tears to her eyes. She had studied and got her license. Nevertheless, her dad and Arnold wanted her to stay at home and be a good little hostess and wife. Oh, she argued with her husband, but soon enough he showed her what happened if she didn't go along with what he wanted. Nobody would ever treat her like that again. Not ever. She knew she sounded like a broken record, but better that, than to ever allow anyone to abuse her again.

It would be nice to stay put though—maybe even apply for work right here. Except, she had to think of Blake and put him first. The memory of the night they'd shared before this nightmare started came floating back. All the sweet kisses and the way his hands trailed over her arms and legs, even the way he gazed into her eyes. He hadn't tried to make love to her because he was worried about her bruised lungs and all her injuries. Just thinking about Blake gave her goose bumps.

She'd never felt like that about Arnold. Actually, nobody had ever made her feel so alive. Sure, in the beginning, Arnold had seemed like a nice guy, but she'd always told him she didn't want to settle down. He'd acted like he understood and gone along with everything she talked about. Even going as far as taking her out to dinner to celebrate when she passed the biology and anatomy tests.

The sounds of footsteps approaching made her stop and look over her shoulder.

Beth Ann smiled. "Hi Ginger, Blake was in pain so the nurse gave him something. He's sleeping now. She said he needs his rest, but he did ask for you before he dozed off."

Ginger studied Beth Ann. She was so pretty with her big, brown eyes and auburn hair that curled in every direction. Nobody would ever guess she'd just had a baby. Her figure didn't show one sign of imperfection.

"Are you okay?" Beth Ann asked.

"Not really. I can't stop thinking about how all of this is my fault." Ginger wasn't sure why she was opening up to Beth Ann. After all, she used to be Blake's fiancée. Except, there was just something about her that rang true. She seemed to radiate trust and gentleness. Somehow, when she walked into a room, you knew she was the real deal.

Beth Ann gave her a gentle smile. "Can we go talk in the waiting area? I went by and nobody is in there right now. Maybe we could have some coffee before I go see Dana."

"Sure." Ginger nodded.

Once they arrived, got coffee, and sat down, Beth Ann took a sip and reached out for Ginger's hand. "I want to let you know how happy I am that you and Blake found each other. He doesn't blame you, and I really wish you wouldn't blame yourself."

"But?"

"No buts allowed." Beth Ann chuckled. "I don't want to seem like I know it all, but I'd say that fate brought you guys together. It doesn't matter how." Beth Ann stopped briefly before asking, "Do you love him?"

Ginger had to gather her thoughts. "Yes," she said. "I do love him. I'm in love with him." A lump formed in her throat. "I think I loved him from the moment I saw him."

"Oh, Ginger, don't you see? That's all that matters. He's in love with you, too. I can see it when he looks at you. I'd like to say something if you don't mind. Even if you do, I'll say it anyway." A slight curve turned up at the corners of her lips. "My husband scolds me when I say that." She got a far-off look in her eyes. "I get away with it though, at least most times. Except when I try to play matchmaker."

"Would this be one of those times?" Ginger found herself smiling. Beth Ann was rather adorable when she spoke of her husband.

"Yes, I suppose it would be, but he's not here. Honestly, I've known Blake since childhood and he always thought he loved me. But how deep can love go when it's only one sided? I love him as my dear friend, and he was there for me when everyone thought Kaylob was dead." Her eyes misted. "Even so, he has a chance to have two-sided love." She glanced up. "That is really special, in my book."

Ginger drifted into silence and thought about Beth Ann's words. Her big question was how Blake felt about all that. Would he want her love? They had only spent a little time together. They hadn't made love again.

That had only happened once. Well, many times in one night. These last few days had been holding hands, kissing, watching old movies, and laughter. Never in her life had she felt so close to a man or trusted him so implicitly.

"Well …" Beth Ann stood. "I should leave you to your thoughts and go check on Dana, then I need to get home to my baby girl."

Ginger stood too. "Thank you, Beth Ann. You've given me a lot to think about."

"You're welcome." Beth Ann crossed over to where Ginger was and embraced her. "If you want a place to stay or a friend to visit, we are here for you."

"I might just take you up on that." For a reason she didn't fully understand, a wave of emotion almost swallowed her.

"Good," Beth Ann said. "Oh, Shawna will be here later. She wanted to come and check on you."

With that, they said their goodbyes and Ginger headed back to Blake. She needed to figure things out. Would she stick around? Should she stay and take a risk that more damage could be done to the people she cared about?

* * * *

Three weeks later, Beth Ann and Kaylob stood in front of their house waving goodbye to the last of their guests. Gram and Nicky were getting ready to spend the next few years traveling in their motor home. Part of her was worried, but she was mostly happy for them. They were so in love and would spend the rest of their lives together. Beth Ann was thankful she and Kaylob had helped them to reunite. It had been one of the best things they had ever done. Nicky and Gram deserved this since they had been kept apart because of Gram's family. Now they had a chance to make up for all those missed years.

Once they were out of sight, Kaylob took her hand. "Alone at last." His voice was deep and husky. "How long do we have to wait?"

"Wait for lunch?" She gave a halfhearted shrug. "I'm not really all that hungry."

"No." He lifted her in his arms and carried her into the house. "Can we?"

"Watch a movie?" Beth Ann said, trying to keep from laughing.

"I'm going to spank you." Kaylob growled and his eyes heated.

"Oh, you want to fool around?"

He sat her down. "Yes," he said, looking down at the ground. "I'm dying here, baby."

She took his hand. "Well, we might not be able to do everything, but I think we can make each other feel good."

"Beth Ann, you're saving my life." He followed her into the bedroom after they peeked in on Kaylie, who was sleeping soundly.

After they made love to each other, Beth Ann glanced at her husband. He had a big smile on his face and was peacefully resting. Yes, he was happy. They hadn't even touched each other for the last three weeks. Although, she had heard some women didn't want to fool around for a long time after having a baby. That certainly was not the case for her. She wanted him as much as he wanted her. Easing herself off the bed, she threw on her robe and sneaked down the hall to check on the baby. She was going to feed her in an hour and keep her awake for the rest of the day. That way, she'd sleep more at night.

Beth Ann closed the baby's door behind her, then went into the kitchen. She saw the chest Gram had left for her on the counter. It was so heavy and there was no way she could move it alone. Gram had said there were secrets in those journals. Beth Ann, wanted to know what kind of secrets. All her Gram had said was there were things about her Great Grandma Ann and her Auntie that were not known and she admitted never wanting to talk about it.

Kaylob was going to have to do it again. The chest was filled with letters from Great-Grandma Ann. Walking over to it, she opened the lid.

"Wow," she whispered. "This thing is full." With that, she decided to go through it with what little time she had alone, she grabbed a footstool so she could be high enough to get inside.

After pulling out stacks of letters, she noticed they were not just from Great-Grandma Ann. They were also addressed to some of her great-aunts and from people all over the world. What was that about? "*Oh my gosh,*" she said under her breath. "*Journals.*" She started pulling them out and wondered if Gram knew about all of these. There were three of them. One was extremely large. She carefully opened up the first one.

Holy midnight. It was incredibly old. She read the first entry. Until that very moment, Beth Ann never knew her great-grandma's name was Rachel Anne Morgan, with Anne spelled with an E.. Everyone had always said Grandma Ann. It must have been a nickname. Like she was Beth Ann. How cool was that? She carefully opened the pages and figured she'd start with the first one. That way she'd follow the trail to get to the secrets.

This journal is the property of Rachel Anne Morgan, born March 31, 1885.

November 2, 1900.

Dear Best Friend,

Yes, my journal is my best friend because it never argues, never tells me what to do, and it listens to all my feelings without judgement.

Things are bad, and I won't be able to see Carlotta because she moved to Europe. There is no way my parents will let me leave the state to go visit my aunt and uncle so far away. My best friend in the whole world happens to be my cousin, and I can't be with her for the holidays. My heart is broken. I wish she could come and stay with us. I feel sad because I love and miss her. We've always spent the holidays together.

Sad and alone,

Rachel Anne

Beth Ann heard Kaylie fussing and knew it was time to place the mementos back in the box. As she did, she thought about how much fun she would have reading about Grandma Anne.

After getting the baby, she settled down to feed her. While Kaylie nursed, she wondered how Blake was doing. He had made a great recovery with Ginger by his side, but his legs were still not working. He was supposed to be going home tomorrow. Well, not home, but back to the place they had been staying before the shooting. She and Kaylob had stopped by almost daily, but they hadn't taken Kaylie to see him yet. They'd do that after he got settled.

As she sat, feeding her precious baby girl, Goldie lay beside her, keeping watch. More than once, the silly girl had dragged her bed to the baby's room and barked at them when they said no. She wanted to stay with Kaylie every minute.

"Hey, sexy mama, what are you doing?" Kaylob's voice was rich and deep. Even after all the years together, it still gave her chills.

"Feeding our daughter. I'm afraid she has your appetite." She glanced down and saw her suckling and smacking as if she hadn't been fed in days.

Kaylob got on his knees and moved closer. He always seemed in awe when she breastfed. "This is the most beautiful thing I've ever witnessed." He seemed captivated.

Beth Ann reached out and stroked his hair. "I love you, Mr. O'Brien."

He got quiet for a minute, then looked up into her eyes. "I've always loved you, and now I can't even describe the depth of my emotions. I know it sounds corny, but it's deeper than a million seas stacked on top of each other."

"Honey, that's not corny. Those words touch my heart." She placed one of her hands across her chest.

"Okay." He kissed her in a way that made her toes curl.

"Kaylob, I'm feeding the baby."

"What?" He got that oh-so-innocent look on his face, and then kissed Kaylie's head.

"You know *what*, Mr. Not-So-Innocent."

"Well, speaking of feeding." He stood and patted Goldie's head. "I'm going to heat up that pasta with roasted garlic sauce and sauté those cherry tomatoes to put on top. I also have a fresh loaf of garlic bread."

"Yum, that sounds wonderful."

"It is. Andria gave me her special recipe. I just love that woman."

Beth Ann arched a brow. "Is that so? Do you want to hand me some pillows?"

Kaylob threw his head back and laughed. "My wife is a cute one and boy, when you were younger, your aim was damn good."

Beth Ann smiled as Kaylob walked out of the room with Goldie on his heels. She did understand what food meant. Never had she seen such a smart dog.

Just the thought of Andria's recipes made her mouth water. She was one of the best chefs at his restaurant. Everything she made was amazing, and her self-confidence was tangible. Many of the other male chefs ran for cover when she got upset. Beth Ann loved to watch her in action.

Kaylob had scored big with her, and there was no doubt about it. Beth Ann thought about the restaurant. She missed singing there and was planning to go back as soon as she could.

There were also times she thought about being in another Broadway play. After winning the Tony a few years ago, she'd gotten plenty of offers. However, there was no way she'd leave her husband and baby girl to tour again. Not to mention, she wanted to be around for Blake. Ginger was by his side every day, even with him growling at everyone. He'd sure gotten good at that. Kaylob kept saying to just give him time and he would adjust.

Beth Ann didn't think he'd get used to being in a wheelchair. This was the man who was America's most eligible bachelor when they were dating. It had to be hard on him emotionally and physically, especially since he was such a perfectionist.

Chapter Four

Blake sat in the wheelchair waiting for Rob, his physical therapist. Why in the world did he have to start so early? He was feeling pretty pissed off anyway, being in the hospital, he couldn't keep his clothes color coordinated and his damn socks hadn't been folded right. But who the hell could he say anything to? The nurses wouldn't understand.

Besides all that, not one tiny bit of sensation had returned to his legs. So much for positive thinking and beating all the odds. At least he wasn't sleeping on that hardboard anymore, or whatever the hell that thing was called.

Ginger waltzed in the door with a big smile on her face. Even in his bad mood, how could he not notice the curvy way her body moved? Not that he'd ever be able to enjoy being with a woman again. Who the hell would want him, being a cripple and all?

"How are you doing this morning?" she asked as she set down some colorful flowers.

"Just happy as a cow with a stud iron stuck to his ass." He met her gaze.

"That good, huh?" She moved next to him, leaned down, and kissed his lips. "I missed you last night." She touched his hair. "Would you mind if I tagged along and watched you work out?"

"Sure, why not? It's a blast to see me fall on my face."

"Oh." Ginger raised both eyebrows. "Do they have you standing?"

"Oh sure, they tried, but I almost fell." He scowled. "Why bother? It's been three weeks and nothing has come back. I'm stuck like this for the rest of my pathetic life."

He watched pain flood her eyes. "Blake, do you want me to go

34

away? This is my fault, and I don't want to make it worse when I come around."

Blake felt like an ass. Of course he didn't want her to leave. He loved having her there with him, but he didn't want her to stay because she felt guilty or sorry for him either. "Why are you staying?"

"Because I care about you and I love being with you." She seemed serious.

"You *loved* being with me. Look at me now. I don't want you to stay because you feel sorry for me or guilty over this whole damn thing. Hell, I'm not even sure if I can ever function again."

"Blake Tanner! Function?" She met his eyes dead on. "Do you mean sex?"

"Yes," he grumbled.

She gave him a sexy smile before moving her hand under the throw. Her gaze clung to his while her hot little fingers moved in a way that made him shudder.

"Jesus," he mumbled.

Ginger cleared her throat. "Ah, I don't think that's going to be an issue." She slowly slid her hand away. "I am staying because I happen to be in love with you, Blake Tanner. All of you." She stared downward and motioned toward the proof of his ability.

Before he could respond, Rob walked in the door and Blake shifted, trying to return to normal.

"So, how is Mr. Sunshine today?" Rob winked at Ginger, and that pissed Blake off even more.

"How does it look like I'm doing?"

"Well, I'd say damn good. You have this redheaded goddess with you." He unlocked the brakes on Blake's wheelchair. "You ready to boogie? Oh, by the way, did they change your bandages, and how are the stitches doing?"

"Yes," Blake grumbled. "they tortured me, and I'm good, so let's get going."

Once they got down to the rehab room, Rob started working with Blake, lifting his legs and demanding that he use his arms to pull himself up. The more they worked, the more Blake wished he could kick someone's ass.

When he glanced at Ginger, it made him feel uncomfortable, but she seemed to be watching with keen interest. For that reason, he pushed away his own feelings.

"Rob," Ginger tilted her head. "Are they still giving him steroids or just muscle relaxants? And do we know how far the swelling has come down?"

Blake noticed what appeared to be shock on Rob's face as Ginger continued.

"I know his vertebrae wasn't involved," Ginger said. "And nothing penetrated his spine, or he wouldn't be here working out this soon."

Rob nodded. "You're exactly right."

Ginger touched Blake's arm. "The steroids are more than likely helping with the swelling and inflammation. I would bet they put him on smaller doses. I would also imagine he wouldn't take them for too long. I also know if the spine was actually injured, it can take months to get to this point."

Rob shook his head like he was removing cobwebs. "Whoa, you've done your homework. I'm impressed."

"No, well, yes." She smiled. "I am a physical therapist, licensed and everything. I just haven't worked in the field yet, except as an intern." She studied Blake. "This could be temporary. I remember that it can last days, weeks, or even months. Rob, I noticed while you were working out his legs," she pointed, "that his toes were moving."

Rob studied Blake's feet. "Can you wiggle your toes?"

"I don't know. Is that important?" He concentrated and was able to move them.

"Excellent. That is a fantastic sign." Rob gave Ginger, and Blake, a high five.

"It is?" Blake arched a brow. "It's really a big deal?"

"Yes, it is," Rob and Ginger said in unison.

Ginger kissed Blake's cheek. "It means you could walk again."

"Well, that is true," Rob said. "But it's going to take some long hours and hard work."

"I'm ready to get this jackass on the trail," Blake said and felt like yelling to the world. "I'm willing to work hard now that I know there's a chance."

So they did. Rob and Ginger worked him hard. Two hours later, he didn't even remember laying his head on the pillow.

* * * *

Ginger took a stroll outside of the hospital and studied the unpredictable weather. Normally, in January, Palm Springs was in the sixties. Sometimes, it was warmer. The sunshine was coming through the clouds and hitting the grass, leaving a trail of sparkles from the raindrops. She found a bench that was dry and eased down, taking a sip of the coffee. It was from the cafeteria, so it wasn't the best, but she wouldn't label it the worst either. Ah, the wind was strong, but it felt good as it gusted against her cheeks. There were sounds of engines starting and people walking with jingling keys.

A few minutes later, she spied a homeless lady walking with a shopping cart. It seemed to be the same woman she saw from the window when Blake was first admitted. The old woman fought the wind as she stopped and rummaged through a garbage can.

"How sad," Ginger whispered and watched the poor lady dig deeper.

She stared at the wedding ring on her finger and wondered, should she?

Before long, the old woman pulled out some kind of bag, which must have had chips or something left in it. She was stuffing the food in her mouth as though she was starving to death. How long had the food been in there? Ginger reached in her purse and pulled out a banana and apple she had brought for a snack. Her mind was made up; she was going to help the woman.

Ginger stood and sprinted toward the lady. Once she got there, she knew what she was going to do. When she paused and cleared her throat, the lady eyeballed her suspiciously.

"What do you want?" she grumbled. "I have a right to go through the garbage." She swallowed whatever she'd been eating.

Ginger reached in her purse. "I just thought maybe you'd want this food." She handed her the banana and apple.

"Oh." She seemed embarrassed. "Thank you." The woman stuck the fruit in her bag and stared at Ginger. "If you don't mind, I need to gather things before the rain starts." She looked up at the sky. "It's going to be a doozy."

"I also wanted to give you this." Ginger pulled the ring off her finger and reached for the old lady's dusty hand. "Here." She handed it to her. "This was very expensive." It was true. Arnold had wanted to show off and had to tell everyone how much he paid for it.

The old woman's eyes widened. "This is a wedding ring. Why would you give me this? Is it stolen? I don't accept nothing that's been stolen." She tried to hand it back.

"No, I promise, it's not stolen. I want you to have it."

"Why?" She stared at Ginger, looking perplexed.

"Because it might actually help me feel better." She sighed.

"Make you feel better?" She shook her head, staring at Ginger in confusion.

"What is your name?" Ginger asked. "I really want to do this for you."

"My name is Mildred, but most people call me, Millie." Her eyes softened. "What's your name?"

"My name is Ginger. It's nice to meet you, Millie," she replied. She saw Millie glance at the faded bruises around her neck. If only she would heal a little faster, nobody would notice. But sadly, her bruises had always faded slowly. Even more so with how bad these were.

"Are you okay, my dear?" she asked, placing her hand on Ginger's arm.

"I will be." Ginger gave her a small smile. "It's going to take some time. Right now, I'm here visiting a sick friend."

Ginger realized how much the older lady reminded her of her grandma who had passed away, except for the outfit. Millie wore raggedy clothes with an old, worn-down pair of tennis shoes.

"Do you have a home?" Ginger asked. Her stomach turned, thinking about this sweet old woman being on the streets.

"I have a nice area, right over there." She pointed. "It has a bathroom and a tree that shades the park bench. When it storms, I can hide out in the bathroom and keep nice and warm." She walked over to her cart. "Look, I have a new blanket and a little portable cooker. I use it to heat up tea and soup." Her shoulders straightened, and she placed her hands on the grocery cart. "I should be going. I don't want anyone to take my place. Thank you again, dear, and God bless."

"Wait, would you like to sleep in my car tonight? I mean it's a couple years old. But it's a Datsun 74' and it's in good condition and the seats go all the way back," Ginger explained.

"No, no, but thank you." She turned and strolled away.

Ginger didn't miss the old woman's limp. A lone tear trailed down her face as she thought about how it must feel to be homeless. How in the world did she end up on the streets? Where was her family?

Ginger turned and went back to her seat, then glanced around. It made her wonder about others as she surveyed the parking lot. What were they going through? Some walked fast and others crept along. Were they coming to visit a sick friend or family member? How many people came to say goodbye to a loved one who might be leaving the world?

Old memories blew in like a whirlwind. It still brought up tears, thinking about the day her grandma passed away. After her mom had received a phone call from the rest home, they had driven out of town to go see her. Her mom had wanted to keep Grandma in town, but her dad didn't.

He had said, *If we spend all her money on a rest home in town, there is no chance of having anything left.* He had pitched a fit about the issue. Ginger had even noticed a few bruises on her mom's face the next day. When she asked her mom what happened, her mom simply said, *"I walked into a wall."*

Ginger had never believed her, even more so when her dad laughed about how clumsy her mom was.

They had driven for over two hours in almost total silence. When they arrived, the nurse out front had told them to wait. Finally, after a long while, a doctor came out and told them she had passed away. Her mom cried. After all, she'd just lost her mother. Her dad had been furious, not because she had died, but because he had pushed a meeting aside. That was the first time Ginger had called her dad a jerk, at least in her mind. While her mom suffered the loss, her dad complained about missing out on a chance to get some new clients. How cold was that? Why did her mom stay with him?

"Ginger." She jumped and looked up.

"Hi Rob, is everything okay?" she asked.

"Yes," he said. "I actually came out here because I wanted to talk to you about something."

"Okay. Is anything wrong?" She felt the weight of his gaze as he stared at her.

Rob glided down on the bench, eyeing her over the rim of his coffee as he took a long sip.

Ginger met his stare. "You're making me nervous. Is there something wrong?"

"No, no, nothing like that." He waved his hand, obviously picking up on her nerves. "I was just wondering—would you like to work here at this hospital? You would be great, and we sure could use someone like you."

Ginger wondered if she heard him right. "Like me?"

He nodded. "I happen to know there are two positions coming up, and I wanted to see if you might be interested. At least in the one where we would work together."

"Are you talking about me doing physical therapy?" She wasn't sure if this was for real.

"Yes, I am." He nodded and gave her a soft smile.

Was he flirting? Just dandy. She'd better clear the air right now. "Rob, I'm not interested in dating or anything. I'm with Blake, at least for the most part."

Rob chuckled. "Well, you are a knockout, but I'm engaged and very much in love." He took another sip of his coffee. "I'm not sure why you didn't follow through with your career, but … I know all three of you were shot by your husband, and I'm sorry."

Her cheeks heated, and damn it, she was blushing. "Soon to be ex-husband … and I'm sorry. I shouldn't have assumed it was for any other reason than professional."

"No problem," he said. "Maybe now that you're divorcing the scumbag, you'd like a fresh start." His eyes went to the area of her wound.

"I guess a lot of people know because it was on the news." She looked away.

"I heard about it when you were brought in," he explained.

"I didn't think of that," she said. "I mean, you are a physical therapist."

"Three gunshot victims in one day tends to get around the hospital fast."

"Oh, right, I can see that. So what kind of job would it be?"

"One of the positions would be for my assistant. After you work for a while, you could have your own patients."

The thought made her so happy that she almost burst. She could earn her own money and do what she loved. "I don't have any experience."

"You could have fooled me from what I saw today. Not to mention, we worked awesome together with Blake."

"We did, didn't we?" She smiled. "Can I talk to Blake about this? He's going to need help when he gets home. I don't know that he'll want me to take care of him, but I hope so."

"Well, that would be perfect," he said. "The job with me won't start until the end of April. As you may have noticed, Laura is pregnant. Her last day will be the thirtieth of April. I'd like you to start on the twenty-seventh."

"Wow! I'd love that. Can I give you an answer tomorrow?"

"Absolutely." He stood.

"Rob," she said. "Will the hospital be okay with this?"

He nodded. "I already went to the top after I left Blake." He glanced around and waved at a short lady who had bleached-blonde hair. "My fiancée is here. I'll see you later."

She watched as he approached her. They kissed, then he took her hand and led her inside. She must be there to have breakfast with him. Glancing down at her watch, she realized how hungry she was. Now that she didn't have a snack, maybe she should go get something. Getting up so early was great. It seemed to make the days longer, but she sure did get hungry sooner.

The excitement of doing what she had always dreamed of gave her tingles. However, just the thought of talking to Blake made a lump form in the pit of her stomach.

What if he got angry and didn't want her to do this? No, he wasn't like Arnold. He would support her, wouldn't he?

A gloomy feeling matching the dark clouds forming in the sky hovered around her. Inhaling deeply, she headed back inside to be with

Blake.

* * * *

Beth Ann walked out and called in Sasha and Goldie. It was starting to rain. "Come on, kids. Breakfast time."

Goldie was up and through the doggie door while Sasha just sat there. "Come on, kitty, it's starting to rain."

A bolt of lightning tore through the sky almost as fast as Sasha tore through the yard. Next, she dashed through the doggy door and Beth Ann had to chuckle. That was the quickest she'd ever seen her move.

Once Beth Ann was back inside, she fed them, then went into the kitchen and washed her hands. Kaylie was in her playpen in the family room, watching the musical mobile. She loved that thing.

Beth Ann moved over by the playpen and watched her amazing baby girl, her heart swelled like the moon.

"Mommy loves you," she said. Never in her life had she imagined loving anything so intensely. She leaned over and picked Kaylie up. "You're Mommy's special girl." She kissed her lips and watched her pucker like she was being fed.

An hour later, she finished feeding and changing Kaylie, then put her down for a nap. The house was clean, clothes folded, and Kaylob would be home in two hours. Now what could she do? Shawna and Frankie were gone for the day. She'd already called Blake. He seemed like his usual grumpy self, not that she could blame him. Losing your ability to walk would make the happiest person have a bad day.

The letters and journals. "Yes."

She went into her bedroom closet and opened the chest, pulling out all the letters first so she could get to the journals. What she wanted was to read the one she had started. This would be fun. She headed to the family room. The flames were barely burning, so she placed another log into the fire. While it caught, she made her way into the kitchen and fixed a pot of coffee, then poured herself a large cup.

This was like buying a new book, only more exciting, because she was related to the writer. She had never met Great-Grandma Anne, but she'd always been told they were a lot alike.

Once she was back in the living room, she sat on the comfy couch and put her feet up near the fireplace. She cuddled down into the throw, ready to take a journey back in time. It was fun reading about the olden days. Compared to how modern everything was today in 1976, she could only imagine how it was to live without the modern conveniences.

She turned to the second entry.

November 20, 1900
Dear Best Friend,
Things are quiet and just not the same. Sometimes living in Franklin can be so lonely. When Carlotta lived here, things were swell. Now, things are hard. I'm living in the depths of sadness.

Mother says I should be patient and not be upset about Carlotta, but how can I? We would be together right now if it weren't for the move. Today, I walked down to the new store in town and bought some material for my dress for the holidays. I didn't really care as much since Carlotta won't be here to see it. While I was walking home and feeling blue, I met a boy in town. His name is Abraham Williams. He was very nice and wanted to see me smile. I have seen him a few times in church, but this was the first time we had ever talked to each other. I need to think of a reason to go tomorrow because I would like to see him again. Father always said it's not proper for a young lady to court a boy before she's eighteen. I wouldn't be courting him, but I would like to know him better. I think my father is old fashioned, but he's such a good provider and I wouldn't want to disappoint him. Father said we get to read a new family book tonight. It's supposed to be really exciting. I'm looking forward to it.

After I left Abraham, I enjoyed the walk home until I saw Old Mr. Wiggins. He tried to tell me I took some milk from his cow. I've never done any such thing. Father said to ignore him because he's not right in the head. When I agreed and said he was crazy as a June bug, Father scolded me and said young ladies don't talk with such language. Why do ladies have to hold their tongue, while men can say anything they want?

I have to go; Mother is calling me to help with dinner. I'll write again soon.

Chapter Five

The phone rang. Beth Ann unfolded herself from the couch and answered the noisemaker. "Hello," Beth Ann said, her tone a bit harsh.

"Hey baby, what are you doing?" Kaylob asked. "Did you get the breakfast I left you in the oven?"

"Not yet. I'm having a cup of coffee and reading my great-grandma's journal. The phone is too loud."

Kaylob laughed hard. "I haven't heard you complain about the loud phone in a long time. It's refreshing. Now, tell me about this journal."

"I think I'm a lot like my great-grandma."

"Uh-oh. I feel trouble." He chuckled.

"Funny, Mr. O'Brien."

"Don't forget to eat, Beth Ann," he reminded.

"I won't. I promise."

"I'm calling for a reason. How would you feel about coming in to sing next weekend? There is a wedding party on Saturday at five and the couple requested you. That's next Saturday, of course, not tomorrow."

"I'd love to, honey. I was just thinking about how much I missed being there, but I don't know what to do with Kaylie."

"Uncle Frankie and Auntie Shawna," Kaylob said. "They've been dying to have her to themselves."

"True. It will give them a chance to practice. Of course, we have the best baby in the world. You know, she hardly ever fusses. She's just so happy to be here, just like her daddy."

Kaylob laughed. "She's amazing, that's for sure, just like her mama."

Once they hung up, Beth Ann heard Kaylie cooing and Goldie and Sasha were roughing around. She'd have to read another day or maybe after lunch when Kaylie went down again. She couldn't wait to read more about Abraham because that was her great-grandpa. How fun was reading about their romance going to be?

She let Goldie outside since the rain had eased up and went into Kaylie's room. It was incredible to watch her lying on her back, babbling and smiling.

"Hello, my baby girl." She bent down, picked her up, and watched a big smile spread across her face. Her little fingers reached up to Beth Ann's mouth. "Oh my gosh, you are the love of my life, just like your daddy." She kissed her little fingers.

"What more could a mother ask for?" Just then a big rumble of thunder hit and made Beth Ann jump. Kaylie must have felt it because her little lip started to tremble. The weather was extremely unusual since they mostly had blue skies.

Beth Ann placed the baby back down in her crib, and she started to fuss louder.

"I'll be right back, honey," she said, but Kaylie wasn't listening.

Beth Ann dashed into the mudroom where Goldie was shivering in the corner, along with Sasha. She closed the doggie door and opened the gate leading into the kitchen. Both Sasha and Goldie ran past her. Beth Ann heard the wind howl like she'd never experienced before. She darted back to a crying Kaylie.

"It's okay, sweetie pie." She gathered her up and tried to calm her down.

Another flash of lightning lit up the entire bedroom. *Bam. Kaboom.* A noise sounded above the thunder.

"Holy living heck, what in heaven's name was that?" she said.

Goldie ran by her side. Sasha came too, but darted under the changing table. This day was not going to be easy after all.

Beth Ann stepped over to the window and saw the big tree smoldering in the backyard. Another bolt of lightning shot across the sky, and a lingering rumble of thunder followed. The sky opened up and drenched everything, making it hard to even see. The rain swept across the grass in a downpour, overflowing the flower pots and drain spouts.

Memories of the last storm she'd experienced swept through her. It was the night Kaylob had told her he was going back to Vietnam. She was madder than a wet hen and left the tiny apartment, walking for hours through the storm. But that was nothing compared to this. At least the rain anyway. A large sound ripped her from the memory.

"Oh, hell." A gust of wind had picked up both garbage cans and tossed them against the house. She decided to call Kaylob.

Next, there was cracking and clanking above her. "What is that?" She held Kaylie close and peered once again out the window. "Holy roof alert," she saw what appeared to be pieces of their roof flying through the air. Next, hail started plummeting down on the patio. The house started to shake, and a howling sound sent chills down her spine. Kaylie bawled, and Beth Ann knew it was because she was picking up on her mommy's nerves.

Goldie started barking and the cat was meowing loudly, which caused Kaylie to get more frantic.

That did it. With the baby in her arms, Beth Ann ran into the bedroom and picked up the phone with Goldie on her heels, woofing louder.

Thank God she got a dial tone and heard it ring. "Seven Nights and Seven Roses," Kaylob answered.

"Honey," she shouted into the phone. "I think our roof is blowing off, and our tree just got hit by lightning." She could hardly hear him, because of Goldie's yapping and Kaylie crying.

"Be home …" was all she heard before the line went dead. No dial tone—nothing.

He was coming home, but now she had to worry about him driving in this mess. Oh no, why did she call him?

In the next instance, she heard glass shatter from what sounded like the kitchen or family room. She held Kaylie closer and knew what she had to do. Without another thought, she ran into Kaylie's room, grabbed a blanket, and put it across her tiny body. She swooped Sasha up in her other arm while Goldie stayed right by her side. Then, without hesitation, she rushed them all into the hall bathroom and climbed into the shower. They all huddled together. Beth Ann was grateful there were no windows, but wished one of the phone cords was longer so it would reach the bathroom. Why hadn't they done that?

"Dear God, please keep us safe and let Kaylob make it home," she whispered as she cradled Kaylie to her chest and rocked her. She started to sing, trying to erase the noise and ease the tension.

"It is no secret what God can do."

* * * *

Blake sat in his room, watching the dark, threatening clouds. In some way, the storm reminded him of what had happened during the shooting. It sent tremors down his spine.

"Blake."

Ginger's voice made him jump, and he hoped she hadn't noticed. He looked in her direction.

"Did you hear?" she said. "One of the nurses told me there is a storm advisory and we can expect some really high winds. She also said some funnel clouds were reported."

"Funnel clouds? That's unusual for here," he replied. "I hope I can still get home today."

Ginger moved over in front of the window. "I hope Millie will be okay." She turned around with sad eyes.

"Who is Millie? Is that your sister?"

"No, no, it's an old lady I met today. She was going through the hospital garbage can." She sighed. "She lives across the street in the park and said she stays in the bathroom for safety. I gave her my wedding ring."

That was another thing about Ginger that reminded him of Beth Ann. She always had a soft spot for homeless people. When they were engaged, Beth Ann was constantly after him to donate. He had to be honest; he hadn't done it as much anymore. Actually, if truth be told, he hadn't done it at all lately.

"Ginger," Blake whispered. "Let's get her into a room until we can get her an apartment. With this weather, I don't want someone you met and obviously liked sleeping outdoors."

"Oh Blake, I wasn't telling you about this for anything like that." She sat down. "I was just thinking about her."

"Let's get her somewhere safe. There is a hotel right next door. Let me make a call while you get her over there. It will be temporary until we can get her settled. So long as she's clean and not on drugs, I'm willing to help."

Ginger leaned over and hugged him. "I don't know what to say. She wasn't high or on drugs. She just seemed like a lost and lonely soul."

"Go on and pick her up," he said. "It's just next door, so hurry and get back here. This storm looks awful, and I don't want you out in it for long. When you get back, could you try to find out when they are cutting me loose? I'm hoping today."

"I hope you can get home, too. I need to talk to you about something, if that's okay?"

Suddenly, Beth Ann and Kaylob flashed in Blake's head. Strange. That had never happened before. What the heck was wrong with him?

"Ginger, could you hand me the phone first? I need to call Kaylob and Beth Ann. Sorry, but something doesn't feel right."

"Sure." She handed him the phone. What looked to be a flash of worry flickered in her eyes. "I believe in ESP," she said as he dialed the number.

"Me too," he agreed. He got a fast busy signal, so he tried again. After four times, he finally gave up. He glanced at Ginger. "I hope they're okay."

"Should I drive to their house and check on them after I get Millie settled?" she asked.

"No, I don't want you out in this weather any longer than you have to be. I'd worry my ass off."

Ginger slyly smiled. "Wouldn't want to lose your ass. I might have to dump you for sure."

He arched a brow. "Oh really? I see how it is … you just like me for a little tail." He looked serious, but couldn't help cracking up.

"I wouldn't call it little." She winked.

"Are you saying I have a fat butt?" He put his hand over his heart and feigned shock.

She shook her head and chuckled. "I better get going, but I need to talk to you when I get back if that's okay."

"Of course it's okay. Just be careful," he instructed before she beat a hasty retreat.

* * * *

The wind rushed so fast and hard that it almost knocked Ginger backward. "Crud!" The blustery weather pierced her bones as she climbed inside her car. "Dang, I'm soaking wet," she complained under her breath, shivering.

The thought of Millie being out in this storm sent a shudder down her back. Once she started the car, the rain and hail pelted at her windshield. Then, with no warning, an avalanche of hailstones hit the hood of her car. The park was only across the street. She needed to get there fast, so she cruised away.

The place was abandoned and lonely. There was no sign of Millie. "The restrooms," she whispered. She got out of the car and made a mad dash down the sidewalk. *Swoosh.* She slid from the hail and tried like heck not to fall on her ass.

Once she made it to the restroom, she froze at the door, feeling jittery. "Just open it," she told herself. Taking a deep breath, she pushed on the door.

"God in heaven." The stench assaulted her. She wasn't sure which was gloomier, inside or out. Millie was lying on the bathroom floor, shivering with the blanket around her. She was using an old handbag for a pillow and faced the bathroom stalls.

The sound of the rain and wind was so deafening that it must have muffled out Ginger's presence. Slowly, so as not to frighten her, Ginger sat down close and placed a hand on her arm. "Millie, it's me, Ginger."

The old woman turned, and Ginger could see her cheeks were wet from tears.

"What are you doing out in this weather, child?" She sat up and nonchalantly wiped her cheeks. "You need to get home."

"I'm here to take you to a place that's safe and warm."

Millie shook her head. "I can't let you do that. You already gave me a ring."

"Please, if you don't, I'm staying right here with you. Then we'll both catch our deaths." She met her gaze. "I won't leave."

Just as Millie started to open her mouth, a rain spout from the ceiling started pouring down. It was hitting the floor and splashing all over.

Chapter Six

"Oh dear." Millie looked around. "You'll catch a death and I'll be to blame."

"Come with me, then," Ginger pleaded. "Please."

"Okay." She nodded. "I'll come with you."

They both stood and grabbed some of her stuff from the cart, what little there was.

Ginger waved for her to follow. "Let's hurry, this storm is getting worse."

Once they stepped outside, a gust of wind tore away Millie's blanket. There was no way to go chasing after it. The storm whipped at them as they inched their way down the sidewalk, carrying bags and small items.

Finally, they climbed into the car and placed Millie's things in the backseat. Ginger started it up, then turned the heater to full blast.

"Oh my dear, that does feel good." Millie stuck her hands, covered in tattered gloves, by the vents. "Now, where are you taking me? I won't go to a shelter. They scare me."

"There's no way you're going to one of those places." Ginger shook her head. "I'm taking you to a hotel. Remember, I told you about my friend in the hospital. He's a good and caring man. He was shot. Right now, he's paralyzed. It would make him feel so much better to help you." She inhaled. "Please let him do this. You would be helping us more than you know."

Millie sat in silence for a few minutes. "Okay, I just don't understand. Why me? Nobody has ever helped me before." Her voice trembled. "Even when ... never mind." She stopped talking. "Thank you

51

and please thank your friend. What's his name?"

"His name is Blake, and he saved my life, too." She reached over and held Millie's hand. "Now, let's get you home."

"Home," she whispered. "Never thought I'd have a home again."

They arrived at the hotel, and Millie's eyes grew wide. "I've found some good things in those garbage bins." She pointed. "This place is fancy. I'm not sure they'll let me in. They've yelled at me many times."

"They'll let you in. I can promise you that," Ginger assured.

When she climbed out, the wind clobbered her again. She went around to the back of her car and checked to make sure her overnight bag was still in the trunk. There wasn't much, but it had some nice lotion and a few personal items. However, she did have some clean pants, two sweaters, and a really warm nightgown with slippers. She was glad to see it was still there for Millie.

Ginger went to the front desk and checked in. Millie seemed concerned with her appearance and stayed in the car. Funny, that was how Ginger had felt when Blake had pulled into the Colony House. Only it wasn't because of the way she was dressed, as much as the feelings of shame from being beaten.

Ginger retrieved the key to the room, finding out Blake had rented a suite with a kitchenette and paid for the entire month. The manager said it was the nicest the hotel offered, almost a thousand square feet, with a living room and a queen-sized bed. They served breakfast free of charge every morning, along with a nighttime buffet. They also offered all kinds of snacks. The manager handed her the tickets for Millie to use for the meals. Tonight, they'd be serving Mexican food with salads and ice cream for dessert.

The minute Ginger went back to the car she examined the little map. Once she figured it out, she pulled to the rear of the building so they'd be closer. They both grabbed Millie's stuff, which consisted of a couple garbage bags and smaller items. Plus, Ginger grabbed her bag from the trunk. They first had to enter a set of glass doors, and then find the correct room.

When they found it, Ginger handed the key to Millie. "Here you go; it's your room for the next month until we find you another place." Ginger smiled and gave her a hug. "Go ahead and open it."

Her poor hands trembled as she struggled to unlock the door. "I feel like I'm dreaming. It's been three years since I stepped foot into a nice, warm shelter. It was a crowded church." She twisted the key. "The pastor let a few of us homeless people stay in a room for a few nights."

She opened the door, and her hand went across her mouth. "Oh, my Lord," she said with a gasp. "I can't believe this." They stepped further inside.

The place was cute. The light tan walls were decorated with pictures of flowers and trees. There was a tan couch and a TV with a coffee table and end tables. There was even a tiny gas fireplace set against the side wall next to the couch. The small kitchenette was adorable and part of the living room, but spread out in an open space. It had a stove and small oven with a normal-sized refrigerator.

"Look." Millie pointed to the coffeemaker. "There's coffee here with creamer and sugar." She moved over closer to it. "I can't believe this." She swept away some tears.

Ginger steadied her emotions. This was something she'd never forget.

Just as Ginger stepped over to open the refrigerator, there was a knock at the door. "Do you want me to answer that? They might be bringing you some extra blankets. I asked them at the front desk, just in case it got chilly, but I had no idea about the fireplace."

"Yes, please." She stood, staring around.

When Ginger opened the door, there were two girls there. They were smiling, their hands full.

"Mr. Tanner asked us to pick up food," the smaller girl with dark hair said.

"And he also said to pick up some freshly prepared food," the tall one said with a mouth full of braces and a big smile. "In case the guest wanted to stay inside."

"Come on in." Ginger opened the door. "This storm is something else." She couldn't believe Blake did this, but then again, of course he would.

They came in, putting the food on the counters and the small dining table. The taller girl opened up a big bag and pulled out blankets. She also took out a white, terry cloth bathrobe and laid it on a chair.

"Well …" The short one smiled. "If you need anything else, just ring the front desk." She set down some cash and a few rolls of quarters. It appeared to be about two hundred dollars. "Mr. Tanner asked us to leave her this. It's two hundred and fifty dollars and some change for laundry." She studied Millie with gentle eyes.

The taller one explained. "The laundry room is right around the corner, and it has soap powder you can purchase in the vending machines. It has about five washers and dryers, and it's pretty available during the week."

"Thank you," Ginger said.

Millie gave them both a small smile that was clearly heartfelt. "Thank you."

"We have to get back to work now. Have a nice day," the tall one said as they left.

Ginger touched Millie's arm. "Let's see what you have." She was excited to see what Blake had done for Millie.

They both started going through the bags. Ginger held up goodies. "Ice Cream and cheese cake." She put them in the freezer. There were eggs and bacon, sandwich fixings, and a fresh baked chicken with large fries. "Wow, you can have a feast tonight. They have more food down in the dining area, but look at all this."

There were grapes and melons, so much fresh fruit and salads. Blake had even remembered drinks. He had ordered all different kinds of pops, along with milk and orange juice.

Once they had all the food put away, Ginger saw Millie sit down with tears filling her eyes.

"I still can't believe you and your friend did all of this for me. I don't know how I will ever repay you."

"You have already repaid me." Ginger sat across from her and reached for her hand. "I have a new friend. Believe me, when we have a chance to talk and spend time together," she inhaled, "You'll understand how desperately I needed someone. I just know we are going to become the best of friends."

"Oh, my dear, I needed you too. Not just for this, but for the loneliness." She swallowed. "I'd really love to take a shower, if it wouldn't be rude. It's been over three years since I took a real one." She seemed embarrassed. "I want to smell normal again."

"Of course. Take your time and enjoy everything." She handed her the phone number to the hospital and the Colony House. "I need to get back to my friend. He's still in a lot of pain, but I'll be checking in on you."

"I will pray that his pain leaves, and I look forward to meeting him. Maybe I could cook breakfast for you when you have some time."

"I will call in a couple of hours to check on you, and I would love to spend the morning with you." The new friends embraced, and Ginger knew they had forged a bond.

Before Ginger left, she handed her the overnight bag. "There are warm clothes inside and some very nice lotion."

Millie smiled. "You are an angel from God." She touched Ginger's cheek.

On her way back to the hospital, she imagined Millie watching TV, eating a big plate of food, and enjoying herself. She'd call her later to check in and make sure she was doing well. Never could she remember feeling so satisfied.

* * * *

When Blake saw Ginger enter the room, there was no missing the happiness in her eyes.

"Oh Blake, I can't believe what you did. You've changed her life." Her lip trembled. "It has been three years since she stayed in a warm place, and that was just a church room that she shared with a lot of other people." Her voice dropped. "They only let her stay for a few nights, and then she was out on the streets again."

"That makes me feel doggone good, darlin. We will make sure she stays in the hotel until we find her a place."

Ginger nodded. "Thank you so much."

"My pleasure," he said and meant it. "So, what did you want to talk to me about?" He picked up his cup of water and took a sip. "I hope it's something else good."

"Well, there are a few things I want to explain. I think it's good news." She fidgeted with her purse and glanced up at him.

"Okay." He saw something in her eyes, but wasn't sure what it was.

She hesitated and seemed lost in thought, so he didn't say anything

55

and gave her some time.

"I told you I met Arnold in college and that's where we dated. He pretended to be a nice guy."

Blake nodded. "I remember you telling me that."

"You heard me tell Rob that I'm a physical therapist, but I only did my internship. I never actually worked and made a living, although I wanted to."

Blake's heart ached; he had a feeling why she'd never worked. But he reached for her hand and stroked it. He said nothing, just let her take a break before she continued.

"I want to do it when you don't need me anymore. I think you know, once I moved in with Arnold, I never got the chance to work." Her voice trembled. "I got offered a job here as Rob's assistant. However, after some time on the job, I could become a physical therapist with my own clients. It's always been my dream." She shifted in her seat and appeared nervous.

"Ginger, is this what you truly want?" He lifted her chin and made her look into his eyes.

"Yes." She swallowed. "I've always wanted to do this."

He motioned for her to move closer, so she did. With that, he gently kissed her lips. "I'm proud of you," he murmured. "You do not have to wait until I'm better. This is your dream, so you need to follow it." The surprise in her eyes told a sad story. Jesus, she thought he was going to be upset.

"Blake," she whispered and kissed him with her soft trembling lips. "You are so wonderful. What you did for Millie and for me is beyond anything I ever dreamed." She melted her lips across his and oh lord, his insides did the hokey pokey.

Okay, cowboy, slow it down. He wanted her and wanted her bad. Hell, he was all talk and no rodeo, but she was melting him into a puddle of lard.

"Thank you, darlin." He was sinking into her serene blue eyes.

"Do you have any idea how wonderful you are?" she asked. "Sometimes, I wonder if you realize how much goodness you have inside."

"No, because I'm not wonderful. You might think I am, but I've done some …"

"Shush," she whispered, placing her lips over his again.

With that, he dissolved into bliss. He was held captive by her mouth with its delicious taste of coffee and something sweet. Never had either tasted so fine.

After a little while, he pulled back to catch his breath. "Why don't you go and let Rob know you can start right away?" He scanned this incredible woman who had touched his heart and soul like nobody since … yes, since Beth Ann.

"They don't need me until the twenty-seventh of April. I can help you until then, and even after, I will work with you, if you want me to."

"I want you to, but I won't let you unless you let me pay you," Blake said.

Her eyes widened. "Are you serious? You are not paying me. Blake, you've already paid me. I am living in your place rent free. Plus, look at all those clothes you bought me and the food. Not to mention what you did for Millie."

Blake shook his head. "I want to pay you, and I won't take no for an answer."

"Blake, if you try that, I'll make you hire someone else."

"Well, in that case, I guess you win since you played that card." He arched a brow. "By the way, is there any way you could find out when they are cutting me loose?"

"I thought they would have come in by now." She stood and smiled. "I'll go ask."

Once she left the room, Blake let out a long ass sigh. That woman was getting to him, and he was beginning to feel like a moth to her flame. What he needed to do was walk again, and make damn sure he didn't get his heart busted up like before. Sometimes, all that glittered brought nothing but pain. Where the hell did that come from? He answered his own question. It came from having his heart ripped out by another redhead. Although, he reminded himself, Ginger was not Beth Ann.

The phone on the end table rang.

"Hello."

"Hi Blake, it's me, Melissa. I just found out about this. I am coming to see you."

"Hi there, little darlin, you really don't need to do that. They say there's a good chance I'm going to walk again. I can move my toes, which I found out today is a good sign."

"Some jealous husband shot you, they said. Blake, you shouldn't be messing around with married ladies. I've never known you to do that before."

"It's a long story," he said. "She wasn't married when I met her. How's it going back home?" He changed the subject.

Blake had known Melissa's dad for years. She had worked for him, tried to come on to him, and even kissed him. She was a cute kid and he really cared about her, but nevertheless, she was too young and only a friend. The bottom line was he didn't have those kinds of feelings for her.

"I have plenty of time to talk," Melissa said. "So why don't you tell me what happened? Afterward, I'll tell you how it's going here."

About twenty minutes of conversation later, Blake saw Ginger walk in the room and tiptoe back out.

"Well, little darlin', I have to get off the phone and find out if they are going to release me today or tomorrow. I'm glad things are going well over there. Sounds like connecting with your old boyfriend might end up being a good thing."

"It has been, Blake. If you need me though, I'll come."

"Thanks, but I'm covered. You take care, and I'll call you with updates."

They said their goodbyes, and Blake exhaled. Now that was some good news. Sometimes, things did work out how they were meant to.

A few minutes later, Ginger walked back into his room.

"Hi." She gave him a look he didn't recognize.

"So, did you find out anything?"

"Yes, they are going to let you out tomorrow morning," she said, her tone curt.

He studied her for a minute and wondered what had happened. Maybe it didn't go so well with the job thing. "Is everything okay? Did something happen while you were gone?"

"No, I just had to wait for a while to see when they would release you." She sat down and didn't look at him.

"I'm sorry you had to wait. I didn't know it would take so long."

After a long time, she met his gaze. "Was the girl you were talking to an old girlfriend?"

"Ah-ha …" Now he recognized that look. The green-eyed monster. He laughed. "Darlin', you have nothing to be jealous about."

"I heard you call her darlin' when I was walking out the door."

"Ginger, I've always used that term with women."

"So it means nothing intimate then?" She arched a brow.

"Well, it depends on how the darlin' is used. There is darlin' friendly, then darlin' hot, sexy, and beautiful."

"Okay." She gave him a tiny smile. "Which one am I?"

He crooked his finger and called her closer. "Let me show instead of tell."

She moved closer to his mouth. "Show me then."

He slid his lips across hers and felt his heart speed up. After a few seconds, he deepened the kiss. Lord have mercy, she was the warm in winter and the sweet taste of honey on a sugarless day.

His brain said, *Hold your horses and slow it down*, but his heart and a few other areas wanted to continue. He forced himself to pull back the reins before he completely lost control. "Ah, darlin.'" He gazed into her eyes. "I think you understand."

All she did was nod and swallow.

"What time tomorrow are we breaking out of this joint? There are things we need to get ready. I'll need to take a bedroom downstairs."

"Johnny already did it all. He moved us to another house suite; I guess that's what it's called. He said it's more open. It has the largest bedroom downstairs with a handicap bathroom."

He felt slapped. The word handicap, hit him hard. As long as he was in the hospital, he looked at himself as injured, not disabled.

"Remember, it's only temporary." It was as though Ginger had read his mind.

He nodded, but inside, he didn't know how to define his life as a handicapped Blake Tanner.

* * * *

Kaylob sped toward home. He needed to get to his family and make sure they were okay.

Up ahead, he saw flashing lights and cars coming to a standstill. "What the hell?"

The water was crossing the road, which of course meant it was flooded. Even so, he was confident he could drive through it.

He tried to go around a few cars, but a police officer in heavy rain gear waved him over.

Kaylob rolled down his truck window and felt the wet wind hit his face. "Officer, I need to get home. My wife called and said the roof was coming off. We have a new baby, and they are home alone."

"Sorry, sir." The guy raised his voice over the noise. He pointed down the road and held his hood, trying to keep the wind and rain out of his face to no avail. "We can't let anyone go through. The road is washed out. Plus, funnel clouds have been spotted. A few have even touched down."

"Is there another way to get in?" Kaylob wanted to ignore the officer.

"Not that I know of. All reports say that none are open. The best thing you can do is turn around and wait this out. Go someplace safe."

"I need to get home. Can't I just try it anyway?" Kaylob leveled a look at him.

"No, sir, I can't let you do that."

Kaylob rolled up his window. He wondered how much trouble he would get in if he did it anyway. A little bit of water seemed like nothing if his family were in trouble. However, he didn't think the police would let him get very far.

The clouds were dark and threatening. Not even a second later, the wind picked up even more. Turning around, he went back toward town. There had been a small convenience store just down the road. He'd try to call Beth Ann from there.

The minute he saw the place, he pulled into the driveway. The pay phone was in use, so he jumped out and fought the wind. The rain smacked him in the face hard, but he continued to pace until the guy was done. Once it was available, he put in the change and dialed. All it did was ring, no answer. Damn it to hell, he felt sick as he tried several more times to get Beth Ann on the phone. He needed to stay calm. Obviously, the phones were down.

Wait, the family who lived two houses down had met him in his driveway last night. Maybe their phone was working. Crap, he had forgotten about booking them in for the party. But that was good news because he still had their number. He yanked it from his wallet.

With shaky hands, he dialed and listened to the rings—five, six, and then seven times. "Please answer the phone." After at least twenty rings, he hung up and ran back to his truck, hearing thunder all around him.

What the hell was he going to do? He ran his hand through his hair while he waited in his godforsaken truck. The storm was getting worse by the minute. The rain pelted his windshield and streaks of lightning lit up the sky.

"Map." He needed a goddamn map. He'd find a street that would take him home. There had to be some old, out-of-the-way roads.

He darted into the store, thumbing frantically through the maps on the counter.

An older gentleman glanced up at him. He had silver hair and a matching mustache, and he was wearing faded, farmer-style overalls.

"Planning a trip?" the man asked, looking at him in confusion. "This ain't a good time to be traveling."

"Trying to find a way home," Kaylob said. "I need to get to my wife. She's out in the Redlands on Palmdale Court, and I'm worried about her. She said the roof was blowing off before we got disconnected. The phone must have died because I can't get in touch with her."

The man shook his head. "Hear they been having some high winds and tornados out that direction."

"That's why I'm trying to get home. We have a newborn baby, and my wife is all alone out there." Kaylob studied one of the maps.

The man met his eyes. "All alone?" He frowned. "Look at this road." He pointed to the area. "I can't be saying it's going to be smooth, but there are no creeks or rivers in that direction, so shouldn't be any flooding in those parts. It's an old road. It has a lot of holes, and it's pretty torn up from what I've been told."

Kaylob leaned closer and saw the tiny line. "That's a road?"

"Yep, used to be the only way to get down there. People don't use it anymore. The only thing out there is the old water company, from my understanding. Do you have flashlights and an emergency kit of any kind?"

"Yes." Kaylob nodded.

"Just take the map. I'll expect you to stop by and let me know what happened later."

"I will," Kaylob shook his hand. "Thank you." He rushed out the door.

Chapter Seven

Beth Ann was still in the bathroom, but she needed to get a few supplies. Staying positive was sure as heck not easy, but she focused on keeping them all safe. She had been using her hand to give the animals a drink from her bottled water. Kaylie was sound asleep, bundled up in her blanket. Goldie was awake, and Sasha was sleeping soundly on the bathroom rug. The lights were not working, so she needed to get flashlights, a bowl for the animals, and everything she could to keep them safe. The thought of being in the dark when it got late was not appealing.

The wind still howled. Thuds and crashes caused the house to vibrate from time to time. She got out of the tub, telling Goldie to stay and watch Kaylie. Quietly, she opened the door and crept down the hall. Her nerves were fried. She silently prayed that the house was not too badly damaged, but more than anything, she wanted the storm to end.

Once she stepped into the kitchen, she gasped. The windows were broken, and water was everywhere. But the place was still standing, so she was thankful for that. Holy trash alert, litter was all over the kitchen.

What she needed were the flashlights and battery-operated radio that were in the mudroom. There was no way they were leaving the bathroom. At least it was large and comfortable where they could stay safe.

They had thought about having some windows put in, and oh boy, was she relieved it never happened. At least the mudroom was intact. She gathered up everything she needed.

Once she set everything down in the bathroom, she ran into Kaylie's room and grabbed as much as she could, along with a few toys. The pinging of something hitting the glass windows made her nervous. There was no way she was going to stay near anything that could break.

Bustling through the house, she grabbed even more things. The adrenaline was surging through her faster than the wind. When she got to the kitchen once again, the storm whipped through the broken glass. A foul smell, almost like rotten eggs, hit her. She grimaced. Gathering some food along with bottles of fresh water, she stopped and tried the phone again. "Darn it." The thing was still dead.

When she peeked out the window at the backyard, her heart sank. It was a flooded mess. There was water up to the first step, and the pool was running over. It was a good thing they had a first-rate draining system around it.

What if the water got inside? There was no upstairs. Wait, there was an attic. She'd pull down the steps and take everyone up there. Relief washed through her as she remembered how solid the floors were. What about bugs and stuff?

"Get over it," Beth Ann said to herself. "There are worse things in life than bugs." She ran to the spare room and pulled down the steps leading into the attic, just in case.

With fresh blankets and a hurricane lamp, along with the radio, Beth Ann felt better. She had everything they needed, except Kaylob. However, she had to keep the faith that he was okay or she would go crazy. The bottom line was that he'd do everything he could to make it home. On the other hand, she didn't want him to put his life in danger, and that was what worried her.

Back in the bathroom, she wrapped the blanket around her shoulders and turned on the battery-operated lantern. It was great and lit up the entire room.

Perfect. They'd never used it, but they'd bought it just in case the power ever went out. It turned out to be a great investment.

Kaylie started moving around so Beth Ann turned on the radio to drown out the wind, which seemed to have died down some. It didn't matter to her. The bottom line was that she was staying put until someone got home. Thank goodness Shawna had brought the kitty to stay with her while they were out.

As she fed Kaylie, a song she knew by Simon and Garfunkel came on, 'Bridge Over Troubled Waters.' That came out a few years ago. Thinking about how far they'd come made her more relaxed until the emergency broadcaster announced there were tornado watches and high wind warnings, as well as flash flood alerts. That sure as heck didn't help. She already knew that, she was living it.

Two hours passed. She needed to let Sasha use the cat box, and Goldie needed to do her business. After she did that, she could bring in Kaylie's playpen. There was plenty of room. Kaylie was cooing and making gurgling sounds as she held her baby rattle, so Beth Ann turned up the music a little louder and crept out the door with Sasha. The poor kitty made a mad dash to the cat box, so Beth Ann waited. No way did she want her to climb under something and not be able to find her. Plus, the wind was whipping through the broken windows. Sasha finished her business and Beth Ann took her back in the room, putting down a little blanket for her. Next, she took Goldie and walked to the front door. It was a flooded mess, too, but not as bad as the backyard. Glancing around, she noticed that the front yard wasn't covered as deeply in water. That was good news; she could carry Goldie and let her do what she needed.

"Oh my gosh, you are getting heavy." She waded through the water and made it under the tree before sitting Goldie on the ground. The poor little thing must have been holding it forever. "Good girl."

By the time she got back inside, she was chilled and her brand new bell bottom jump suit was wet up to her ankles. The first thing she did was grab Kaylie's playpen and bring it into the bathroom, with Goldie's help. She was such a good dog. She was right by Beth Ann's side the entire time, even when she changed into some dry clothes and shoes. Only once did Goldie bark at the wind blowing through the broken window. It was as if she knew why they were staying in the bathroom.

When they'd bought the house, Beth Ann wondered why anyone would need such big bathrooms, and she'd griped about the size. From this point forward, she'd never complain again.

The sounds of pellets hitting outside echoed through the walls. Holy crap, would this ever end? Next, the wind started howling. It sounded like a freight train was coming. She grabbed Kaylie, then jumped in the shower and closed the door. Her main goal was to be sure Kaylie and the animals were safe. Just as she turned up the radio, a tornado warning came blasting out. She cradled her child and prayed it would not hit their house.

* * * *

Kaylob had gotten turned around for over an hour, but he was pretty sure he was on the right road this time.

The rain came down in buckets, flooding his window and making it hard to see. This left him with no choice but to drive a mere ten miles an hour. Not to mention, the road was old as hell, eighty-percent dirt and twenty-percent asphalt, with giant-sized holes. At least it wasn't flooded, not yet anyway.

There wasn't a house in sight, and he hadn't seen one other vehicle. As he thought about it, he realized the only person who knew he had left in this direction was the old man at the store.

Maybe that wasn't so wise. He slowed and veered to the left, seeing what appeared to be a funnel cloud, trying to touch down.

"Holy hell!" Golf-ball sized hail clunked the windshield of his truck. He stopped and was ready to outrun the damn thing when it turned in the other direction.

Another twenty minutes had passed when he spotted an old, industrial building of some type. At least there was a truck out there, and it looked to be in running condition. As he passed the building, he saw another car parked with a yellow light on the top, it was at least ten plus years old. Maybe a 65' Ford truck. Some signs of life were better than none. He wondered if someone was in the building and if they might have a phone.

When he rounded another corner, there was a guy in a yellow truck heading toward him. Kaylob stopped and rolled down his window; the other guy did the same.

"Hey there, buddy," the guy said. "Not a good road to be on today. Are you lost?"

"Not really." He held up his map. "I'm trying to get home to my wife. We live in the Redland's, and she is home alone with our new baby."

"Whereabouts in the Redland's do you live?"

"On Palmdale drive."

"Man, I really don't think you can make it, That's still a long ways." He frowned. "There are trees down on the road, and nobody's out here. It's only used by farmers for grazing and grain. It's not safe; even the cows are in their barns. There are things blocking the road, and I thought I just saw a tornado."

"I saw it too, but it went another direction. I'll go on foot if I have to."

"If you're going to do that, you should park your truck here. But I would advise you to wait this storm out."

"Can't do that." Kaylob shook his head. "I'd crawl on my knees to get to my family."

"Okay, pal. I have some rain gear in the back. Park your truck inside the gate, and you can come back for it. Do you need me to call someone for ya?"

"Yes, that would be great." He nodded. "If you don't mind, I have a friend who might be able to help. Even if he can't, I want him to at least know where I am."

"No problem. What's your name?"

"My name is Kaylob O'Brien."

"Nice to meet you, Kaylob. My name is Skip. Let's get your truck inside the gate."

The guy was great. He gave Kaylob the rain gear and some boots. That would help keep him dry. He thanked Skip and headed on his way.

The wind was blowing hard as he trudged down the broken-up road. He wondered why the hell nobody had fixed it. Potholes and cracks were filled with mud and water, which was not easy to walk through.

Time passed, and things got extremely worse. Even with the heavy-duty gear on, the wind chill and rain battered his body. The water stung his eyes, making it hard to see anything, but he continued forward anyway. Every now and then, a gust of wind would almost knock him backward, until one finally knocked him on his ass.

The echoes of trees cracking and making a swishing sound drew his attention. He wanted to make sure there were no tornados.

When a tree limb hit him in the shoulder and the side of his head, he yelled into the storm. "Damn it!" The thing almost knocked him out. He tried to pick up his pace, but the rain hitting the hood and his feet did nothing but slow him down.

"I just want to get home to Beth Ann and my baby girl," he mumbled out loud.

He walked for another block or so when the hail started pummeling him. It sure as hell didn't feel good.

A few times he had to make a mad dash under a tree to dodge the stinging pellets. He had no choice and had no idea how long he had stayed under those trees waiting for the hail to stop. He needed to keep going, and he'd been through much worse.

Just thinking about his Vietnam days brought back memories of the POW camp. This was nothing compared to the torture and hardship he had gone through during those dark days. Hell, they had buried him in the dirt, beat him black and blue, and broke fingers and ribs. He had survived the abuse for over two years, so he could sure as hell make it through this.

He lifted the wet map and tried to figure out how much longer he had to go. It looked like another ten to fifteen miles. At this rate if he kept stopping, it was going to take forever and would be dark by the time he got home, hell it was already getting there. He was sure relieved that he had a flashlight.

A blinding flash of lightning slashed through the sky and hit the ground, making a god-awful rumble. He prayed that neither he nor the trees got hit. At least, not the ones close by. With so much water on the ground, that might give him a shock.

"Yikes!" A snake slithered across the ground right in front of him. Okay, he was a tough guy, been through Nam, but damn it to hell if snakes didn't give him the creepy crawlers. He stopped and made sure the thing crossed the road. The last thing he wanted was to step on it or tangle with the creature.

Lights bolted through the sky again, and then a long *kaboom* rumbled under his feet. He froze as Shaffer flashed through his mind. The pain slammed into him. Once again, Walt was dying in his arms. "Not now," he yelled into the almost dark sky. He didn't have time for flashbacks and wondered if things from that war would haunt him forever. Shaking off the memory, he once again tried to pick up his pace.

After a while, Kaylob was weather beaten, hungry and exhausted, but he stayed strong and fought to keep going. Just as he took another step, he noticed there was water crossing the road. Wasn't that great? He was going to have to go through that shit to get across or go around it.

* * * *

Blake had been down at physical therapy again, working out for a good part of the afternoon. He'd spent time in the pool, which felt great. While swimming, his world almost seemed normal. At least his arms worked.

He'd sent Ginger down to get some information from the nurse. He was exhausted and laid his head down on the pillow, but the ringing of the phone drew his attention.

"Hello," he answered.

"Is this Mr. Tanner?"

"Yes." He wondered who it was.

"My name is Skip Waymire, and I work for the Regional Urban Water district out in the Redland area."

Strange. Why would someone from that water company be calling him? Oh crap, he sure as bacon hoped his townhouse hadn't flooded.

"Okay," Blake said and waited.

"You're a friend of Kaylob's, correct?"

"Yes."

"He wanted me to call you and let you know that his wife and baby are stranded in the house. He's out in this storm, trying to get to her, and left his truck here."

"He's on foot? Good God, what was he thinking?"

"Well, sir, from what I could gather, the roof of their house was ripped off and he was worried about tornados. She was home alone with a new baby."

"Shit, I don't like the sound of that. Thanks, Skip. I'm calling in some favors right now. I'll handle this." Blake grabbed his pen and a piece of paper off the hospital tray. "What road is he on?"

"Old Mountainside Road, which does go to Palmdale. His truck is here at the old water district," he said. "Thank goodness we still do some work from here. We're only out here two days a week, and today was one of those days."

"Thanks for calling, Skip. Do you have a phone number there or anywhere we can reach you?"

Skip gave him his phone number and once again, Blake thanked him for calling.

The minute Blake hung up, he reached over and pulled his address book from the side drawer. After he dialed the number, he waited for someone to answer.

"Hello."

"Hey Johnny, glad you're answering the phone. Are you able to leave Dana alone?"

"Sure can, boss. She's fine. Plus, her best pal is here."

"We have an issue, and we're gonna need a few feet on the ground. Some big-ass trucks, and I mean big, that can make it through flooded areas."

"Where we going?" Johnny asked. "Would a helicopter be better?"

* * * *

As the afternoon faded away, Kaylob shivered at the drop in temperature. The clouds were getting darker, and the rain had only eased up a couple of times. The water on the ground had slowed him down and he'd had to take way too many breaks. Trudging through the flooded area had left him weak and hungry. He didn't even have a snack. What was he thinking, not grabbing the candy bars from his truck?

His mind was playing tricks on him. He kept seeing houses when it was only trees and telephone poles. At one point, he thought he'd seen a shadow lurking at the base of a tree. But it was just his imagination.

The light was almost gone, and he wondered what Beth Ann was doing. Did she have power? How bad was the house damaged? He didn't care about anything other than her safety. He'd give up every cent he had to keep his family protected.

Why had he thought that working in Riverside was okay when they lived so far away? He had been a selfish asshole and put the popularity of his restaurant first. Shit, what an idiot. None of that mattered at all without Beth Ann and Kaylie. Even their dog Goldie, and the kitty that belonged to Frankie and Shawna were part of his family now.

After another hour of walking, he tried to look around, but darkness surrounded him. What if all the power was off? How would he see the houses? If the lightning would stop blinding him, he'd probably be able to see them just fine.

Hell, with all the rain, even the flashlight on the map was making it hard to see. It was a good thing it had a plastic coating. He heard a loud beating sound over the wind.

"What the heck?" He glanced up and saw a helicopter. Jesus, they must be rescuing someone. Maybe he was close to home. He watched them shining a light on the ground just ahead of him. *Wait.* They were pointing it right at him. He wasn't breaking the law, and they better not try to make him go back. He'd fight if he had to.

He ignored it and kept moving. After a few minutes, the damn thing was landing right on the road and having a hard time from the wind.

He watched, wondering if they were going to tell him to turn around. No way, he'd stand his ground. He hadn't come this far to be sent away. Screw that!

Once it landed, the door opened. A guy started running toward him. He was ready for a battle, and he took a stance.

"Kaylob." He heard a guy yelling his name.

* * * *

Beth Ann had given up hope that Kaylob would make it home. Maybe he would make it tomorrow. The evening had set in, and the storm had calmed down a bit so they had climbed out of the shower and made room on the floor. At least, nothing was pounding against the walls anymore. Thankfully, Kaylie was toasty, and Beth Ann was wrapped up in the comforter from their bed. She had food and a toilet, but no running water because of being on a well. Thank goodness they had those bottles to drink.

She had made the last trip outside with Goldie a while ago, and the water had receded in the front yard. Not a lot, but she didn't have to get so wet. She was grateful for the sweaters and warm sweats. The whole situation could have been worse, and it seemed that the beast of the storm was over. Her sweet dog and Sasha had warm blankets, too. They were buried underneath, both snoozing. Kaylie had fallen asleep nursing and was bundled up like a little angel.

Her stomach flipped upside down with worry about Kaylob. She tried to think positive. He more than likely couldn't make it down the roads and went back to his restaurant. If only the darn phone would work.

She turned down the radio and fluffed up her pillow. Maybe just for a few minutes, she'd lay her head down and try to get some rest. Never had she been in a storm this big. It had lasted the entire day. She closed her eyes and never felt herself drift off.

Sleepily, she opened her eyes and heard a noise. "What was that?" Sitting up, she almost bumped her head on the garbage can. She grabbed the flashlight and listened. What now? Was that a tornado? It sounded almost like a helicopter, but it had to be the wind again. She turned up the radio and heard a new song 'Muskrat Love' by Captain & Tennille. The music did nothing to calm her fragile nerves, she laid her head back down. Not even a second later, Goldie was up and barking, which woke up Kaylie.

"Goldie, no honey. We'll be okay." She went to the door and tried to calm her, but it did no good. She was scratching and wanted out.

"There is nothing out there, just blustery weather," she said to no avail. Goldie wouldn't listen. Maybe she wanted to go pee again. Darn it, she hated to walk through that water when it was dark.

"Beth Ann!" She heard the sweetest voice ever.

Oh my gosh. "Kaylob."

She ran down the hallway and saw him running toward her. "Baby, you're safe." He pulled her into his arms. Goldie was running around, wagging her tail and barking.

She glanced over toward the front door and saw Johnny. "Was that a helicopter?" Beth Ann asked as she released Kaylob.

"Yes." Kaylob nodded. "Compliments from Blake." He reached down, giving Goldie a hug and kissing her head.

"Where's your truck?" she asked. "You're soaking wet."

"That's a long story and yes, I need to change. Right now, I'm just glad to be home."

"I'm glad too," she said and smiled at Johnny. "I wish I could offer you some coffee. I do have bottled water."

He laughed. "No need, Mrs. B. I'm just glad you're safe."

"Where's my baby girl?" Kaylob asked.

"She's in the bathroom." She waved for them to follow.

They all went down the hall using Kaylob's flashlight, then walked into the lightly lit bathroom with Kaylie in her playpen, staring up at her mobile.

Kaylob bent over and touched her head. "My baby girl." His lip trembled. "I was so worried. I can't pick her up yet. I need to change."

Johnny cleared his throat. "She's a doll face." He grinned. "Well, do you guys want to go into town and stay in a hotel?"

"No," they said in unison.

Beth Ann added, "We have a cat and our dog." She stroked Goldie's head.

"That's no problem; we can take them too."

"We can camp out here tonight." Kaylob shook his head. "Hopefully, we'll hear from Frankie and Shawna, if the phones ever start working. If they can't get through they might call you guys."

"Okay, if they do, I'll let them know you're safe. It looks like the worst is over. Give me or Blake a call when your phone is back on," Johnny said.

"Sure thing." Kaylob shook his hand. "Thank you again for coming to find me. It was pretty rough out there."

Johnny nodded. "See you two's later." He kissed Beth Ann's cheek and left the house.

Beth Ann heard them take off and wondered what the neighbors would think. She prayed everyone had managed through this storm. "I hope the people around here are safe."

"From what we saw when we came in, it looked like some downed trees and lines, but the houses are all still standing. I hope Shawna and Frankie found a safe place to stay."

"I'm sure they did." Beth Ann took his hand and called Goldie in the bathroom.

"Why don't you go and change before you freeze to death?" she said to Kaylob.

"Good idea." He leaned down and kissed her gently on the lips. "I can't tell you how much I worried, but once again," he waved around,

"You proved that you are amazing at survival. I'm proud of you."

Beth Ann felt herself blush a bit. "Thank you, honey, but I was scared."

"But look what you did here. You kept everyone safe."

Chapter Eight

Beth Ann awoke to the sound of hammering and opened her eyes. It must be Kaylob doing something because he wasn't next to her. He had held her all night. Every time Kaylie stirred, he was up checking on her.

Since they were kids, Kaylob had always been protective. Now Beth Ann was the same way. She'd do what she had to do to protect her family.

"Burr." It was a bit chilly. She wrapped the blanket tighter around her shoulders. Kaylie was making cute little sounds, so Beth Ann stood and picked up her precious bundle. She was dry and warm. Kaylob must have changed her and been really quiet, or she was just so tired that she slept through any noise.

Once again, she heard the banging noise. She headed out to the kitchen to see what was going on.

It didn't take her long to find out. Kaylob was using plywood to board up the kitchen windows. He also had a fire going. She almost sailed over to the flames. Holy wow, it felt good.

Goldie and Sasha were running around and playing, like they knew everything was going back to normal. They had both been through a lot from the storm too, poor babies.

Beth Ann walked around while she held Kaylie, surveying the rest of the house. Other than the kitchen, things were almost normal. There were some leaves and twigs scattered about in the formal dining and living room. But nothing that couldn't be cleaned. The kitchen, on the other hand, was a flooded and muddy mess. Debris was strewn around the counters. Leaves covered the floor with some pieces of the tree. Even some garbage had blown inside.

"What a mess." She glanced around. The paint had been chipped off the wall in some areas. "What the heck is this?" She picked it up, realizing it was a piece of their roof.

A few minutes later, she saw Kaylob put the last piece of plywood across the window. The lights were still not on, but at least he got the place sealed up.

Kaylob walked in and washed his hands with bottled water. "Hey, baby, that will stop the wind. Let me see my baby girl." He leaned in for a kiss and took Kaylie in his arms. "Look how precious." He smiled at Beth Ann. "I love you both so much."

"We love you too, honey." She stood on her toes and gave him a kiss. "Now, I'm going to get the playpen for Kaylie and feed her, then get to cleaning this kitchen. What a mess."

Kaylob nodded. "I think our insurance will cover to have everything professionally done. Plus, they will have to get the roof fixed."

"That's good, but I'd like to at least get some of the stuff off the floor and counters wiped down."

"I'll help." Kaylob looked around. "I hope the road will be open soon and the power back on. According to our neighbors, however, the road is washed out and they don't know how soon we'll have power again. Could be a few more days. Holy hell …" Kaylob's eyes got wide.

"What?" Beth Ann asked.

"I think Shawna has a generator. I remember her saying that she bought one because when she was picking out her paint for the kitchen, some guy told her that every house should have one. I laughed at her, and now the laugh is on me. I'm going to go check in her garage."

Sure enough, an hour later, Kaylob hooked up a backup generator. It was great and turned on the fridge and the water pump. They even had a few lights and the water heater. The thing was still in a box, but it had instructions on how to use it, thank goodness. They didn't need heat with the fireplaces. They had never used the one in the formal living room, but tonight, they would.

Throughout the day, they kept checking the phone. Beth Ann knew her family was more than likely worried sick, and she had a feeling that Frankie and Shawna were staying in a hotel somewhere in town.

All she and Kaylob could do was wait it out and clean up. By early afternoon, Kaylob had heated up some casseroles and a lot of pizzas. He had divided them up between the neighbors and left to go deliver them.

A while later, Kaylob walked into the mudroom. "Baby, I'm home."

Beth Ann approached the doorway and watched Kaylob pulling off his muddy boots.

"It's all delivered and the kids were especially happy with the hot pizza." He glanced up and smiled.

"I bet they were. So is everyone okay?"

"Yes, a little shaken up. But good. They kept saying how sorry they were for not checking on you." He set his boots on a towel. "If anything like that happens again, they'll come and make sure you're okay."

Beth Ann nodded. "That's good to know."

An hour later, the guy three houses down brought some tarp for the roof. He owned a large construction company and helped Kaylob put it in place. It was starting to rain lightly and it would help to prevent water damage, so long as no super high winds kicked up again.

The house was warm, they had food and water. If the storms would just stay away and the roads would open, things could get back to normal.

* * * *

The next morning, Ginger left the hospital and was excited to go see Millie. When she had called her and said she was coming for breakfast, there was no missing the excitement in her voice. Funny, she sounded younger.

Ginger pulled up to the hotel and the darn wind was blowing with a vengeance. Once she arrived at the double glass doors, a lady was standing there and let her in.

"Thank you so much," Ginger said with a smile and started toward Millie's hotel room. Wait a minute … something about the lady made her turn around.

Their gaze met and clung to each other. "Millie?" Ginger couldn't believe it. She looked so much younger, maybe in her early fifties, with lovely chestnut hair and golden highlights.

"Yes, dear." She had a sparkle of laughter in her green eyes. "It's me."

"Wow. You look incredible." She couldn't believe what she was seeing. "Millie, you have green eyes."

"Yes dear, they've always been a hazel green with specks of gray." Millie chuckled.

"I thought they were gray," she explained.

Ginger was amazed at how she looked, dressed in a paisley skirt with a tan blouse and a bow on the front. Her hair was neatly trimmed. She had some light makeup on and a touch of peach lipstick.

"You are beautiful." Ginger swallowed.

"Well, thank you, dear. I guess I clean up pretty good." She opened her arms to Ginger. "Now, I can hug you and feel like a normal person." They hugged and released.

Ginger couldn't help but stare. "I didn't bring those clothes over, were they yours?"

Millie nodded. "I was able to wash and clean some of my own clothes. I had these before I became homeless." Sadness seemed to fill her eyes. "I couldn't wear them because they were moldy and smelled bad from getting wet. But I kept them in plastic, in my grocery bag. I had to wash them three times to get the odor out."

"Well ..." Ginger threaded her arm through Millie's. "You smell wonderful now."

Together, arm in arm they almost skipped down the hallway. The minute the door opened, Ginger got a whiff of something wonderful. "Wow, something smells great."

Millie waved toward the kitchen. "It's all ready. I made gravy and biscuits, omelets, and hash browns."

"It looks wonderful." Ginger glanced around and noticed there was also orange juice with fresh coffee and all the condiments. "This place is so clean. If I cooked all this, I'm afraid the place would be a mess."

Millie chuckled. "I actually had fun cleaning up."

Ginger picked up her fork and took a bite. "Oh heavens. This omelet is scrumptious." She meant it. It was the best she'd ever tasted. "What did you do? I've seriously never tasted anything so good."

"Oh, just some special spices and a few little secrets." Millie smiled.

"Did you used to cook a lot before you were homeless?"

"Yes, I worked for a small restaurant for many years and stopped to raise my ..." She swallowed hard, then picked up her coffee and took a small sip. "Well, I'm just so happy you're enjoying breakfast."

It was clear she didn't want to talk about her past, so Ginger let it drop. The one thing Ginger knew was when someone had been hurt, they had to talk about it on their own time frame.

"I'm afraid I'm not a great cook," Ginger admitted. "I can cook some things okay, but I'm so limited in how many dishes I can make."

"Well, you know what they say. Practice makes progress." She smiled.

Ginger nodded. "I'll have to remember that. I've never heard anyone say it that way before." She could feel Millie staring at her.

When their eyes met, Millie's softened. "Do you feel like telling me about those marks on your neck?"

So while they ate breakfast, Ginger shared every detail with her new friend. She also told her about Blake. "He's the most wonderful man I've ever met." Ginger sighed.

"Well, Blake sounds like a good man." Millie took another sip of her coffee. "I am so proud of him for helping you, and I don't even know him. I'm also grateful for what he's done for me."

"He's something else, and I know you will love him when you meet him."

"Well, my dear." Millie took her hand. "It sounds like you do." She paused. "Love him, I mean."

Ginger nodded. "I do. From the first moment I saw him."

They ended up having a wonderful morning. Ginger was sure there would be many more. There was no doubt in her mind that Millie had a long history. Maybe someday, she'd be able to share.

As soon as she got Blake settled comfortably, she would invite Millie over for dinner. Right now, she had to go help get everything set up for his arrival.

* * * *

It was damn near evening when Blake was released from the hospital. The minute he and Johnny stepped outside, the paparazzi surrounded him. "Shit." He glanced up at Johnny as the damn idiots started flashing their cameras. "You were right; we should have gone out the back way." Blake shook his head in disbelief.

Johnny had warned him, but Blake thought it would just be a couple of reporters. He hadn't expected anything like this.

"Mr. Tanner, Mr. Tanner, is it true you were involved with a married woman?" They swarmed him like a bunch of hungry hornets.

"How long has the affair been going on?" A guy blocked their path and clicked his camera, blinding Blake with the flashing lights. "How do you feel about being called a homewrecker?"

Blake covered his forearm over his face. "Do you mind getting the damn camera out of my face?" If Blake could walk, he would have punched the asshole right between the eyes.

"Her husband is the one who shot you—is that right?" someone yelled. "Where is his wife staying? Are you in love with her?"

Christ all mighty, his world was spinning out of control. "I have no comment. Y'all have a nice day." He gritted his teeth.

Johnny shoved the one reporter out of the way. "One more click and I'll shove that camera up your ..." he said and glared. He rushed Blake to the van.

That didn't stop them. "Mr. Tanner, will you walk again? What's your relationship with this married woman? Is it true you met in a bar? Where are you staying?"

Johnny stopped and glared again. "What part of no comment don't you get?"

When they finally got in the van and closed the doors, the snakes were still snapping photos. He'd never been so ecstatic to get away from them in his life.

Relief washed over him when Johnny pulled into the driveway at the Colony House. He drove around the back and pulled into the private parking. The sign read La CASA Residence. Thank goodness, paparazzi were not allowed on private property. It didn't appear they were followed, but one never knew when they were slithering around.

Blake stared at the building they pulled up to. "I've never seen this one."

"That's because it's brand new, and they finished everything while you were in the hospital. I think you'll find it perfect." He parked and turned off the engine.

Blake saw two people step out front—one was Ginger and the other was a tall blonde. "Great, a welcome home for the handicap." That was when he saw Frankie and Shawna walk out too.

They all smiled and waved. The minute Johnny opened the door, Blake could feel the wind had picked up again, but before he could say anything, Johnny got his jacket.

"Here you go boss." He helped him put it on.

"This place is gigantic." Johnny lifted him into his wheelchair. "It has four bedrooms, three baths, and the master suite is on the bottom floor and handicapped, without looking like it." He smiled. "It also has a baby grand piano, two fireplaces, and Ginger plays beautifully. I'm surprised she hasn't done anything professionally. The back has a private pool and hot tub." He arched an eyebrow. "You have one nurse, one physical therapist to help Ginger, and a private cook and housekeeper. They are going to whip you back into shape."

"Sounds like a real orgy," Blake said sarcastically.

Johnny cracked up. "Well, boss, look at the blonde standing with Ginger. Maybe you'll enjoy her whip."

"Don't let Dana hear you say that. Where is she?"

"Still putting some of your clothes away that she picked up from the townhouse."

Frankie and Shawna approached while Ginger stood on the front porch talking to the blonde.

"Hey, there buddy." Frankie shook his hand and his gorgeous wife leaned down and kissed his cheek.

Shawna straightened up. "Thank you, Blake, for helping Beth Ann and Kaylob. We were so worried. Johnny told us they are home safe with some minor damage to their house. I guess ours is still standing."

"No problem." He winked. "I still can't figure out how Frankie landed you." He chuckled.

"Me either," Shawna teased.

"You must mean how she landed me." Frankie pulled her close, and they both laughed. "We tried to get home," Frankie said. "But the roads were closed. I hope it's okay that we stayed here. We just rented a suite and are going to stay over there." He pointed. "In Suite A2 until the roads open."

"You could have just stayed right here again," Blake said.

"You have a house full, and Shawna is still experiencing some morning sickness. So we needed to get a room to ourselves. As a matter of fact, she needs to go lay down."

Blake studied Shawna. She did look a bit green and extremely pregnant.

"Okay," Blake said. "I'm glad Beth Ann and Kaylob are good. Shawna, I hope you feel better soon."

"Thank you," she said. Her eyes seemed to be pleading with Frankie.

"Okay, thanks again, Blake. Sorry, but I need to get her in the room."

Blake and Johnny watched as they hurried toward the other side of the building. Frankie was holding Shawna's back, then paused and picked her up into his arms. "Twins must be tough to carry around," Blake said and worried.

"She didn't look like she felt good at all," Johnny replied.

Before Blake could respond, Dana came running out the door. "You're home. Yay!" She gave him a giant hug and kissed his cheek. He was surprised to see her shed a few tears. "I've missed you, Blake."

"I've missed you too, little darlin." They hugged, and Blake pointed at her new haircut. "Cute."

She touched her new style. "Johnny loves it."

Johnny released the wheelchair brakes. "You bet I do. Let's get you inside. It's starting to drizzle again." He pushed Blake up the ramp.

The minute they entered, Blake was surprised. There was nothing about the place that came across as disabled. The fireplace was on and flames flickered, bathing the room with a special glow. Prints of flowers decorated the walls, making it feel like a home. The couches were overstuffed and set across from each other near the fireplace. Johnny pushed him across the hardwood floors with ease, and placed him near the flames.

"This place is really large," Blake said as he looked around.

After a few seconds, Blake noticed almost everyone had joined him in the living room. He could feel them studying him. Hell, he just wanted to stand up and tell everyone that it was all a practical joke and his legs worked fine. But he couldn't because his goddamn legs wouldn't do shit.

Ginger finally broke the ice. "Dinner smells divine. It's Steak Diane, twice-baked potatoes, and some sautéed mushrooms, along with asparagus."

Blake nodded. "Sounds great."

Johnny took Dana's hand. "Actually, boss, we were going to go back home tonight, but if you need us, we'll come right back. We want to check on Dana's house and make sure it's still standing."

"Sure, go ahead. If I need you, I'll call."

After he said his goodbyes to Dana and Johnny, the blonde lady came around the corner.

"Everything is all set up for you tonight, Mr. Tanner," she announced, her tone professional.

"Excuse me, let's start this over. Call me Blake. What's your name?"

"Oh, sorry," Ginger spoke up. "I should have introduced you. This is Krista. She is your private nurse and will be here all the time. She is living in with us."

Krista stuck out her hand. "Hello, Blake."

"Nice to meet you, Krista."

She nodded. "I am going to retire to my room, but when you're ready for bed, I'll return."

"Don't you want some dinner?" Ginger asked.

Krista shook her head. "I'm afraid the cook fed me earlier, and I ate way too much." She glanced between Ginger and Blake. "But if you need any help, please call me."

Blake gave her a nod. "Will do."

Ginger walked behind him. "Let's go eat. By the way, the other lady you saw is your private housekeeper, her name is Samantha and she likes to be called Sam. She's in the kitchen right now and a very nice lady too." She released the brake and pushed him into the formal dining area.

"Glad to have something besides hospital food." He inhaled the incredible aroma.

Ginger stuck her nose in the air. "No kidding. Marty said he wanted to do all the cooking for you and knows what you like. He said you use to hang out here a lot."

"I did. There was a time I didn't have my townhouse, and this was

83

my second home. Well, actually my first. Marty always took good care of my meals."

Ginger grinned. "I'm going to let him know we're ready."

A while later, Marty carried out the food. It was every bit as good as usual. Blake knew he shouldn't eat too much, but after being in the hospital and ingesting the food there, he couldn't help himself.

When they finished eating, Ginger stood. "What would you like to do?" She started gathering the dishes and turned to face him.

Blake met her gaze. "I'm thinking I should have gone to a special hospital. Maybe coming here was not such a good idea."

"Why?" Ginger sat down in the chair again.

"I want to be honest, darlin, and the truth is, I'm not sure how you will feel about me, if you work with me."

"I feel how I feel, Blake. I told you in the hospital. I'm in love with you."

"Yes, you did." He worked up a smile.

"Blake, you've never responded to that. How do you feel about me being in love with you?"

"I don't know, Ginger. Love scares the shit out of me."

She reached out and touched his hand. "I understand. I'm just glad you know how I feel, and I'm glad you didn't say it back. I don't want you to say it because you feel obligated."

"Don't worry, I would never do that. Besides, I do have deep feelings, but I'm not ready to talk about anything like that right now."

"Got it." Ginger nodded. "No pressure. We don't have to bring it up again until you're ready, or ever. I do want to share about Millie. Blake, she looks amazing. She's not even as old as I thought she was."

"That's great news. I can't wait to meet her." He smiled. Blake didn't know what to say about anything else other than Millie. He wasn't ready to look into his heart yet. Right now, he just needed to worry about healing his body, and that was all he could focus on. Not to mention, he'd be having some stranger helping him into bed. Usually, when a strange woman undressed him, it had been for other reasons. Especially some tall, leggy blonde with piercing hazel eyes.

* * * *

Ginger awoke to the sound of her alarm clock with a new sense of purpose. Today was Saturday, and the first early morning she'd be helping Blake. At least as a physical therapist. Soon as she was done, she was going to call Millie and check up on her and figure out what day they could invite her over.

Taylor would be Blake's head physical therapist. Johnny and Dana had hired him after interviewing about a hundred others. She was hoping to learn a lot since he'd been doing this for twenty-five years.

When Ginger had rolled him into his bedroom last night, there was no missing the uncomfortable look in his eyes. She couldn't help but wonder how he'd done with Krista.

Right now, she needed to get up and prepare for her day. She sat on the edge of the bed and took a deep breath. Her heart was filled with so much happiness. One big reason was her new friends, new job, and Blake. Then for no good reason, her mind shifted to Arnold, who would hopefully be in prison for the rest of his life. Tears stung her eyes when she thought about her baby sister, Gina telling her, *"Father went to see Arnold in prison and is helping pay for his defense."* This was still just as hard to accept now as it was weeks ago. Why would her so-called father blame her because Arnold shot people.

Their dad had called her a harlot for seeing another man. He wouldn't listen, nor did he seem to care that Arnold had beat her and locked her up. Even when Gina had tried to tell him about the burn marks, it did no good.

Ginger had some big questions; like where was her dad getting all this money? Since when did he ever have that kind of cash flow?

The biggest disappointment was her mother. She had actually called and begged her to give Arnold another chance. How dare she say he was going to get therapy and anger management? Right, go back to a man who beat her on a regular basis. She had a feeling her dad was there, telling her mom what to say.

Now that Arnold was in jail, she was safe and so was her family. There was no way she'd ever go back to him. All she wanted was a divorce and a fresh, new start. For the first time since she could remember, she was ready to soar free, spread her wings, and fly. Nobody would ever keep her down again.

The truth was, she might also have to divorce her parents. At least she had her sister. That meant a lot. Her grandparents were gone on both sides, but now she had friends and they were like family.

However, what if Arnold got out and came after her?

Okay, enough. She stepped into the warm, inviting shower. Ah, it felt so good. "Only positive thoughts."

Once she climbed out, dried off, and got dressed, she headed downstairs to the rehab room. They had replaced the furniture with all the things Blake would need to physically work out his body. Afterwards, they'd get him in the enclosed pool out back. This place had it all and then some.

There was a knock at the door. The housekeeper hurried to answer it.

It was Taylor, the physical therapist. He carried a leather bag and appeared extra tall today.

"Good morning, you're bright and early," Ginger greeted.

"I like to get here a tad ahead of time to get everything set up." His smile reached his chocolate brown eyes.

Ginger waved him into the extra-large room.

He glanced around and set his bag down. "This is great." He ran his fingers through his sandy blond hair. "Looks like they got a lot done, and it appears we have the tables and all the rehabilitation equipment we need."

Ginger nodded. "I'm excited to get started." Before she could finish, Marty came in carrying trays of food.

"I'm going to set this down at the little breakfast table and be on my way," Marty said, just as the housekeeper came in with a tray too.

"Wow! Thank you. Blake should be here any minute." Ginger was grateful.

"You're welcome," Marty said as he got everything ready.

"It does smell scrumptious." Ginger inhaled the aroma. "Yummy."

Marty and the housekeeper nodded, then exited the room. A few seconds later, she heard the sound of Blake's wheelchair.

"Good morning, Ginger, and you must be Taylor," Blake said. "This is Krista, my private nurse."

"Hi, Krista. Mr. Tanner, it's great to meet you." Taylor stepped forward and shook his hand.

"Please, call me Blake. Y'all are trying to make me feel old." He chuckled. "Krista, would you like some breakfast?"

"Yes, but would it be okay if I took it to my room? I need to make a few phone calls."

"Of course," Blake agreed.

After the wonderful breakfast and relaxing for a bit, they got ready to work with Blake. Ginger felt like someone was jumping rope in her stomach. She was a fist of nerves.

Taylor glanced between Blake and Ginger. "Okay, Blake it's been thirty minutes, so, we are going to start with some chair exercises today."

Blake nodded, and Ginger helped Taylor transfer him into the chair. She could see him wince, which made her heart sink. Could she do this with him? What if she made him fall or didn't do things right?

Chapter Nine

Blake felt a sharp pain in his hip when they transferred him, but he tried not to show it. However, he was pretty sure Ginger had noticed.

"Okay," Taylor said. "We are going to start by you sitting upright with your feet planted flat on the floor."

Ginger got down and helped to place his feet in the right direction. "There you go."

Taylor pointed. "Now, fold your hands over your left upper thigh. Ginger, you'll need to keep his knee bent this time, until he can do it."

"How long will it be before I can do it on my own?" Blake asked. He wanted a date and wanted it now.

Taylor shrugged. "Well now, that all depends on you."

"You really expect me to do this shit?" Blake snarled. "I could say it's no problem, but that would be a big hat and no cattle."

"Well, cowboy, we need to get the cattle," Taylor said, sounding calm and patient. "I want you to try to flex your hip and lift your thigh upward, while simultaneously pressing your hands down on your upper leg. If you can't do it, then we do it for you to help build those muscles back up. We have to retrain your hips."

"Retrain my hips." He puffed out. "Just what the hell does that mean?"

He felt like pouring a glass of whiskey and getting drunk. "To hell with this." He scowled and let out a deep breath. He couldn't move anything.

"Come on, Blake." Taylor smiled. "You have to at least try."

After about twenty minutes, Blake looked up at the ceiling, folded his arms, and sighed.

Ginger gave an exaggerated groan. "Oh jeez, knock it off, Blake

Tanner." She rolled her eyes.

The thought crossed his mind that he could just quit for the day. They couldn't make him do anything. So he let them do most of the work and kept sighing.

After what felt like an hour of torture, Taylor's voice went up a notch. "Blake, tighten your abdominal muscles and try to raise your own leg. Stop letting Ginger do it for you."

"Does it look like I can lift my leg?" Blake shot back. "Not everyone in this room is muscle bound." He glared at Taylor.

"You're not trying and if you don't, this is going to take us forever. You've already had physical therapy for weeks. Show me what you've got and stop being a pansy," Taylor demanded.

Ginger stepped back and arched a brow, placing her hands on her hips and nodding in agreement.

"Wait, I could just say screw this and not do it period," Blake said, raising his voice.

"So you can stay in this wheelchair and feel sorry for yourself?" Taylor stood his ground.

"Screw you. In case you haven't noticed, I'm paralyzed."

"Okay, cowboy. If that's all you want is to stay in this woe-is-me attitude." He shrugged. "You can keep acting like this and stay in the wheelchair. We can't force you to buck it up and act like a man."

"Kiss my ass and go to hell." Blake used every bit of his strength. Jesus, it was hard, but for the first time, he was able to lift his leg. Not very much, but he did it.

Ginger let out a squeal. "Look at that." She pointed. "You did it."

Taylor winked. "See, I knew you had it in you."

Damn it to hell, Blake felt tears fill his eyes. He wasn't about to cry, so he swallowed. "Thanks guys, I was acting like an ass."

Ginger bent down and kissed his cheek. "I'm proud of you." Her eyes sparkled.

"Now," Taylor said. "Let's get this cowboy back on the horse again." They all laughed.

After another two hours of working out and swimming, Blake felt like he was going to pass out. Every bit of him was worn out.

"Okay, it's been a long morning. I'm ready for lunch and a nap,"

Blake said. "You two beat me up today."

Taylor stopped and gave him a pointed look. "You ain't seen nothing yet. Remember, you are doing a set of fifteen repetitions on each leg, three times each, before today is over."

"What?" Blake frowned and said a shit load of curses under his breath. "I think I've done enough for one day."

Before they could finish the argument, Blake heard a voice he recognized. Being that he'd brought her here with him a few times, the front desk knew her well.

"Blake, darling, I just saw the newspapers and read about you in some magazine. I went to your place and found out from your neighbors where you were." Celise crossed the room and threw her arms around him.

He about swallowed his tongue and had to find his voice. Not to mention the fact that Ginger's eyes were shooting daggers. Even more so when she hugged him, pulling his face right smack dab into her busty chest.

"Celise, what a surprise." He gave his best innocent look and a half shrug to Ginger, who had her hands on her hips.

"I have my suitcase. I am going to stay here and help out." She straightened up and glanced around. "Oh, hi, I hope I'm not interrupting something. You both must be his physical therapists." She glanced between Ginger and Taylor. "I'm …"

"Celise, I heard," Ginger interrupted. She continued with a sarcastic tone. "We were doing physical therapy, but we're done for a while. Blake was just getting ready to eat and take a nap. Weren't you, darling?"

Blake's heart raced while sweat formed on his brow. He was pretty damn sure it wasn't from working out.

Celise ignored the remark and turned back. "I also wanted to pick up a couple of my dresses that I left at your townhouse. But that's not a worry, I have plenty." She turned and smiled at Ginger. "I'm here, what can I do to help? Where can I put down my bag? I'll stay as long as needed." She leaned down and placed a big, wet kiss on Blake's mouth.

Taylor interrupted. "I'm heading out." He held his bag and wore a sly grin. "See you later this afternoon." He turned and left.

Celise glanced at Ginger. "Oh, I suppose you have to head out also. But don't worry; I'll take really good care of him." She ran her fingers down his neck. "He just needs some tender loving care, and well …" She chuckled. "I'm certainly good at doing that."

Blake removed her hand, but she ignored it.

Blake wanted to run away, with Ginger glaring between him and Celise. Even though he didn't have much sensation, he sure as shit felt something crawling down his spine.

When Celise kissed his cheek again, he could smell the scent of musk she always wore. Springing back the memory of the time she showed up at his townhouse with nothing underneath her coat. She had helped him forget all about Beth Ann. The woman had a way with her fingers and that mouth. He glanced at her lips, remembering all she could do.

"Uh, well, it's like this. Ginger stays here full time, and I have a nurse and housekeeper. There aren't any spare bedrooms."

"Oh, no problem, I'll stay in your room. I'm sure the hotel has a spare bed or something. I could always try to sleep in bed with you."

Ginger's eyes narrowed. Blake had to do something fast. "No, I'm really good. I have all the care I need."

"Oh, but darling, there are other things that you need."

"What I need is for you to leave, and I'll call you later. It's very nice of you to want to help, but right now, I'm covered."

"Oh poo," she pouted. "I'll just have lunch with you then, and I'll come back later."

Blake gave Ginger a half shrug and watched her hands drop from her hips.

"Well," Ginger said. "I guess my job is done here for a while. I'll go tell the nurse and the cook to get lunch ready for the two of you." She whisked around and left the room.

"I'll go wash my hands and freshen up." Celise kissed his lips again and vanished.

"Shit," Blake said, along with other words that inundated his brain. Ginger was pissed, and he was in a pickle.

Celise had left town to be with her sister who was having a baby. They had spent a few weeks off and on together, mostly in bed. Their relationship had been a sex thing and nothing more. Of course, it had always been hot and steamy. She did things to him he wouldn't soon forget. The fact was that he'd always loved sex with her the most—until Ginger.

Ginger didn't have the overall knowledge that Celise did, but she had something damn special. A tenderness, and heart as big as a full moon. There was also that stubborn streak and a flare in her style. Even the way Ginger walked into a room took away his ability to think straight. He had deep feelings for Ginger and none for Celise. He liked her as a person, a friend with perks. The truth was, if he hadn't been America's most eligible bachelor with a private plane, she wouldn't have glanced his way. Whereas Ginger didn't know who the hell he was. She had liked him for him, well, maybe for a few other assets. He smiled. Now, as he watched Celise strut back into the room with her long legs and her oh-so-fine body, he knew there was only one thing he could do.

He met her gaze. "Celise. We need to talk."

* * * *

That afternoon, Beth Ann watched Kaylie sleep and could hear Kaylob outside cleaning up the yard. He was trying to get rid of some of the tree branches from the storm. The power had come back on, and she was sure as heck happy about that.

Beth Ann heard a car pull up and a familiar voice. "We made it home finally." It was Frankie.

"Yay! They're home." Beth Ann hurried out on the back steps, but the wind slapped her a good one, so she ran inside to the family room by the fire. She'd wait for them to come in.

Goldie was barking and wagging her tail, while Sasha just sat by the blaze, not wanting to move. Beth Ann could have sworn Goldie was trying to tell her that her parents were home.

"Goldie, be quiet. Kaylie is sleeping."

Shawna walked in. "Where's my favorite sister-in-law?" she called out. "I need to take off my shoes. It's still a muddy mess out there, and that wind is ferocious."

Beth Ann went into the kitchen, watching Shawna put on a pair of slippers she had left there. When she glanced up at Beth Ann, she smiled.

"I'm so glad I left these here, and I'm happy you're okay." She moved over to Beth Ann, and they embraced.

"I was worried about you guys," Beth Ann said as she released her.

"What an awful storm. We ended up spending one night in Blake's room, at some really fancy Ritz, before he got home. That place even has a baby grand piano and an entertainment room."

"Sounds like Blake—he always liked that stuff. When we were together, he used to get upset with me for going to second hand stores." She laughed.

"Really?" Shawna tilted her head.

"Yeah. One time, we had to go on TV and explain why I did that. The paparazzi were always spying on me. It was awful."

"I couldn't handle that." Shawna frowned. "It was hard enough living at home in the castle. People expect you to dress a certain way and be all refined and classy."

"Let's get some coffee and get a snack." Beth Ann laughed then pointed. "Then let's sit in the family room by the fire. Kaylob boarded up the kitchen windows, but it's still drafty."

"Wow, the glass was broken. How scary. I heard you were here by yourself, and Blake had to help Kaylob get home."

"Yes, it was pretty scary, but your generator sure helped while the power was out."

"I'm sorry you went through that, but I'm glad you were able to hook it up."

"We were all okay," Beth Ann said. "But I'm worried about you. You're a little pale."

"I know. I've been throwing up again. Almost daily." She left the kitchen and went into the family room. "Blake looked good though. He told us he moved his legs," she said from the next room.

"Wow! That is good news. Ginger is good for him." She picked up the coffee and cookies, placing them on a tray and carrying it into the family room.

"Well ..." Shawna arched a brow while Beth Ann set everything down and sat next to her on the couch.

"What?" Beth Ann asked.

"There was another girl there named Celise when we stopped to say goodbye. She was having lunch with Blake. I knew the minute Ginger answered the door that she didn't look happy. The girl was tall, dark, and stunning."

"Oh, I remember running into her once at a dinner party. She had a thing for Blake, but many other women did."

"Was that hard on you?"

"No." Beth Ann shook her head. "I really didn't pay much attention, and I knew he'd never cheat. Although, if that had been Kaylob, holy tantrum alert." They both cracked up.

"Well, we left, but Frankie got in the doghouse about it." She huffed.

"Uh-oh, what did he do?"

"He said he'd hate to be in Blake's shoes and have to choose which one of the foxes he wanted to be with."

"Oh, that guy. He speaks before he thinks," Beth Ann said.

"Yes, he knew he put his foot in his mouth by the look on my face. He corrected himself and said, 'Oh, I meant Blake. I'd never have a hard time choosing my wife over any other woman.'"

"I'm sure that's true, however, Blake better be careful. Ginger doesn't seem like the kind of lady who will play games or put up with that stuff."

"I agree. She's been through enough and put up with way too much abuse." Shawna's eyes fell. "I hope Blake realizes that." She took a sip of her coffee and a tiny bite of the cookie. After she swallowed, she said, "Thank you, this is great. Speaking of Ginger, did you hear about what she and Blake are doing for a homeless woman? Her name is Mildred. I was in tears when Ginger told me the story."

"No, tell me." Beth Ann wanted to hear. She'd always had a soft spot for people who had no home. She knew darn well what that felt like.

By the time Shawna was done sharing, Beth Ann's eyes held unshed tears. "I think I just grew more in love with Ginger, and I'm so proud of Blake. Even with everything he's going through, he took the time to help a stranger." She swallowed hard.

Shawna nodded. "I know. Now, tell me about your adventure before I start crying again."

By the time Beth Ann finished sharing her story, Frankie and

Kaylob entered the room.

"Hi guys," Beth Ann said.

Frankie crossed the room and gave Beth Ann a hug. "I'm so glad you stayed safe. Where is Kaylie?"

"She's down for a nap, but she should be waking up soon."

"Our house looks great inside, but the yard is a mess. At least the power is working fine," Frankie said. "We have pieces of your roof and other debris all over the place."

"We didn't see anything out of order except the yard," Beth Ann said. "There's a whole pot of coffee. Want me to get you guys a cup?"

"Actually …" Shawna stood. "I need to go lay down. I didn't sleep well last night."

Beth Ann noticed she looked shaky on her feet. "Shawna, I think you need to go back and see the doctor. Want me to make you an appointment? If Frankie has to work, I'll take you."

Kaylob nodded. "You do look a little pale, sis."

"I agree," Frankie said with a flicker of worry in his eyes.

Shawna gave Kaylob a kiss on his cheek. "I'm just tired and need a long nap. This whole storm thing was stressful, but yes, I should see the doctor. Thank you, Beth Ann. That would be great."

"True and this was a bad one," Beth Ann said.

"Come on, Sasha," Shawna called her kitty that was still in front of the fire. The cat lay without a care in the world.

Frankie turned and met Beth Ann's gaze. She could see the concern glide across his face. "Thank you, Beth Ann. I do have to return to work on Monday, and I really want her to go see the doc."

"No problem." Beth Ann assured, but she had a sense of worry, too. "Why don't you just come and get Sasha later? She hasn't wanted to leave that fireplace since Kaylob got it started."

"Alright." Shawna laughed. "I can tell how much she missed us."

Kaylob turned around and stared at Beth Ann after they were gone. "I hope everything is okay."

"I think it is." She moved closer and wrapped her arms around his waist. "Remember how tired I got with one? She's carrying two and just had to stay away from home for a few days. By the way, I asked Lillian about your birth father's blood pressure and issues in the family."

"And?"

"She said your dad never did, but her father had issues. I guess he had a sweet tooth too."

"That's good to know." He glanced around. "We're all alone, and Kaylie is sleeping."

"Well, Mr. O'Brien, can I take advantage of you?" She stroked his arm.

"Oh, you better." He scooped her up and carried her back to the bedroom.

Once he put her down, she kissed his lips. "What about all the work outside? I don't want to use up all your energy."

"Believe me, baby, where you're concerned, I have all the energy I need and then some."

* * * *

One week later, Blake sat in the workout room waiting for Ginger and Taylor. Krista, his nurse, had helped him and done a great job. She was a fine-looking woman. However, these days the only person he cared about was Ginger, and she hadn't spoken to him much at all. Maybe it was because of Celise, but he'd sent her packing.

More than likely, she was through with his sorry ass. He couldn't blame her because his cheese had slid off his cracker, and that was putting it mildly. Just thinking about the night in the hotel with Ginger made him sweat. One night with her had been the hottest thing he'd ever experienced.

They had stayed up almost all night and, hot damn—*six* times. When had he ever been with someone that many times in one night? The answer was easy—never.

Nobody had ever stayed on his mind like she did. He couldn't forget the way he had made love to her against the wall, with just his touch. Jesus, she had come unraveled so fast and hard, it blew his mind just thinking about it.

With all that passion, why in the world did the word commitment feel like a noose around his neck? There was no way in hell that he was blaming her for the shooting. Arnold was a sick man, and Ginger had nothing to do with his insidious behavior.

The last few days she'd been acting like an employee, not even eating meals with him, opting to take them in her room instead. Thinking about losing her made his chest tighten.

"Good morning, Blake," Ginger said with a cool tone. "I hope you're feeling well this morning."

Their eyes met. "And how about you?" Blake asked.

"Really well, thank you. I just got off the phone with Millie. She's made some new friends at the senior center and is doing really well. She said she fits in more now and doesn't feel so embarrassed."

Before he could reply, Taylor walked in. "Good morning."

Blake grumbled. "What's so good about it?"

"I can see your spirits are high again this morning. So, why don't we get started?"

"Do I have a choice?" He frowned.

Ginger snapped. "Oh brother! Stop your whining, and let's get moving."

Blake saluted and let out a long sigh.

Once again, he moved his legs and they even went higher.

"Look at you," Taylor said with a big smile. "You're going to be walking sooner than you thought."

Ginger nodded and gave him a small but sincere smile.

Blake was fully aware that his legs were much stronger. He was surprised he was able to stand and take some steps. Even if it was for only a few minutes, he felt proud to do it.

Three hours passed, and he was starving. Funny how doing these workouts made him hungrier than hiking or running ever did.

"Blake, this was a good day," Taylor said with a grin.

"You did great." Ginger picked up her bag. "I'll see you this afternoon."

"Ginger ..." She paused, but didn't turn around, so he continued. "Would you like to have lunch with me today?"

"Oh, thank you, but I have so much to do. I'm also going to meet Millie for lunch a little later." She swept out of the room.

"Oh man, you pissed someone off." Taylor looked toward the direction she left. "None of my business, but I do know an angry woman when I see one."

"No shit," he said. He stilled when he heard footsteps. Hoping it was her, he turned to look. Disappointment hit hard.

"Are you ready to take a shower?" his nurse asked.

"Sure, in about ten minutes." He tried his best to smile.

"I'll come back then." She nodded and left.

"I'll see you later, Taylor. Thanks for the workout."

Taylor moved across the room. As he was about to leave, he stopped. "You're welcome, and Blake?" Taylor turned around and stared at him.

"Yes." Blake waited.

"Flowers are good. Also, saying you're sorry might help. And inviting her new friend over for dinner might win you some big points." Taylor arched a brow. "See you later." He left the room.

"Flowers, sorry?" he complained out loud. He could invite Millie over for dinner. That was a good idea, since he wanted to meet her anyway.

However, why should he say he was sorry? He didn't do a damn thing. It sure as beans wasn't his fault that Celise decided to stop by. There was nothing serious with them. They were just good in bed together. What was the problem with that? He rolled himself over to the small table, opening the drawer to pull out his address book. Flowers were listed under gifts for clients. He never sent women flowers. Hell, he'd never even given Beth Ann any. He'd bought her a lot of gifts. But what was it about flowers and women? Did they really like that?

He dialed the number, but he hung up before they answered. What if she thought he wanted a commitment? Blake had grown accustomed to his life as a bachelor again. Well, he had been a little lonely on Christmas day. The truth was that he really cared about Ginger.

Ah hell, he dialed the number again. This time, he let it ring. "Wind Song Florist."

Blake spent the next ten minutes ordering the flowers. The florist asked what he wanted the card to say. He was lost for a minute, but decided to keep it simple.

Please forgive me and have dinner with me tomorrow night.

Now, if she would accept the peace offering and they could start enjoying each other's company again, he'd be a happy man. He missed having her around like before.

"Blake," Krista said. "Did you still want to shower first or have lunch? Would you like to eat in here or in the dining area?"

"I'll just have it in here. Afterwards, I'd like to take a shower and a nap before I work out again."

Krista nodded. A few minutes later, she brought back a tray of fresh homemade soup, a slice of bread, and a glass of lemonade that had little berries floating around inside. Why'd they do that? He had to make sure he didn't choke on the dang things.

Krista helped Blake into his bed after he showered. Once his head hit the pillow, he didn't remember falling asleep. Later on, he heard a voice and his eyes opened.

"Are you ready to work out or do you need a little more time?" Ginger lightly asked.

"No, no, I'm ready." He sat up. Realizing he'd done it too fast, he went backward. "Crap." His head was spinning.

Ginger was by his side in an instant. "Are you okay?"

"I just got up too fast." He tried again. This time, it was better.

"Maybe we've been working you too hard." Her eyes were filled with concern.

"No, I want to get back on my feet." He moved his own legs down on the floor. All he wanted was to be able to walk again this year.

"Thank you for the beautiful flowers." She leaned over and kissed his lips.

"You're welcome. Does that mean I'm forgiven?"

She nodded and kissed him again. Only this time, he used his hands to pull her closer. "I've missed you," Blake whispered, wanting to bury his nose in her neck. He loved the honey smell of her skin and the taste and feel of her soft, silky lips. "I was thinking we could invite Millie over for lunch or dinner. Whenever she wants to come. She's always welcome here."

"Oh, Blake, thank you. I'll call her. I've missed you too." Her eyes sparkled.

"Ahem." Blake glanced up and saw Kristi in the doorway. "I'm here to take you to the workout room, but I can come back later." She turned to leave.

"No." Ginger stood. "He needs to get started."

"Darn and I was just having fun." Blake laughed as he watched Ginger blush.

Chapter Ten

Kaylob sanded the last place on the fence where the wind had damaged the paint. He stood and admired his handiwork. That storm had done a number on some areas around there, and he enjoyed fixing it himself. The insurance company said they'd have someone do all the repairs, but he didn't want to go back to the restaurant right now. He wanted to be with his family.

The fact was that he wanted to get out of his lease and find a restaurant closer to home. He'd been wanting out of Riverside for a while. The business was good and he sure as heck hoped his staff would follow him, but if they didn't, he'd find new people. Nothing was more important than his family.

He needed to talk to Beth Ann and tell her that he wanted to move. Surely, she'd support him, right? She was painting inside. He'd better go check on her to make sure she wasn't drowning in the bucket. He laughed. She didn't know the first thing about painting, but she was adamant about the fact she could do it.

Dusting himself off, he entered the living room and could smell the paint. Shawna had Kaylie with her now that she was feeling better. After seeing the doctor, Shawna had found out she had a vitamin B deficiency. They had given her a shot and pills to take home. Thank goodness. It was nice to see her rosy cheeks had returned.

He followed the sound of Beth Ann singing and knew she was in the kitchen, so he tiptoed to the edge of the door and listened. She was singing a rock and roll song by John Fogerty and holy shit, she had a powerful voice, even more so for someone so little. He listened to the words and watched her shaking her sweet bubble bootie.

"Oooh! Ah! Well, a-here-ee-yup, a-here-ee-yup, a-here we go. Four in the mornin', justa hittin' the road. Here we go-oh! Rockin' all over the world! Yeah."

He laughed. "Hey, baby." She turned and blushed. Jesus, she was gorgeous and cute as hell. "Nice song." He winked.

"I'm having fun." She gave him a sexy grin.

Damn, she had paint on her face, in her hair, and all over her body. Goldie was on the floor sleeping, with drops on her as well.

"Look at the walls. What do you think?" She put down the brush, climbed off the ladder, and stood back, staring at her job. "Not bad, huh?"

He had to admit it looked damn good. They'd taken a page from Frankie and Shawna, only they'd chosen a lighter yellow with white crown molding. The molding would be done by professionals.

"I'm impressed, Mrs. O'Brien. You continue to blow my mind." The smile that spread across her painted face was priceless. He'd loved her smile since childhood, but now it was more sophisticated and womanly.

"Thank you." She crossed the room and put her arms around him, staring up into his eyes. "I love you, Mr. O'Brien. How is that fence coming along?"

"I just finished sanding the last part. Now I have to paint." He examined her face and tried to restrain a laugh.

"What?" She looked at him questioningly. "Did I make a mistake?"

"No, baby girl. You did a great job of painting." He touched her nose. "You missed a spot though." He moved his finger to her lips, then leaned down and tasted the bottom one.

"Kaylob, don't start anything, Shawna is taking care of Kaylie. What if they need us?"

"We could try a quickie. We've only done that once or twice." He leaned down into her neck. "Please."

She backed up with a sultry look. Slipping off her shorts, she hiked herself up on the counter. "Okay, Mr. O'Brien, come and take advantage of me."

His knees halfway buckled. "You are so beautiful. I want to eat you up," he said as he started raining kisses on her inner thighs.

She laid back and moaned his name. *Whoa, afternoon delight.* His childhood sweetheart knew his number.

It didn't take long for her to go over the edge and beg for more. With that, he gave her all of him. For the next twenty minutes or so, they were lost in the passion of their love. They laughed when Goldie barked. She was more than likely confused at what they were doing.

While they were in the shower, Kaylob heard the phone ring. "I better get that because it might be Shawna." He rinsed quickly, grabbed a towel, and ran to answer it.

"Hello."

"Hi Kaylob, it's me, Lisa."

"Hey you, we just about have the place back to normal after all this time. That storm was a biggie and it's taken us forever to get it cleaned up."

"That's what Beth Ann told me." Her voice cracked. "Kaylob, I have some bad news. I don't know if I should tell Beth Ann on the phone, or if you should tell her."

"What is it?" He could hear her crying. "Lisa, you're making me nervous. Is it her parents?"

"No, no."

"What's going on?" Beth Ann said while she dried her hair with a towel.

"Lisa, just tell me. Beth Ann is right here."

He heard her take a deep breath. "Denny was killed yesterday afternoon," she cried. "I can't believe she's gone."

"What. How?" His head was pounding from the news. He and Denny had never been that close, but he cared about her because she was one of Beth Ann's best friends.

Lisa inhaled. "They were doing a photo shoot. She was on the edge of a high cliff in the Cayman Islands. They said it could have been … a gust of wind blew her off into the water or it caused her to tumble and maybe lose her balance. They actually don't know what happened, because they weren't taking pictures at the time, they were on break. They never found her body. It took hours to get someone to search for her." She paused. "By the time they got there with the rescue team, there was no sign of her."

Tears pooled in his eyes as he inhaled deeply. This was awful news.

When the hell was life going to give them a break? This would shatter Beth Ann's heart.

"Oh, Kaylob, we were going to spend two weeks this summer with Beth Ann, and Denny hadn't even seen the baby yet."

"Okay, someone better tell me what's going on." Beth Ann demanded. "I can see by your face that this is bad."

"Lisa, let me call you back, okay?" He hung up the phone and turned to his wife. "Baby, sit down on the bed with me, okay?"

"What's wrong?" She already had tears in her eyes.

"Oh, sweetheart, there is no easy way to say this. Denny died yesterday in a horrible accident."

Tears rolled down her cheeks. "How … oh my God." She covered her mouth.

"She was doing a photo shoot, and they think the wind blew her off a cliff. Speculation is that she lost her balance. Nobody saw it happen, because they were on break. They haven't been able to recover her body because of the sea, and it took them a long time to start the search."

"Kaylob, no." She shook her head. "She can't be gone."

"I'm so sorry." He wrapped his arms around her. "What can I do?"

"I don't understand. Why?" Kaylob watched her lip tremble and her eyes filled again.

"What can I do, baby?" She fell into his arms and wept like he'd never seen her do before.

* * * *

Beth Ann woke a few hours later. She had cried herself to sleep, and her heart still felt like it had been stomped on. Denny was gone. She looked over at the old photo on her dresser. It was of Lisa, Denny, and Beth Ann, all dressed up for the party at Harry's pool hall. Her mother had taken those photos of her first Halloween in Novato.

Beth Ann rolled off the bed, went to her dresser, and picked up the picture. "Oh, Denny, we didn't talk much the last few years with your modeling schedule, but I thought of you every day." She held the picture to her heart.

How in the world would they ever find her in all that water?

"You'll never meet Kaylie and she'll never meet her Auntie Denny," she mournfully said. She went to the table and picked up the phone.

Lisa answered on the first ring.

"Lisa, I can't believe she's gone," Beth Ann cried.

"Me either. Her family is here right now, along with Gayle and her mom. Oh, Beth Ann, they are devastated, and to not even have her body … I hope they find her, but they don't seem to think they will because of how long it took to get help."

Beth Ann and Lisa cried until they had no tears left, the phone call ending with Beth Ann wiping her eyes. Their childhood friend was gone. All they had were the sweet memories and the love they would forever carry in their heart.

The memory of their childhood flooded around her, and she heard Denny's voice from years past. *"Beth Ann, come jump in from the deep end. Beth Ann, don't stand there all day. Let's get moving, girl."*

That August before she left Novato for Riverside, four friends, Lisa, Beth Ann, Gayle, and Denny, stood under the summer moon and held hands.

Denny had glanced around at all their faces. "Let's all connect pinkies." So they did. "Repeat after me. We swear to always stay friends. Every year, we will get together and have girlfriend time. No matter where we go, or how far away, we pledge to be the best of friends for always."

They all repeated the lines and cried that night, knowing that their lives were moving in different directions. But even so, they had remained in touch. Denny had been there when Jackie, Kaylob's mom, had called to say he was missing and presumed dead. During the wedding, she and Lisa had been her rocks.

"Gayle," she whispered. "You must be hurting so much too." All of them had lost a very special person.

The bedroom door opened, and Kaylob walked in with a tray of food. "I brought this to you. Shawna and Frankie are keeping Kaylie tonight. Frankie was pretty torn up when I told him. When you get a chance, you might want to call him."

"I want to eat out in the dining room and watch the stars come up. She was a star, you know."

Kaylob nodded. "I know, baby. She was and will always be." His eyes got misty.

"I need to call Blake," Beth Ann said. "He was close to the whole family. Denny's brother, Stephen, was one of his best friends."

"That's right. Do you want to call before or after you eat?" Kaylob asked.

"I'd better call now. I'll eat after I talk to him." She picked up the phone and dialed.

"Tanner residence," a friendly voice answered.

"Hi, is Blake available to talk? This is Beth Ann."

"He's right here, Beth Ann."

She heard the lady take the phone to him. "Hey beautiful, when are you bringing that little girl to meet her Uncle Blake?"

"We were going to do that later this afternoon, but something has happened." Beth Ann inhaled and tried to calm herself.

"What is it? I hope you can come anyway. We have a new friend named Millie and she's going to be here."

"I heard about her, but Blake …" She paused and took a breath. "Denny was in a horrible accident, and she's gone." She felt her voice tremble.

"What do you mean gone? As in dead?"

"Yes," Beth Ann voice shuddered.

"Jesus H. Christ. When and how?"

Beth Ann told him everything. He was torn up. For the first time since she ended their engagement, she heard him cry.

"I can't believe she's gone," Blake said.

After a good twenty minutes on the phone, they decided to see each other. They could use some time together and seeing Kaylie might just help. Also, she'd get a chance to meet Millie.

Beth Ann had one giant-sized question. Why would God take Denny?

* * * *

Blake sat in his room, his heart crushed, after getting off the phone with Stephen, one of his childhood best buds and Denny's brother. Jesus, his baby sister was gone. How did someone deal with that kind of loss? Blake thought about Denny's parents, Gina and Fred, and his stomach almost turned. This had to be unbearable. He hadn't spoken to them on the phone, but he could hear the cries in the background.

After hanging up, he had to fight to maintain his emotions.

"How are you doing? I'm so sorry about the loss of your friend." He glanced up to see Ginger, staring at him with sad eyes.

"It's a lot to take in. I need to get off my ass and start walking."

She moved closer. "Want to do anything else? Maybe go for a walk in the park, meet someone new? It's nice to see the sunshine after the winter we've had."

"No, but thank you. I really want to get my legs moving and be able to do things on my own," he explained. "Meet someone new?" He stared at her.

"Millie is downstairs." She stood and placed her hands on his wheelchair. "She wants to meet you. Honestly, with all this going on, I forgot we invited her over. Should I tell her this is a bad time?"

"No. I'm looking forward to meeting her and I didn't forget." He wanted to use his arms when he entered the room. "Just let me push myself though. I want to impress her." He winked, fighting to get rid of his sadness.

The minute he rolled into the room, he saw her standing by the window. She turned, and his heart warmed. Her gentle smile and kind face seemed oddly familiar. "You, of course, are Millie," Blake reached out to her.

"And you, my dear boy, are Blake." She took his outstretched hand, but moved in for a hug as well. "Thank you from the depths of my soul." She kissed his cheek. "I feel like I know you already."

"Funny …" Blake stared into her forest-green eyes. "I feel I've seen you before."

"I think I have one of those faces." She glanced around the room. "This place is stunning."

"Thank you, Millie. It's good for now." Blake couldn't place her, but he was sure he'd seen her before. Where, he hadn't a clue.

As the afternoon drifted by, they had all enjoyed an early dinner. Millie stood. "I should be getting out of your hair and let you get to your workout. It's already dark outside. It gets dark so early now."

"Please, don't leave." Blake really wanted her to stay. He couldn't figure out what it was, but he felt connected to her.

"Are you sure? I don't want to wear out my welcome."

Ginger stood. "You can watch him work out. We love you being here and the late afternoon workout is only an hour."

Blake nodded. "We do, and you're not going to wear out your welcome."

"Okay," Millie agreed. "I'd love to."

One hour later, he stopped. He was sweating and used his hand towel to wipe off his face. He had done more than he'd ever done. Millie had touched him a few times, and he could have sworn her hands had magic. It was as if a healing energy went through him. Was he losing his mind? How could she have helped him that much from just a touch?

As he sat there pondering the idea, he heard footsteps. It was Beth Ann and Kaylob with the baby. "It's about time you brought this little girl to meet her uncle Blake." He held up his arms and took the baby.

"Here, meet your uncle Blake." Beth Ann pulled her hands away.

Ginger smiled and moved closer, peeking down at her. "She's precious."

"Thank you, Ginger." Beth Ann smiled.

Blake looked over at Millie, who was almost glowing. "Millie, this is Beth Ann, Kaylob, and this little darlin," he looked down at the most beautiful child he'd ever seen. "Is their baby girl, Kaylie."

Millie crossed the room, greeting Kaylob and Beth Ann with a hug. "I'm so very sorry for your loss." She touched Beth Ann's arm.

Beth Ann's eyes shone with tenderness. "Thank you, Millie, and it's so nice to meet you."

Millie hugged her again, then came and stood by Blake.

The minute Kaylie opened her eyes, Blake dissolved into a puddle of mush. "Well, look at you," he said. "The boys are going to be knocking all over your door." He glanced up at Kaylob and winked. "Your poor daddy."

Kaylob actually frowned, and everyone chuckled. "She won't be dating at all until she's at least thirty."

"Right," Beth Ann said just before she and Ginger laughed.

Blake studied Beth Ann's weary face while he was holding Kaylie and saw the pain in her eyes. Before he could say anything, her lip trembled so he handed Kaylie back to Kaylob.

"I'm sad too, darlin. Life won't be the same without her."

"I'm going to take Kaylie for a little change," Kaylob announced. "Okay, if I use your bedroom, Blake?"

"Sure, help yourself to anything." He waved toward his room.

"Let me go with you and help. I want a chance to hold her. Do you want to come, Millie?" Ginger touched the baby's head.

"I'd love a chance to hold this precious child." Millie smiled.

Once the three of them left, Beth Ann leaned down and placed her arms around Blake. They had both loved Denny, and this was a big loss.

Beth Ann touched his hair. "I'm sorry, too, Blake. I know how bad this hurts you."

"Jesus, she was such a big part of my heart. These last few years, I was a shitty friend. I hardly ever called her." He wiped away a tear. "I loved her."

"I know." Beth Ann kissed his cheek, and that did it. Their silence shared everything.

Beth Ann arched back up. "I have an idea."

"What?" Blake asked.

"This summer, on her birthday, let's throw a celebration of her life. Let's rent a house on the ocean and spend a weekend with friends, in memory of Denny."

"That's a great idea," he said, and then added. "I should be walking by then. I will rent the biggest house I can find. Or two next door to each other."

"We'll help. I'll talk to Kaylob." Her face lit up.

"About what?" Kaylob asked as all of them walked back into the room.

Beth Ann held out her arms and took the baby. "Ask if you'd be okay with us doing a celebration of Denny's life on July ninth. That was her birthday. We could go in with Blake and rent a vacation house on the ocean."

"Of course I'm okay with doing that," he said. "That sounds like a great idea. By the way, that's some piano in the other room."

Blake smiled. "Ginger is an amazing player."

"Really?" Beth Ann touched her arm. "I'd love to hear you."

Ginger nodded. "Only if you sing."

"Deal." Beth Ann agreed. "Do you know *The Way We Were* by Barbra Streisand? I think it would be good for a tribute to Denny."

"Sure do." They all went into the entertainment room where the baby grand was. Millie sat down on the oversized chair and brushed the hair out of her face. "What a treat."

Kaylob cuddled Kaylie in his arms, Blake sat close to Millie near the fire, and Beth Ann sat down on the bench with Ginger.

Ginger gave a nod. With one note, she made magic fill the air. As her fingers glided across the keys, Beth Ann joined in harmony.

The truth was the song wasn't just about Denny to Blake. It reminded him of what he and Beth Ann had been together. Blake would always remember the good times. He glanced over at Millie and when their eyes met, he wondered if she was reading his mind. Even more so, when she reached her hand over to his and held it tightly.

"Memories, like the corner of my mind."

Beth Ann's voice had power and elegance. The room became enchanted, and Blake couldn't help but stare at Ginger and Beth Ann.

The look in Kaylob's eyes was pure and everlasting love. Even the baby seemed content. The two women he cared about the most were taking his breath away.

Memories floated back to his and Beth Ann's childhood. He could see her smile and the way she pushed the hair out of his eyes. The days she and Denny dressed alike. They were both cute as hell.

Damn, he had been in love with Beth Ann. Maybe a part of his heart would always belong to her. Watching the way she gazed at her husband and child made him know that although the memories were lodged there, they needed to be put away in a special place. It was time to move forward and let the past stay asleep.

Beth Ann hit all the notes, and her voice was full of strength. *"Could it be that it was so simple then? Or has time rewritten every line."*

Ginger and Beth Ann together were beyond anything he imagined. Kaylob seemed completely taken, which left no doubt the man was utterly smitten with his wife. By the spark in Kaylob's eyes, one would think he'd just realized that he was in love with her.

Hearing Beth Ann perform one of the great songs by Barbra Streisand was spellbinding. She was able to match note for note, and it obviously got to Kaylob because he swiped away a tear.

"If we had the chance to do it all again. Tell me, would we, could we? Memories."

Blake saw movement out of the corner of his eyes and, sure enough, Johnny, Dana, and even the staff were all there, being seduced by the enchanting melody of the two redheads.

"What's too painful to remember, we simply choose to forget, so it's the laughter we should remember."

Would he do it all over again? Would he have spent a year of his life engaged to Beth Ann and endure the pain and heartache?

Millie released his hand and leaned closer. "Yes, you would do it all over again."

Chills ran down his back. He knew that Millie had been through her own tragedies. Yet, she could feel his emotions. Almost like she was reading his thoughts.

After the song ended, the room exploded in applause. Beth Ann and Ginger stood and bowed, then stared at each other with a look he didn't recognize. But it seemed like a newfound friendship had emerged … and a close one at that.

A few hours later, everyone had left and Johnny had driven Millie back to her place. Blake was going to see about finding her a real home, and soon. He was looking forward to spending more time with her.

Blake noticed Ginger was quiet and staring out the window. "What's on your mind?"

"I feel bad about your friend, and I didn't even know her." She turned to him. "What a strange thing to have her life wiped away so fast."

"She was so into her world as a model, but you know, she loved it. She left home and hardly ever went back," he explained.

"Where did this happen?" Ginger asked.

"Over in the Caymen Islands. A place I know well. She was just starting to make a name for herself." Pain pierced his heart. "This was one of her biggest shoots; she sent me a letter when she got the job." He glanced down at his hands. "I got cards and letters, but we hadn't spoken in a while. I hadn't written to her for almost a year." He paused. "How do I ever forgive myself?"

Chapter Eleven

The end of April came roaring in, and things were warming up in Palm Springs. Blake was now standing and slowly walking on his own with a cane. It was still hard, but at least he was back at work part time, which gave him a sense of purpose.

Ginger had taken the job at the hospital and loved it, spending almost every day with Millie. They were becoming the best of friends. However, Blake and Ginger were strangers in the night, passing by and not spending much time together. She had seemed distant lately and he wasn't sure why.

Tonight, he had talked her into dinner. He was looking forward to spending the evening with her. The one thing he needed to know was where they were taking this relationship. He slipped on his dinner jacket and stood in front of the mirror. Okay, he looked pretty darn good. A few more pounds would help, but that would be back on soon enough.

Blake thought about her upstairs, getting ready, and wished he could go tell her to grab her stuff and move into his bedroom. Maybe tonight at dinner, he'd invite her to come back to his room. She'd been so darn quiet lately.

Her divorce with Arnold was going to be final next week, and the trial was set for the middle of May and hopefully this time it would happen. It had been one delay after another. First Frankie pushed the date out, due to some information about another woman Arnold had abused. They were trying to get her on the stand. Then, Arnold's team had something come up, so there was another delay.

The hospital had been totally supportive with Ginger, and said she could take three weeks off to attend the trial, or longer if needed. Frankie was helping to build a solid case against Arnold, and Blake sure hoped the clump of dirt bag would be locked up for life.

He moved into the formal living room and heard her coming down the stairs.

When he glanced up and met her eyes, he about dropped to his knees as his gaze clung to all of her. Her white wrap around dress hugged in all the right places.

His heart thrashed against his rib cage. "Wow." He pulled his eyeballs back in their sockets. "You look fantastic."

"Thank you, Blake. So do you." She gave him a charming smile, but something was missing.

Once they headed out, Carl, his backup driver, took them to a new place on Desert Drive, just down the street from where his townhouse was. Mexican food was something she said she loved.

They arrived at the restaurant, and he couldn't help but stare at the bright orange tile roof and awnings that matched. "Guess they don't want you to miss this place." He chuckled.

Ginger nodded in agreement.

The minute they entered, the aroma of onions and garlic fanned its way through the air. The smell made his stomach growl in anticipation.

A short, dark-haired hostess picked up two menus and motioned for them to follow. They sat down in a burnt orange booth with a tile tabletop and she placed the laminated list of options in front of them.

"The special today is Botana Grande, a wonderful combination of taquitos, quesadillas and garnachas. Served with guacamole and sour cream topping."

"Thank you." Blake nodded. "We will need a few minutes to look things over."

She smiled and left.

Blake studied Ginger. "Are you okay, darlin?"

"Yes, well, no. We need to talk," she spit out.

The hostess returned with chips and salsa, along with two glasses of water. They both picked up their menus and studied what was there.

A few minutes later a waitress came up with a smile. "What can I get for the two of you tonight?"

"I'll have the fiesta plate. With extra salsa, please," Blake said.

Ginger nodded. "That's sounds good. I'll have the same with ice tea, please."

The young girl with dark brown eyes and blonde hair nodded. "Great choice." "Anything to drink, sir?" She looked up from writing and asked Blake.

"I'll have the iced tea also."

Once she left, Ginger folded her hands on the table and started to speak when a young guy came over and set down their ice tea with a lemon perched on the side.

"Thank you," Blake watched as the kid nodded and left. "So want to try this again?"

"Yes," she said, and continued. "Blake, I really want to move out on my own, and well, I might want to live with Millie. I appreciate everything you've done for me, and I care deeply, but I need my own space."

Blake felt slapped. "What did I do?"

"Oh, you've done nothing. I just realized that I've never been on my own. I need to be alone and heal from everything I've gone through."

"So, you want to break the whole thing off then?"

"Break what off, Blake? You know you don't want to settle down, and we both know you will never commit again."

Blake swallowed. She was right about that. He didn't want commitment, but he sure as shit wanted her around. "When did you want to move out?"

"Soon, if you don't mind. You're walking and doing great now. I really need to do this for myself. With the money I've been able to retrieve from the savings account, I can get something."

"Okay, I won't stand in your way. Did you find a place?"

"No, but I did get offered a full-time job working on my own and having my own clients after the trial. Plus, they want me to travel to Denver, Colorado every month starting in September to work with their sister hospital. It's good money, and I think it will be fun. I figure Millie could watch the house while I'm away."

"I'm proud of you, Ginger," Blake said and meant it. "You'll go far, I'm sure of it, and it sounds like a nice plan having Millie there with you."

Tears filled her eyes. "I hope we can keep in touch."

"Oh, you betcha, darlin. I wouldn't want it any other way." His heart sank down into his stomach. What a dipshit he was. He had deep feelings for her, but he couldn't commit. Just the word gave him a dry throat and made him dizzy as hell. What a damn fool.

Why was he so afraid? Was it that he wanted to keep all the women in his life? He knew the answer to that. He hadn't even been seeing that many women after the first night with Ginger. None of them measured up. As a matter of fact, before he was shot, he hadn't gone that long without sex since high school.

Just then, the waitress showed up with their food. "Here you two go. Be careful because it's hot." She set down the plates. "Hope you enjoy."

The rest of the evening was spent in near silence, just idle chatter about how good the food was. When they got back to his place, Ginger kissed his cheek and headed upstairs. That was it. The thing between them was over. Maybe it was for the best. Was it possible she'd met someone else? Someone who could offer her a life with children and commitment?

That night, he tossed and turned. All he needed was to try to talk to her one more time. Why did she have to move out? It made no sense. Getting up, he stretched his arms over his head. He needed to get ready for the day and try to push Ginger leaving out of his head. Oh, to hell with it. He needed to go talk to her now.

He walked up the stairs slowly and knocked on her door.

"Come in," she said.

When he stepped inside the bedroom, she was sitting up in bed. From the looks of it, she hadn't gotten much sleep either. Blake crossed the room and sat down next to her. "What can I do to keep you from moving out? I care about you and well …" He reached for her hand.

"Blake, I told you I love you, but …" Tears fell down her cheeks. "I can't stay here and live with you when I know it's one sided. I can't do that to you or to me. But if you feel up to it, when the trial takes place, I'd like you to be there."

"Of course I'll be there and I just can't respond to love yet. Why don't you at least stay here until it's over? I don't want you going through this alone. Plus, I have to give witness anyway." He pulled his attention away from their hands and stared into her electric blue eyes.

Jesus, they swallowed him whole. His heart skipped a beat, and he was in fear of it exploding. Next, he found himself hankering to kiss those full sensual lips, so he eased his mouth across hers.

"Okay," she mumbled close to his mouth. "I'll stay until the trial is over."

Lord have mercy, her lips were warm, voluptuous, and tasted like pure honey with a dash of lemon. He deepened the kiss and was a goner. After a few minutes, he paused to catch his breath. "How do you taste so good first thing in the morning?" He pulled back and saw a smile twitch in the corners of her mouth.

"Lemon and ginger water." She pointed to her nightstand. "It's good for you."

"Hmm …" He moved his mouth back to hers. "It sure is—I'm feeling better already. As a matter of fact, I think I'm healed."

She giggled. "Blake …" She glanced deeply into his eyes. "Come to bed with me."

The emotion that flowed through him warmed his soul. "Oh, darlin, I thought you'd never ask." As she slipped off her nightgown, he realized just how much light she had brought into every corner of his life. Those dark, lonely places were now filled with brightness.

Could he let her just walk away?

* * * *

Beth Ann sat at the breakfast table and watched her husband squirm. Something was up, and she knew it. He hadn't squirmed like this since he told her he was going back to Vietnam. Oh shit, what had he done? She put down her spoon and stared at him.

"Okay, Kaylob Shawn O'Brien, what in the world have you done?"

His mouth was full, and he was giving her an innocent look. How well she knew that expression. She got up and moved onto his lap, as she had done a million and one times. His arms went around her and, as usual, he buried his nose in her neck.

"Kaylob," she said, cupping his face in her hands. "What's going on?" She forced him to look into her eyes. Could any one man be as handsome as her husband? He was big all over and just built.

He studied her face and cleared his throat. "I haven't done anything

117

yet, but I've been looking into something and I need to talk to you about it."

"So long as you're not going back into the military, I'm sure we can handle it." She smiled.

"Oh no, nothing like that, baby." He touched her nose, and happiness leaped into his eyes. "I'm supposed to resign the lease on the restaurant, and the landlord has been calling. Honestly, I've been avoiding him." He wiped his mouth with the napkin. "I want to move out this way, and Blake is scouting the area. He called me yesterday to tell me he found a couple of places that he thought would be great."

"Really?" Beth Ann held his gaze. "When were you going to tell me about this?"

"Right now, of course. I don't want to go see them without you. I haven't looked at anything yet. Both places are like five-to-ten minutes away from here, at the most."

Beth Ann placed her arms around his neck. "We could be out of Riverside and close to home."

"Yes." He nodded and glanced at the dog sleeping on the floor in the kitchen.

Beth Ann stood. "Let's call Blake and tell him we want to do this."

"I'll call him now." He stood and kissed her, then crossed the room to the phone.

She watched as he dialed the number.

"Hi, is Blake available? This is Kaylob," he said to someone on the phone.

"Oh, alright." He chuckled. "Will you have him call me, when he is …? Yes, of course. How are you?" Kaylob asked. "Glad to hear it, and I sure wouldn't want to disturb him …" He paused, listening to the other side. "Thank you, and you too. Bye."

He turned and grinned at Beth Ann. "Uh, apparently he has a *do not disturb* sign on his bedroom door, and she really didn't want to bother him."

"I hope he's busy with Ginger and nobody else," Beth Ann said, and added, "You shouldn't be so flirty on the phone."

"What?" Kaylob tilted his head.

Before they could finish talking, Frankie came barging in the door.

"I'm taking Shawna to the hospital. She's having contractions. It's early, but the doctors warned us this might happen." His eyes were wide.

"Should I come with you?" Beth Ann asked.

"No, just come on and follow us. I will make it to the hospital with my wife." He arched a brow at Kaylob.

"What's this, pick-on-Kaylob day?" He glanced at his wife and watched Frankie tear out the door. Kaylob stared at Beth Ann. "We promised when this happened, we'd call Uncle Jack and Lenard. They wanted some time with Kaylie." He stood, his face stressed. "What did you mean flirty on the phone?"

"Oh, never mind, you can't help it that your voice is so deep and sexy." She gave him a gentle kiss on the cheek and watched his grin spread. "I have to go call." She went to the phone and dialed the number, but there was no answer.

"What do we do now?" Kaylob asked.

"We'll just take her with us and try them again. I'll put Goldie and Sasha in the mudroom with food and water. They'll be fine for a few hours. We can come back and forth to check on them if we need to."

"Sounds good," Kaylob agreed.

Beth Ann was impressed with how calm Kaylob stayed as they drove. It didn't take them long to pull up to the hospital. Once they were inside, Kaylie was looking all around. She was becoming more alert at her surroundings.

"Look at how big she's getting, Daddy," Beth Ann said.

"She is, and she's also the most beautiful little girl in the world." He touched her nose as she made a gurgling noise at him. "Look at Daddy's girl trying to talk." Kaylob glanced at Beth Ann.

"She's a daddy's girl, alright." Beth Ann chuckled.

Hours later, after finding out both babies' heartbeats sounded healthy and they would more than likely be fine, Beth Ann finally got in touch with Jack and Lenard. They came by, picked up Kaylie, and took her home, so they could care for Sasha and Goldie too. Not long after the guys left with Kaylie, Frankie walked out into the waiting room with a smile on his face.

"I have two girls, and they are both healthy," he said with tears in his eyes. "They are gorgeous and a little small, but perfect. They are not identical; they are fraternal. One has dark hair like me and the other is a blonde like her mom."

Kaylob smiled. "Let the party begin."

The two girls, Daisy with blonde hair and Violet with dark, were born on April 28, 1976 and weighed barely four pounds each. Frankie was a proud papa, and Shawna was glowing. They appointed Beth Ann and Kaylob the godparents, just as they were with Kaylie.

* * * *

A few weeks later, Frankie informed Beth Ann and Kaylob that he'd be gone long hours due to his first criminal trial, which involved the shooting. He was worried about Shawna and wanted them to watch over her. He had hired a part-time nanny, but still, she was tired all the time. Having the twins had taken a lot out of her. Beth Ann was worried because, once again, she was so pale and seemed weak.

Three times, Kaylob and Beth Ann had taken the babies and kept them all night. They were precious, and Kaylie was just fascinated with them. Daisy was quiet and hardly cried, whereas Violet was a little louder, but not enough to make Shawna as tired as she seemed. The minute she heard from Gram, she was going to talk to her about it and see if she had any ideas.

Beth Ann went into the laundry room to get the vacuum while Kaylie was down for a nap. She had a lot to do today. The weekends they didn't do much, so Mondays were always busy. The minute she started cleaning the living room, the phone rang and made her jump.

Holy nerve damage. When was that phone ringing going to stop bothering her? She'd never liked a loud phone, but this was more about the past and the creepy calls she'd received for so long. Even after all this time, it sometimes still gave her a chill down her spine and she half expected to hear Peter's creepy voice.

"Hello." She waited.

"Hey darlin, how's that little Kaylie doing?" Blake had taken a big liking to their baby, as Kaylie had with him. Funny, she might be an infant, but somehow, Beth Ann could see a special sparkle in her eyes when Blake held her.

"How are you, Blake?" Beth Ann asked, and added, "She's fine, down for her nap, or she was. I think I hear her talking to Goldie."

"Her own special language." Blake chuckled. "I'm doing well. I was wondering if I could talk to you alone this week, or today, or maybe right now?"

"Sure, come on over," she said.

"Where is Kaylob?"

"He's actually downtown, looking for some bark for our yard. He was mad at himself and said he measured wrong. The storm did a number on our yard, and we are finally getting a chance to get it all fixed since the weather is nice."

"Well, Ginger is meeting with Frankie and his team before court. I can't stay long; I need to join her before the trial starts. But I also needed to talk to you about something."

"Sure, come on over."

After they hung up, Beth Ann continued vacuuming and wondered what he wanted to talk to her about.

* * * *

Blake pulled up to Beth Ann and Kaylob's house and noticed the place looked incredible, like an all-American couple lived there, with the American flag blowing gently in the breeze. Actually, they did. He stepped outside to a warm, sunny day. Wow, figures, Kaylob would be doing this himself. He noticed the bark had been added around the multi-colored roses and flower gardens. He remembered Kaylob outside working on the yard in Novato, making that little place look pretty darn good.

Blake got a rush of guilt, thinking of the mean things he'd said to Kaylob growing up. Crap, had he ever apologized? There was no way to deny he was a punk back then, mainly because he was angry at the world. All except with Beth Ann … he'd been in love with her forever. She had always been able to see the truth in his eyes. Which was that his childhood sucked. His parents were cold and uncaring. Everyone else thought he had the perfect life, but she knew better. *That being said, there was still no excuse to have taunted Kaylob*, he thought, mentally kicking his own ass.

Speaking of kicking ass, he sure as hell hoped Kaylob didn't kick his. Maybe he should have asked Kaylob first. Shit, what an idiot. This was a dumb thing to do, and he knew it. Nevertheless, he climbed the stairs.

"Okay." He arrived at the front door. "Pull it together." He knocked lightly, almost ready to run away, like a kid playing ding-dong ditch.

Beth Ann opened the door. Damn, she looked gorgeous, but then again, she always did. However, since Kaylie was born, she looked even more amazing, and he tried like hell not to stare. She had filled out in all the right places.

"Blake, are you okay?" Beth Ann tilted her head. "Come in."

With his hand clutching his cane, he entered the living room. He felt sweat dripping off his neck and knew it was from nerves. "I'm here because I need to ask you a giant favor, and of course, you can say no, but I really need this. I could have asked Kaylob first, but I don't feel like being punched."

"What in the world are you talking about? Kaylob wouldn't punch you over a favor." She laughed. "You're acting really nervous."

"Oh, he might." Blake sat down.

Beth Ann seated herself next to him and placed her hand on his arm. "Blake, what is it?"

"Can you kiss me?" he blurted out.

"What?" She leaned over and kissed his cheek. "There. My goodness, Blake, what's the fuss?"

"No, can you kiss me? Really kiss me." He felt a lump in his throat.

Beth Ann stood. "What? Kiss you for real? Why? I can't do that."

Blake felt his face heat. "I know it's crazy. I'm sorry. I should leave. I need to get to court before the trial starts. Just forget I said anything." He stood and felt stupid. What had he been thinking? Of course she couldn't kiss him. That was insane.

Beth Ann's forehead wrinkled with confusion, and he could see that she thought he'd lost his mind. He headed toward the front door. "I'll call Kaylob later."

"Blake, what is going on?" She stepped in front of him, blocking the door.

He swallowed and met her gaze. "I think I might be in love with Ginger. And, I just needed to test something."

"Test something?" Beth Ann repeated with questioning eyes. "What are you talking about?"

"I need to see how I feel about you. I don't want to get into a commitment if I still have leftover feelings. It wouldn't be fair."

"Leftover feelings for me?" Beth Ann studied his face.

"Just forget I asked. It was so dumb. I'm sorry."

Beth Ann gave him a soft smile. "Kiss me, Blake." She stepped closer.

"Really?" He swallowed hard, almost afraid of what he might feel.

"Yes." She nodded.

Blake examined her eyes. There was a sparkle, and he wasn't sure what it meant. Was it laughter?

Without another word, he placed his lips across hers and she gave him a tender kiss back. It was sweet with a taste of coffee and chocolate, just the way he remembered. And for a second, he felt a sense of loss, but he also felt something else.

After a few seconds, he pulled away and stared into her chestnut-brown eyes. "Wow!" he said and grinned at her. "I do still love you, but …"

She brushed his hair across his forehead, like she had been doing since childhood. "Blake, you're already *in* love with Ginger. We're friends now, and I'm happy to help you know that."

Blake's heart exploded. By god, she was right. What they had now was a type of love that was connected to a wonderful friendship. "Thank you, Beth Ann." He hugged her and grinned. "Do you think Kaylob will kill me?"

She chuckled. "No, he'll be amused. We trust each other."

"Whew." Blake took a step back. "I don't feel like getting beat up, and I don't want to lose his friendship. He's one of my best buds now."

Beth Ann pointed. "Go to your Ginger. You two are perfect together." She shooed him away, but not before he kissed her on the cheek.

Just as he stepped off the front porch, Kaylob pulled up in his truck. Shit, he felt his heart sink. What if he did get mad? He'd tell him, and then run like hell into the car. That would be a good plan if he could run.

Kaylob stepped out of his truck, and Blake could see all the bark in the back.

"Hey, Blake, I thought you were at the trial today." He walked toward him.

"I'm on my way now, but I needed to see Beth Ann to ask a favor."

"Oh …" Kaylob tilted his head. "What did you need?"

Blake stepped closer to the car. "A kiss. See ya later." He hopped in his car and waved.

Kaylob stood there with his mouth open, staring with a blank look.

Shit, I'm a dead man, Blake thought, half laughing and half afraid as he drove away.

Chapter Twelve

Seconds later, Beth Ann heard the front door open. Blake must have forgotten something.

It was Kaylob instead, staring at her.

"Hi, honey. You just missed Blake," she said.

"Oh, I saw him. A kiss, huh?" Kaylob arched a brow and crossed his arms across his chest.

Beth Ann told him the whole story and waited for him to say something—anything. She had been sure he would understand.

"So, you were kissing another man ... and that man was your ex-fiancé," he said, looking into her eyes.

"Yes. He asked nicely, and you know what a matchmaker I am."

"Well, you know there has been this woman who has been dying for my kisses, so ..." He paused. "I guess I'll have to be a nice guy and give her what she wants."

"Oh really?" Beth Ann placed her hands on her hips and gave him a speculative look.

"Yeah, she's some sexy redhead, and I know she's dying for me to kiss her." He swung her up in his arms.

"Is that so? Do I know her?" She pretended to be mad.

"I think you do." He kissed her gently before setting her down.

* * * *

Ginger sat around the table, staring at the three attorneys who were helping Frankie with her case. Mostly, Frankie was in charge. Even though this was his first big case, he seemed confident. They were taking notes, passing around the pictures showing what she looked like when she was beaten, and going over last-minute details.

Frankie cleared his throat as he slipped some of the things into a folder. "Are you ready for this today?" He met Ginger's gaze.

She nodded and swallowed the ball of nerves caught in her throat. Having to face Arnold again made her stomach flip, more than once. They had reviewed the nature and purpose of the proceedings, including the courtroom modus operandi and what to expect.

If she could shake the fear of messing up, she'd feel better. Frankie had told her she had handled direct examination perfect. However, she hadn't been staring into the eyes of the devil.

Another thirty minutes went by as they talked about strategy and witnesses.

Finally, Frankie stood. "Let's do this." He paused and stayed with Ginger while the others left ahead of them.

"You're going to be fine, I promise." His eyes flashed pure confidence with no hints of doubt.

"Okay." She tried to sound unafraid, but knew she failed. "I hope Blake gets here soon. Tomorrow, Millie is coming to support me too."

"I heard about Millie from Shawna. I'm glad she'll be here tomorrow. Would you like to call Blake? It will be a while before you go on the stand, if it's today at all. We have opening arguments."

"No, he'll be here. He said he would." She knew it in her heart. As they stepped out into the hallway, she spotted Blake walking toward them. He was limping, but moving fast and using his cane.

"Sorry, I had to stop by and talk to Beth Ann," he said, catching his breath when he took Ginger's hand. "I'm not as fast these days."

She smiled and squeezed his fingers. "I'm just glad you're here. Don't rush like that again. You don't want any kind of setback."

"Yes, ma'am." He kissed her cheek.

Frankie placed his hand on Blake's shoulder. "You're right on time. Just a reminder, you might be called today. Are you ready?"

"Yes." He clutched Ginger's fingers a little tighter, and there was no missing his sweaty palms. Of course he was nervous. Her deranged ex-husband had almost killed him. More than likely, Blake didn't really want to be here. He was here for her and because he had to be.

Once they got in the courtroom, Ginger noticed Arnold sitting down front. He was next to two attorneys with her parents close behind. There was no pushing back the tears filling her eyes.

How in the hell could they do that? What kind of parents protected a man who had beaten their daughter and tried to kill her? Never mind that they were paying for his attorney.

She leaned towards Blake's ear. "That's my parents."

Blake placed his hand on her back and led her to the wooden chair where Frankie nodded for her to sit.

Ginger leveled a look at her dad. There was no way she'd let the ass intimidate her. Her dad continued to stare at her with fury flickering in his eyes, whereas her mom's eyes fell and her lip trembled.

Ginger's heart broke, but she squared her shoulders and lifted her head high, refusing to show him or Arnold one ounce of weakness. *Screw that.*

A few minutes later, the bailiff announced, "All stand, Judge Thomas presiding."

"Please be seated," Judge Thomas said with an authoritative voice. "Good morning, ladies and gentlemen, calling the criminal case of the People of the State of California versus Arnold Reid Parker. Are both sides ready?"

After both sides said yes, the judge continued. "Will the clerk please swear in the jury?"

The voices of everyone faded, and a flood of worry plagued her. She remembered the way Arnold burned her hands and all the things he had threatened her with. Her mind was filled with the horror he had inflicted. What if they didn't find him guilty due to the plea of insanity? What if he got out and tried to hurt her sister? There was no doubt he'd try to kill her and Blake. Next time, he might just succeed. They had to put him away because she never wanted him to cause pain to others again.

Looking at her parents, sitting behind the man who had so brutally beat her and held her hostage, made her sick. How could any parent justify that? Her dad had always been controlling and hateful to her mother, and now she was seeing firsthand just how awful he was.

Frankie stood and drew her attention back into the courtroom.

"Ladies and gentlemen of the jury, my name is Frankie Dean Russo, prosecutor for Palm Springs, California District 2399. On this day, May 15, 1976, it is my pleasure to represent the people and my client, Ginger

Roberts, in the shooting that took place on, December 27, 1975. I intend to show that the defendant." He pointed toward Arnold. "Arrived at 2134 Desert Lane with the intent to kill his wife, and all those around her.

"I will produce witnesses who heard him yell at the scene that he was going to finish the job." He moved closer to the jurors. "At the conclusion of the case, we will ask for a verdict of guilty." He pointed once again to Arnold. "The evidence will leave no doubt in your minds that this man is a danger to others. It will be clear that Mr. Parker has no remorse, that he left a man paralyzed and shot two others, one being his wife. In addition, we will show proof that Mr. Arnold Reid Parker held his wife hostage and beat her for one solid week."

Ginger watched as Frankie moved closer to her with sadness in his eyes. "Ladies and gentlemen of the jury, this case is about a man who could not control his anger. This is a man whose evil deeds got the better of him, and he had no regard for his wife or others. You will see evidence from photographs taken by a doctor of the burn marks Mr. Parker deliberately inflicted upon his wife and how he beat her black and blue. He not only left marks on the outside, but she was also injured internally as well. Not to mention the emotional damage he inflicted."

He glanced down at his legal pad and several of the female jurors were obviously taken in by his good looks. Two of them smiled at each other in a way that told a story. He continued. "I will be calling another female who will corroborate the fact that she was injured and had to hide from Mr. Arnold Parker." He took a deep breath. "You will hear testimony from the family of one young lady that was too afraid to be here today. She now lives out of state due to her fear of Arnold Reid Parker. I intend to show you that this man is not insane, but malevolent with malicious intent. I implore you to find Arnold Reid Parker guilty of three counts of attempted murder as well as kidnapping and domestic abuse. This man needs to be locked up for as long as the judge can allow, according to the law." He nodded then continued. "Thank you, ladies and gentlemen of the jury, for listening to my opening statement."

The other attorney stood. "Good morning, ladies and gentlemen of the jury. My name is Brandon Carls, and it is my privilege to represent Arnold Reid Parker in this case before you today." Brandon was a tall, older man, with white hair and serious blue eyes. "You've heard Mr.

Russo's explanation of what he says should happen and why. What he failed to inform you of is all the facts. Such as Ginger Roberts, Arnold's ex-wife." He pointed toward Ginger, and her heart sank. "She pushed him over the edge by flaunting her affairs." He stepped closer to the jurors. "This caused my client to temporarily lose his mind. I intend to show how she did this, with no regards to how bad it hurt him. Her promiscuous ways drove him to do things that were outside of who he really is. Even her mother and father are here today, supporting Arnold instead of their daughter. Why you ask? Because they know the truth. My client." He moved toward Arnold, but kept his eyes on the jury. "Worked hard every day and would come home to his wife, who compared their intimacy to other lovers. So yes, my client did things that he shouldn't have done, but it was by way of insanity."

He darted a look at Ginger. "So we would ask you to keep an open mind, listen to all the evidence, and return a verdict of not guilty, due to temporary insanity." He took a long breath and glanced down to the floor. "I implore you to think of what that might do to you, if you had loved someone since college, who day after day, shattered your heart and soul. Thank you for listening to me today. I'm sure by the time we're done, you will see how my client is a decent man, who worked hard and tried to give his wife everything she wanted."

He moved across the room and sat next to Arnold.

Ginger's stomach turned. Would they believe that? What proof did she have that she hadn't done those things? Frankie placed his hand on top of hers, and then leaned closer. "It's all fine. There is no way the jury will buy that."

She tried to smile, but knew she failed.

* * * *

Beth Ann laid Kaylie down for a nap, while Kaylob was out working hard in the yard again. It had taken longer because of the restaurant and getting the house touched up. At least the inside was done. Wow, imagine that, she had time to actually take a break and do something indulgent for herself. Shawna had a daytime nanny, and all the chores were done. The thought crossed her mind about Blake and Ginger at court and this being Frankie's first big trial. She was sure everything was going to be fine, and she was really proud of him.

The journals and letters were in the bottom of the closet. She had wanted to read more, but she hadn't had time.

Once she opened the closet door and saw the cedar chest, she pulled up the top. Inside were three journals. Maybe she'd have time to go through a few of them today and catch up with Great-Grandma Anne.

There was one extremely large journal embossed with the date 1940; she'd save that one for last. Wow, her great-grandma Anne must have written it when she was around fifty-five years old. She placed it back inside and lifted the other smaller one. Heading into the family room, she plopped down and started to read.

March 20, 1901.

Fresh fruit and new birth bring forth the heralding of spring.

I love to watch all the plants and trees warmed by the sunlight. Perhaps the closest to my heart is the subtle smell of the sweet newborn blossoms. As I gaze outside my open window, watching the curtains ripple from the breeze, I can't help but feel there is something exquisitely lovely about the morning dew, splashing like a rainbow across the flowers. Hearing the symphony of birds and the ruffling of the leaves as the wind carries them about brings out emotions in my heart.

The world is a big wonder of adventure. Someday, I shall travel it. I will sail the seas and set my sights on springtime in other cities and possibly even countries. My father says it's wonderful; I love to read and have gained knowledge from my books. He also says everyone should see as much of the world as they can. Father believes you gain a kind of wisdom that you cannot find in reading. I'm not sure I agree with him, although I would never say that out loud, for that would be disrespectful. However, the thought of travel brings out my imagination of many hillsides and oceans with ships that sail the green waters of faraway lands.

Now on with new thoughts.

I know it's been forever long since I shared, but I just wanted Carlotta to come back home, and I was too sad to write. Why did they have to leave Franklin and move so far away? They could have at least stayed in Tennessee.

The Season of Forever

In addition to the splendor of spring, something has helped me out of the gloom. And I have to write about it, or I'm surely going to explode from holding in my feelings.

I am enjoying Abraham Williams, and I really like him. When I go downtown, we've been spending time together. Mother and Father have not met him yet, but unquestionably, they will like him since he has all the manners of a truest gentleman, and he is nothing like some of the boys in town. Nor is his family. Mother says some of them are heathens and have never stepped foot in a church.

Abraham carried my groceries home the other day, and his cheeks turned red when I told him thank you...

* * * *

March 21, 1901
I was tending to the chores when I heard someone knock on the door. "I'll get it, Mother." I ran to the entry and swung it open.

"Hi, Rachel Anne." Abraham gave me a soft smile and held up two fishing poles. "I was wondering if you wanted to go fishing with me? You said you love to fish," he drawled, and I wondered if my accent was as strong as his.

"I do. But I still have at least another hour of chores. My father is out of town, and Mother needs my help."

"Oh, alright, but if you want to come and join me later, that would be swell."

"Hi there," my mom said as she dried her hands on a towel. "Who is calling on my daughter?" she asked Abraham with a sparkle of laughter in her solid brown eyes.

Once I glanced back toward Abraham, I turned toward my mother and saw an odd look on her face. It didn't take me long to understand when I caught the color of his cheeks. Watching my mom trying not to laugh at his tomato color, made me come close to laughing too.

"Hi, Mrs. Morgan, I'm Abraham Williams." He paused, and stuck out his hand.

She shook it. "Nice to meet you, Abraham." She released his hand and brushed the brown hair from her eyes.

Mother always wore her hair up in a tight bun. The only time it was loose was at night before she went to bed. So, seeing her brush the strands that had fallen loose from cleaning and cooking was a change.

"Drats, I'm sorry for being such a bonehead and well ..." His face brightened even more. "I just wanted to ask Rachel Anne to go fishing and see if it would be okay. There will be no other adults present, but I thought it might be okay since it was just fishing." He shuffled his feet and glanced down toward the floor.

I looked at my mom, and then back to Abraham. "It's okay, you didn't know I was busy, or that my father was not here. Maybe another day."

"I think today would be fine." My mother grinned. "Rachel Anne, you've worked hard and these chores can wait. However, a fish might not." She chuckled. "I insist that you bring a basket of lunch food. I don't want either one of you starving to death."

"Okay, Mother, that sounds terrific." I turned and ran toward the staircase, then swung around and almost lost my balance. "I'll be right back." I couldn't help but notice that Abraham's lips twitched at the corners.

He had the most handsome olive skin that made his thick, black hair look almost blue when the sun shone on it. I didn't want him to think I was staring, so I whisked up the stairs and ran into my room.

I changed into my new swimming and outdoor attire, which was a dark navy blue harem skirt. I had heard them called bloomers, but Mother had said that was not proper. I ran my hand down the wool material and buttoned the navy blue top. Father had said it looked pretty with my strawberry-blonde hair. I have the best father in the world. The last day he was home, even though he was tired, he sat with me and listened to all the stories about my new friend, Abraham. He was happy I wasn't as upset about Carlotta, even though it still broke my heart.

I glanced at my image. Although I didn't want to be vain, I couldn't help but notice how fashionable and grown up I looked. Next, I placed on my hat, and then my shoes.

My mother and father had given me the new garments as an early birthday gift. What surprised me was how father had pushed extra hard for me to have it before he left. I would be turning sixteen in eleven days and sadly, he wouldn't be home. It made me wonder where he had gone and what kind of business trip it was. Whatever kind had called him away, it seemed awfully important. The other reason my father had wanted me to have the new clothing was because the threads were loose on my old one. The last thing he would want was for my skin to be exposed. He didn't approve of such things.

Once I arrived back down to the living room where Abraham was waiting, I picked up my parasol. "Mother, when should I be back?" I called out.

"Before dark, dear. Be safe and have a good day," my mother's voice rang from the kitchen.

As we made our way to town with fishing poles in hand, we did so in a comfortable silence. The funny thing about being at ease with someone was that most times, you didn't have to speak any words because sometimes words were said without your mouth moving.

Although, I wasn't good at not moving my mouth. I rather liked to chatter. Father had always said I was exceptionally good at it.

We arrived at the heart of town, and people were all around. Most were busy doing their daily activities. Little Gordon was laughing while playing fetch with his big black dog. He was a redheaded daredevil and a wild child.

There was the sound of chopping and horses clomping down the street.

Five brick-and-iron storefronts lined the footpath. Further down, was the train station and I could see the stationmaster doing his daily routine. Near the railway, stood the feed store, along with a new warehouse. The place was growing. Pretty soon, Mother had said it would be a big city. I'd never been sure what that looked like because I have never seen one.

"Abraham, have you ever seen a big city?"

"Yes." He stared blankly, as though he was trying to figure out what made me ask. "Only once and well ..." He stopped and chuckled. "I don't really remember. I was only three, but I'm sure I thought it was truly something."

We both laughed and I continued. "My mother says Franklin is growing into a big city. She said in the next few years, we might have at least two more stores."

"I saw a big city in a picture book once. This place ain't nothing but a speck of dust compared to what that looked like."

"Really? We do have five shops in town." Right then, the roar of a new buggy came flying down the street. "And look at that buggy, Mr. Curtis is driving." He was stirring up all kinds of dust. I coughed and waved it away. Then, with no warning, the thing beeped, which caused me to jump and let out a tiny scream.

Abraham laughed. "That's not a buggy. That's a 1900 Bradley Gasoline Runabout. People in the city have a lot of gas-operated ones and electric too. I heard Mr. Curtis talking to Mrs. Tess, and he told her there were at least twenty, running around the city."

"Twenty? I can't imagine. What city?"

"Boston, and from what I recall in the pictures, there were shops lined down two streets."

"Someday, I hope to go there." I sighed. "I want to see the world and all the cities."

Abraham nodded. "Me too."

As we made our way to the end of town, I couldn't help but gaze at the banks of blooming rose bushes that lined the sides of the road. I needed to remember to pick one before I headed back home. I could imagine rose bushes planted in the yard under my bedroom window. What better way to rise in the mornings than to have roses greeting you.

"Oh, Abraham, just look at how spectacular the day is," I said. "I don't even mind the light breeze that feels cool when it skims my face."

"It is lovely." He gave me a soft smile. "Just like you."

That statement made my face start to burn, so I kept my thoughts on other things.

The gentle wind also brought a scent of something which made my mouth water. It didn't take long to figure out why my stomach was churning—we were approaching Curnock's Bakery.

We both came to a standstill and whiffed the air.

"Rachel Anne, I want some of whatever smells so good." He stuck his nose high in the air. "Let's go see what they have. I have a few cents saved." He pulled it from his pocket.

I was surprised that he was able to buy us each a slice of shortbread with cherry filling. We both took a bite, and the spongy texture and the

*feel of the cherry burst with flavor across my tongue. I closed my eyes
and swallowed. "This is so good, Abraham."*

*"Let's save it for later." He took his handkerchief and laid his slice
in the middle. "Do you want me to wrap yours too?" he offered. "It's
sparkling clean; my mom washes them in hot water and hangs them in
the sunshine."*

"Yes." I nodded. "I'd like that very much."

*Once we left the town, we entered Old Man Floyd's pasture. It was
pretty the way the meadows sloped down with trees and wild flowers
scattered the area.*

*"Abraham, isn't this lovely?" I bent down and touched the soft
leaves of a purple wildflower.*

*"Yes, it's spring and everything is blooming. But do watch where
you step because those cows left patties everywhere."*

*We both glanced around and laughed as we took giant steps to
avoid them.*

*Old Floyd was good about letting the kids in town use his land to get
down to the river. If he didn't, the walk would have been another mile to
cross around the backside of town. For that, I was thankful.*

*We made our way down to the fishing and swimming rest. The area
had dragonflies skimming across the water and little dandelions floating
everywhere.*

*I pointed. "If you use your imagination, you can see fairies riding
on the dandelions."*

He chuckled. "And where might these fairies be going?"

"Oh, to the party, of course."

*"To the party?" He had another blank look. "What party would that
be?"*

*"Well, everyone knows about the party. It's Mr. Toadmasters'
seventy-fifth birthday."*

We stopped and stared at each other, then broke out in laughter.

"We must not be late," Abraham said seriously.

*Off in the distance, I could hear the croaking of a frog. "See, he's
already calling on us."*

Abraham nodded. "I can hear him."

I paused and heard the melody of a bird, which made me want to search and find the little creature. If only I could see where it was perched, I could imagine he was singing just for us.

Together, we pulled out the wool blanket that my mom had packed, each taking a corner and laying it on the grass.

"That will help keep the bugs off our food and us," I said, meeting his gaze.

All of a sudden, I felt a rush of scorching heat crawl across my face and couldn't imagine it away. His eyes were the most fine-looking green eyes I'd ever seen. He had specks of silver twinkling inside. It made my legs weaken like mush.

Abraham grinned, then turned and pointed to the water. "I'm hoping to catch some big fish today," he whispered, turning back and studying me again. "You're the sweetest girl I've ever met, Rachel Anne. I love the way your blue eyes match the sky, and your complexion is like ivory and peaches." He ran his finger down my cheek. Turning abruptly, he headed toward the water with his fishing pole in hand.

Oh, my heart was beating so hard, I was sure it would explode.

I stumbled backward, tripping over my own feet and landing right on my buttocks. I placed my hand across my heart and hoped he hadn't seen me fall. But as I dared to catch his eye, he was looking right at me with a crafty smile. So I closed my eyes and imagined I was sailing on a glamorous boat from the banks of the Charles River, even though we were really on the Tennessee River. In my mind, I could see how magnificent everything was. I was enraptured in the beauty and silence of the area.

Instead of falling on my bottom, I had just crash-landed in New England, on an estate where a party was being held in my honor.

Chapter Thirteen

The phone rang, pulling Beth Ann away from Great-Grandma Anne's story. She was laughing hard. She loved it and didn't want to put it down. But she had to answer the loud noisemaker.

"Hello," she answered, trying not to sound irritated.

"Hi Beth Ann, this is Frankie. We are on break. Could you go check on Shawna for me? Can you let her know I've been trying to call, but the line is busy?"

"Sure, how's it going?"

"Don't know yet. Ginger is really nervous, but Blake is here, and I can see that makes her feel better."

Beth Ann heard him sigh and knew that sound. "What is it, Frankie?"

"Her parents are here, and they are supporting this jerk. How could they? I mean, he tried to kill her, and beat her black and blue! I feel bad, putting her on the stand first. But we need her testimony."

"Oh my gosh, Frankie, that's awful. I can't imagine how they could rationalize that. I bet Ginger will be fine. She's a strong lady."

"She is, but I feel she needs to cut all ties with them."

"As much as I love family, I'd have to agree. I'll go check on Shawna right now."

"Did I disturb you?" Frankie asked.

"No, nothing I can't jump back into. I'm reading journals from my great-grandma Anne. She was a character."

"You'll have to share some time. Thanks, Beth Ann."

After she hung up the phone, she went to the door and called outside. "Kaylob, can you come in the house? I have to go tell Shawna that Frankie is trying to call, he thinks her phone is off the hook."

"Sure." He grinned as he walked up the steps. "I was coming in to

137

get a snack anyway." He rubbed his stomach. "I'm starving."

"Kaylob, we just ate breakfast." She glanced up at the clock. "Two hours ago."

"Exactly, it's been hours."

"You could have some fruit, or I have celery and carrots chopped up." He gave her a look that told her that he had no intention of touching that. And lately, it did no good to argue because he'd just eat junk food anyway.

"I'll be back in a bit." She arched a brow, and he smiled.

Once she got into Shawna and Frankie's yard, she saw Goldie and Sasha were stretched out in the sun, cuddled next to each other. They were so darn cute that Beth Ann had to lean down and pet them.

Shawna stepped outside. "Hi, is everything okay? I was just coming out to check on the kids." She laughed and pointed toward Sasha and Goldie. "Those two are in love."

Beth Ann nodded in agreement. "Frankie has been trying to call you, but the phone's been busy and he was worried."

"Oh darn it. I bet Sasha knocked it off the hook again. Thank you." Shawna took a couple steps back up the stairs. "How is everything coming along with the yard?"

"Really good."

"Tell Kaylob to come and do ours next." She glanced around and laughed. "I better get that phone hung up."

Beth Ann made her way back into her yard and went into the house. Stepping into the kitchen, she saw Kaylob sitting at the table with an entire pie in front of him.

"Kaylob Shawn O'Brien, what in the world are you doing?"

He glanced up with his charming, innocent look. "Eating some pie because I burned off all the calories from my breakfast. I've only had one bite."

"I see." She took the pie away. "I saw how much was there. My gosh, you've already eaten half."

"I guess I took a bigger bite than I thought." He did a half shrug and feigned innocence.

"Right." She put the pie back in the fridge. "You know you have to be careful. Honey, you have high blood pressure." She moved over to the table and gave him her best stern look.

"Come here." He pulled her on his lap. "Oh baby girl, you smell so good. I could eat you." He buried his nose in her neck, like he'd been doing since they were teens.

"Later, Mr. O'Brien. And, if you're a good boy, I'll give you a special dessert that will make you forget all about that pie." She wiggled on his lap.

"Grrr! You're my little tiger lady."

Beth Ann stood. "Guess what I've been doing."

"What?"

"Reading the journal from my great-grandma Anne, spelled with an e, which I never knew. I also didn't know her first name was Rachel. She was so interesting."

"So her name was Rachel Anne? Sounds like Beth Ann."

"I know, but she was an extremely dramatic person."

Kaylob laughed. "No, you've got to be kidding me."

Beth Ann knew by the impish grin on his face what he meant. "I'm not dramatic." She put her hands on her hips. "Well, not usually."

"I'll let you get back to your journals while you can. I'm going out to finish working. I have the backyard to tackle afterwards. We are also going to look at four new places for the restaurant this weekend. I've been thinking that having two locations might be a good idea."

"That would be nice, honey," Beth Ann agreed.

He smiled and placed a sweet kiss on her lips, then headed outside. Just as she turned to go back to her reading, Kaylie cried out.

"Well, so much for reading time," she whispered.

* * * *

Ginger sat on the witness stand in the shabby courtroom with dull tan walls. Her nerves sent beads of sweat down her back. She glanced around, ignoring her parents and Arnold. They had sworn her in, so she took a deep breath and reeled in her emotions. The jurors' faces were engraved with seriousness, but they seemed curious and she could see them watching her. Ginger took note of how all of them were crammed into a dreadfully tight space, which might not be so hot for their mood.

Frankie walked up in front of her and glanced down at the yellow legal pad in his hand. "Can you state and spell your entire name?"

"Ginger Madeline Roberts." She also spelled it.

"Would you also give us your age and what you do for a living?" Frankie requested.

"I am twenty-five and employed as a physical therapist at Palm Springs Hospital."

"Miss Roberts, can you explain to the court why you're here today?"

Ginger went into detail about her life with Arnold and all the beatings.

After what felt like hours, she had tears sliding down her cheeks and was trying to catch her breath. "The beatings got progressively worse over time." Her voice broke. "One time, he broke two fingers. I told everyone I slammed them in a door. The truth was, they were slammed in a door, but not by me. He also pulled a lot of my hair out by dragging me through the house, and more than once, he kicked me in the ribs and stomach." Her pulse quickened, and she blew out an audible breath.

"Miss Roberts, do you need a break?" the judge softly asked.

"No, I'm okay." She wiped her eyes with a tissue that Frankie had handed her and sipped on the water that cooled her parched mouth.

"Miss Roberts," Frankie said. "I know this is difficult, but can you explain to the court how you ended up at Blake Tanner's house on December 25th, 1975? Please state how the day started, how you escaped, and how you made it to Mr. Tanner's house."

"Objection, Your Honor," the other attorney called out. "There has been no proof that she had to escape."

"Overruled," the judge stated. "Mr. Parker has admitted to this. So let's continue."

The attorney sat down, and Frankie continued. "Go ahead, Miss Roberts." Frankie nodded. "Give us the incidents of that day from the beginning to the point you escaped."

Ginger inhaled and turned her eyes toward the jury, just as she'd been instructed to do. "I woke up that morning around six a.m., still tied up, but with a severe stomach ache. I thought at the time I might have the flu, but soon realized it was from," she paused and took in another deep breath. "All the punches to my stomach. I told him I had to vomit and didn't want to do so on the floor. I asked for a garbage can. He threw it at my head, and it almost knocked me backward." Ginger tried like heck to control her trembling voice, but failed. "I proceeded to throw up. He made it clear that I was gross for doing such a thing in front of him. After a few more minutes of vomiting, he let me use the restroom and told me to stay in there until I was done. I couldn't seem to stop, but after about thirty minutes, it finally eased up. All I wanted to do was lie down." She glanced at Frankie, and then back to the jury.

"When I got back into the room, it appeared that Arnold had passed out on the couch. I said his name to see if he was trying to trick me, but he didn't answer. So I put on my shoes, ran to my room, and got my overnight bag. It had Blake's address and some cash inside. On the way out the door, I grabbed my purse, which thankfully had my keys in it."

"Miss Roberts, can you explain how you knew where Mr. Tanner lived?"

"Because she was fucking him," Arnold yelled out and stood. Ginger watched one of the other attorneys pull him back down.

The judge hit his gavel against his block. "Mr. Carls, please refrain your client from outbursts." The judge hit his gavel again.

"Yes, Your Honor." Mr. Carls leaned close to Arnold and said something.

Ginger took another sip of water. "I ran into Blake at Seven Nights and Seven Roses restaurant. I had met him a few days earlier at another location. That was the day he saw the bruises on my arm and my hairline. He wanted to help me and offered his place. He said I could use it, even if he was out of town. He promised I would be safe there."

Ginger felt her stomach flip. She knew that this was the part that would make her look bad. Running to another man would make it appear like they were having some long, drawn-out affair.

She swallowed and continued with the whole story. By the time she was done, she was exhausted and needed a break. Thank God, the judge agreed to a recess.

* * * *

Blake decided to go stretch his legs while Frankie went over some stuff with Ginger. Man, he was dreading getting on the stand, but knew his time was coming. Once he glanced around, he saw Ginger's dad

141

glaring at him. He stared right back and gave him a look that he knew showed just how disgusted he was. Screw them, He wanted to punch her so-called-father right in the face, but refrained because he didn't want to appear insane.

He headed to the men's room. Once he was done and stepped out into the hall, her mom and dad were there.

The man had the nerve to move close to Blake. "You need to stay away from our daughter and let her work things out with her husband. They could get through this, if you'd butt out."

Blake drew in a long breath and met Mr. Roberts eyes dead on. "Look, Mr. Roberts, I can see you think the sun rose today, just to hear you talk." Blake clutched his cane tighter. "But I can damn well guarantee it didn't. Neither I, nor Ginger, care to hear what you have to say."

The asshole had the nerve to step even closer, so Blake propped his cane against the wall.

"I don't know what's wrong with you people. You must have some kind of screw loose if you think your daughter should be anywhere near that maniac." Blake glanced at her mom. "Did you not hear how he tortured her, beat her, and put her down? Jesus All Mighty, he used her hands as an ashtray for his cigarettes." He saw her mom's eyes fill with tears. Well, at least she seemed to care.

On the other hand, her dad didn't even flinch. Once again, Blake stared straight at him and glared. Sure enough, the idiot stepped out of Blake's space. And that was a good thing because he was close to pummeling the son of a bitch.

Her mother covered her mouth. Blake could see she was about to burst into tears. "If you'll excuse me, I've got to get back to the courtroom. I need to be with the wonderful young lady who used to be your daughter."

He stormed off, not looking back and not wanting Ginger to be a witness to her father's uncaring attitude. Although he was pretty sure she was fully aware of what an asshole this man was.

Once he entered the courtroom, he didn't see Frankie or Ginger, so he took a seat and hoped everything was okay. After another ten minutes, they all walked in. Ginger glanced his way. He gave her his best encouraging smile and turned to see her parents walk in and take a seat by Arnold. How in the hell could her mother sit through this?

The judge came in, and everyone stood. Ginger went back on the stand and was told she was still under oath.

The other attorney stood and walked toward her. He glanced down at a legal pad and seemed to study it. "So, Miss Roberts, can you tell us where you were on the evening of August 2, 1975?"

Ginger paused for a long moment. "I left that evening before Arnold got home. He had called me on the phone and yelled for fifteen minutes, all because I didn't cook what he wanted."

"Where did you go?" he asked again.

"I went downtown to a bar called Dragon's Nest."

"Could you give us details of what went on at this bar called Dragon's Nest?"

"I went there to have a drink and was considering not going home at all. I didn't feel like being beat again." She held her head high.

"You lying bitch, you wanted to cheat!" Arnold yelled out.

Once again, the judge pounded his gavel against the sound block. "Mr. Carls, please keep your client quiet. I don't want to ask again."

Blake wanted to stuff his fist down Arnold's throat, but he knew he needed to stop wanting to punch people. He had a pretty good idea what was coming next, and his stomach took a dive.

"Miss Roberts, isn't it true that you didn't go home the night in question? As a matter of fact, you stayed out all night." He raised his voice. "So you could have sex with your lover."

Frankie stood. "Objection, Your Honor!" He glared at the other attorney. "There is no proof that my client had a lover."

"Sustained," the judge said.

He turned to Ginger again. "Tell us what happened the evening in question, Miss Roberts."

"I sat at the bar, ordered a glass of wine, and took a sip. I saw Blake walk in, just as I held up my glass."

"Would that be Mr. Blake Tanner, who is now in the courtroom?" He pointed. "Who is one of America's most eligible bachelors and a well-known playboy. Can you admit, Miss Roberts, that you recognized who he was and wanted him?"

Frankie stood again. "Objection, Your Honor, counsel is leading the witness. My client did not know he was a playboy, nor did she have any idea he was America's most eligible bachelor. Mr. Tanner's lifestyle is not on trial here."

"Sustained," the judge said and arched a brow at Mr. Carls. "Stick to the facts, Mr. Carls."

"Okay, tell us what happened once you saw Mr. Tanner."

"I went over and asked if I could sit next to him. I had no clue who he was."

"What did he say?" Mr. Carls asked.

"At first, he seemed a little reluctant, and then he nodded for me to sit."

"What happened next, Miss Roberts?"

"I made a pass at him. I just wanted to feel tenderness and passion …" She swallowed. "Even if for only one night. I wanted this before I married a man whose biggest thrill was beating me." A tear slid down her cheek.

"I see, so you thought it would be a one-night stand?"

"Objection, Your Honor. He's leading again."

"Overruled. He's stating what is on record," the judge said. Frankie sat back down, clearly upset.

"Yes," Ginger said, adding, "I was tired of being treated so roughly. I wanted to know what making love felt like before I married the abuser."

Blake started to squirm. He never thought his sex life would be open to the public.

"So, Miss Roberts, what happened after you made a pass at Mr. Tanner?"

"We went to a nearby hotel together," was all she said.

Mr. Carls stepped closer. "And you had sex all night. And isn't it also true that you threw this up in your husband's face, over and over again … all the while continuing to sleep with Mr. Tanner, even after you were married? You made this poor man go crazy …" He pointed to Arnold and raised his voice. "All due to your continued affairs."

Frankie stood, and all hell broke out in the courtroom. "Your Honor, he is badgering and leading the witness, and trying to intimidate her." He stared at the judge, and then said, "This questioning and deliberate disrespect is out of line."

The judge agreed. "Mr. Carls, do not try that again or you will be called into my chambers."

"Yes, Your Honor." Mr. Carls gave Frankie a stare down.

Blake had never heard Frankie raise his voice to that degree. He knew that it was going to take everything he had to maintain his own cool.

"Did you tell your husband of your encounter with Blake Tanner?" Mr. Carls asked and continued. "Did you try to hurt your husband with information about Mr. Tanner?"

"No," Ginger said softly. "He was a monster and cruel, and I never even brought up Blake. Arnold had no idea how to make love to a woman. Even the way he did that was hurtful and abusive." Ginger raised her voice and glared at Arnold. "He was a pig."

Arnold's attorney got closer. "You had more than one lover. Isn't it true that you taunted Mr. Parker with it?"

"No!" Ginger said, clearly shaken. "I hated him and never wanted to marry him, but Blake was the only one, and it was only once."

"Objection, Your Honor," Frankie yelled.

The other attorney turned and shot back at Frankie, "You can't object to that!"

"Yes, I can," Frankie fired back.

"Now, now, Mr. Russo, your green is showing." The other attorney snickered.

The judge hit his gavel. "Gentlemen, stop this. Stick to the facts at hand, Mr. Carls. This is not a theatrical event, and I will not have these outbursts in my courtroom."

"Yes, Your Honor," he said, then paused and stumbled backward in front of Ginger.

The next thing Blake saw was her crazy ex-husband heading toward her.

"I'll kill you, you are a lying bitch." Some of the jurors screamed, and Blake got up. The sounds and activity blinded his view of Ginger. He was on his way up to the stand, but before he could get there, two police officers had Arnold on the ground, while Frankie, along with

Arnold's attorney, were shielding Ginger.

"Let me up, you fucking pigs. She deserves to die!" he yelled. "I'm not crazy. She's a fucking slut. You heard her. She screwed another man while engaged to me, and we know she continued after we were married. I want to kill the bitch, and I will as soon as I get out of here. So what if I knocked her around? She deserved it."

The judge pounded his gavel over and over on the sound block. "Remove Mr. Parker from the courtroom. Members of the jury, you are dismissed for the day. Please stay in the designated room and wait for further instructions. No need to rise. I need to see both attorneys in my private chambers." He stood and exited the courtroom.

Ginger's parents rushed toward the door, obviously in a hurry to leave. Blake wanted to say something so bad, but he didn't. Instead, he saw the pain etched on Ginger's mother's face, along with streaks of tears. Blake felt bad for her being married to such a complete asshole. Maybe she should think about leaving him. The next thing he saw was Frankie with the other attorney heading out, but not before Frankie caught Blake's eyes and nodded toward Ginger.

She was sitting with her head in her hands, still in the witness seat. One of the officers seemed to be trying to soothe her. Blake had to get to her. Hopefully, he could take her home.

* * * *

Back across town, Kaylob was finishing up the front yard. Beth Ann loved the view of him working shirtless while she fed Kaylie on the front porch. She was married to a hunk, even if he was getting a tiny belly on him. To her, he was the sexiest man alive.

Goldie sat next to them, watching the butterflies that sailed around, landing on different flowers. All of a sudden, she heard Denny whisper, *"I'm okay, Beth Ann."* Shivers moved down her spine. Was it possible for people who crossed over to make contact? She'd never believed in those things, but look at what happened when Kaylob was in Vietnam, she'd seen the location. Oh, it made sense, because she'd been thinking of her childhood friend since her death. She missed her with all her heart. They had wanted to all get together and have a celebration of Denny's life, but it hadn't happened yet. With Ginger's trial and Blake still recovering and using a cane, the timing was off. They needed to do that soon. It would help all of them with the loss. After a few more minutes of watching her husband and feeding Kaylie, she saw Carol and Shelia had pulled up.

Holy, panic attack, today was the day they were going to take Kaylie for the entire night. This would be the first time she and Kaylob were away from her that long. Beth Ann realized she hadn't even packed her overnight bag. Carol was one of her best friends and had been her dance teacher at the Lakeside School of Performing Arts. She was still just as beautiful now as she was then. Her dark mocha skin and black eyes were radiant. Wow, she had a shorter afro than she'd ever seen her wear. It looked good on her.

"Hey there," Carol called out, and Shelia waved. "We're here to pick up our niece." She smiled.

Beth Ann stood, and Kaylie started kicking her feet just from hearing her Auntie Carol's voice. They were totally in love. Next thing Kaylie did was reach out her arms.

Carol came up on the front porch and took her. "How's my big girl?" She gave her a kiss on her neck.

Beth Ann swallowed. "Are you sure you want to keep her for the entire night? She's a handful now."

"Oh, stop it, you know we're going to have fun." She laughed. "You're such a mama."

"Where is her suitcase?" Carol arched a brow. "We bought all the food and drink that you told us she takes. We have bottles and diapers, so we are all set."

Shelia got done talking to Kaylob and stepped up on the front porch; she looked striking with a yellow flowing shirt and white shorts. Her blonde hair had grown out a few inches and her blue eyes sparkled. "How's our baby girl. Is she ready?" Kaylie stuck her little hands out to Shelia and giggled.

"She's ready. Not sure her mama is." Carol laughed.

"I'm okay," Beth Ann lied. "I'll just call every fifteen minutes."

Kaylob put down his shovel and came bounding up the steps. The minute he glanced at Beth Ann, he sighed. "I knew she'd have a hard time with this." He walked over and put his arm around her. "Baby,

Kaylie is going to have fun. You can get some rest and reading done."

Beth Ann nodded, but felt a large lump in her throat. "Okay, it's just I've never been away from her before, not for a whole night. She stayed with Auntie Shawna and Uncle Frankie, but I could take a few steps and go see her." She sighed. "I do have her overnight bag in the room. Let me go pack it."

Kaylob kissed Beth Ann's cheek. "She's going to have so much fun."

Twenty minutes later, Carol and Shelia placed Kaylie in a car seat and took off. Beth Ann stood there like a big baby with tears tracking down her cheeks.

Kaylob turned her to face him. "Baby girl, if you feel that bad, you can have them bring her back tonight."

"I might." She laid her head on his chest. "I'm not good at this separation thing." She glanced up into his eyes.

"Ah, of course." He kissed her head. "Nobody is ever going to take her away from you, Beth Ann. She's our daughter."

"I know." She nodded and realized that even today, her childhood and all the losses in her life still affected her.

About an hour later, Kaylob went back to working on the yard and Beth Ann strolled in the house to a ringing phone.

"Hello." She knew she sounded sad.

"Is this Elizabeth Ann O'Brien? The one that I haven't seen in a long time? Who is the Tony winner? I hear she's also a mother now."

"Mitch! Oh my goodness, it's so good to hear your voice."

"Ditto, my sweet."

Mitch had hired her for her first and only Broadway show. He'd been like a dad while they traveled the road for six months. That time had been bittersweet though. Kaylob was missing, presumed dead, and she had gone after her dreams without him. However, Blake had been there for the last few months of it, which had helped.

"Mitch, are you back in town?" Beth Ann asked. "I'd love to see you."

"Yes, been back for a couple of weeks. I wanted to come and see you too. However, it's not just for pleasure." He cleared his throat. "I have a new show called Midnight Red, and Elizabeth, the music is made for you."

"Oh Mitch, I can't travel again and be away from my family. I couldn't bear to be away from my baby girl and Kaylob."

"I have great news, sweetheart. You wouldn't have to travel, and hell, I'd hire a babysitter to be on the set with you. It's going to be right in Palm Springs at the new Desert Springs Theater, and we get to use the place for rehearsals. We will be the opening show. You should hear the reviews about your voice and just how powerful it is. They say it's even better than when you won the Tony."

Her hand went across her heart, and she inhaled deeply. She really would love to do a show again, if she didn't have to leave her family.

"When and what would I be doing?"

"Just singing, no dancing. There would be dancers around you and you'd need to move around the stage, but not like before. We are in the process of finding a wonderful pianist to play for you."

"Really?" Beth Ann had a brilliant idea.

"I promise we will only get the best, and rehearsals won't start for another three to four months. And you wouldn't need to be there every day. Three times a week at most, until two weeks leading up to the show, and then we might need you five days. It's scheduled to go on for three months, maybe longer. But there is talk of putting it on TV or a Variety show. Beth Ann, if you and Kaylob wanted to stay there while you perform, we have a house suite. It's part of the package for the main stars."

Beth Ann inhaled. She wanted to do this, but she would need to talk it over with Kaylob. "I have an idea. Can we get together and talk?"

"Can you give me a hint about what you're thinking?" Mitch asked.

"Yes, we might want to stay if it's only three nights a week. We have a pet. But I'm thinking about the pianist. I want to talk to you about someone. You have to hear her play."

"Okay, we can talk about that. In the meantime, can I come over this evening? I'd like to talk to you and Kaylob, get an answer, and go over everything with you both. I'll need to get your new address, and pets are allowed." He chuckled.

"Yes, that sounds wonderful, and that's great news about animals being allowed."

They said their goodbyes and hung up. Now she had to find a minute to talk to Kaylob before Mitch showed up, but she needed some time to roll it over in her mind. Was this what she really wanted? Three days a week and long hours. She knew training, even for singing in rehearsal were hard days.

Right now, she needed to check on Kaylie and maybe read for a while to calm down. She also needed to stop worrying that every time Kaylie was gone she wouldn't come back. Nobody would ever take her away. After she got off the phone with Carol and heard Kaylie laughing in the background, she decided it was time to read. Should she talk to Kaylob first or wait?

No, she'd wait until he came in or at least take some time to unwind and collect her emotions. TV—Broadway show. "Holy Midnight Red," she whispered.

The journals were still on the end table in the family room, so she got herself a cup of sun tea and settled down to have some. Goldie was out front with Kaylob, watching him work, and Sasha was at her house. Goodness, she might actually be able to read in peace and maybe get to know the family she never knew. She was excited to uncover the family secret. Would this journal lead her to hints of what those were?

Beth Ann read the last line again, where Rachel Anne had fallen down.

* * * *

I got up and collected myself the best I could, after falling on my backside. What a fine spectacle I put on. I brushed my clothing off, even though there was nothing to remove but humiliation. Which in truth, couldn't be swept away with one's hand. After a few minutes, I stiffened my shoulders, picked up my pole, and headed down to the water's edge. Threads of gold skimmed across the river and danced like fine jewels. I'd actually never seen any, but could imagine they were stunning. The flowers that surrounded the river were splashed with every color of the spring. I tossed my line in the water.

Today, I would catch a very large fish and show Abraham that girls could do just as much as a boy. When I had told him last week that I liked to fish, he smiled and said girls could fish, but of course, they didn't really catch them like boys.

He glanced my way, and I was sure I saw a spark of laughter in his eyes.

A while later, after I'd thrown my line in the water, I felt it dip down and knew I had caught something. "My heavens," I called out, bursting with excitement. "I've caught myself a fish."

Abraham ran over and helped me to get it in with his net. "Wow, Rachel Anne, you did it. This is a good size, and it's a big mouth."

The day went on with the wind blowing chilly air across the river. There was something miraculous about today. I was sure I'd heard my father whispering, telling me how to catch a fish. It was as though he was there, guiding me. A shiver went up my spine when I caught the next two fish. I could have sworn I heard my father say, 'Way to go Anne, my girl'. He always called me Anne when he was being affectionate. He had often said he wished they had named me Anne as my first name.

Abraham seemed excited each time I caught a fish. He had only caught one, so before we left, I shared one of mine with him.

"That might make a nice dinner tonight. Do you cook them or does your mother do it?"

"My ma cooks them. I will catch and clean them, but no cooking for me," he said and added, "When I get married, I want my wife to be the cook."

"What if she can't?" I asked.

"Then she'll learn. That's a woman's job," Abraham said as though that was the law.

"Someday, those rules just might change," I said sternly.

He held my gaze and tilted his head. "I hope not."

As we strolled back through town with four fish on the line, I got an odd feeling and noticed people staring at our catch and nodding. There was a silence that seemed sad somehow. We weren't too far down the road when I saw Doctor Willis hurrying along the street in his wagon.

"Rachel Anne!" he called out and halted in the middle of the road. "You need to get home. Your mother needs you right away."

"Why?" I could see by the look on his face that something was dreadfully wrong.

"Get in and I'll drive you home."

I handed my fish to Abraham and saw worry emerge on his face. "Take these home to your family," I said and jumped in with Doctor Willis. The last thing I saw was Abraham, standing in the street, watching the doctor drive away.

Doctor Willis reached out and touched my arm as he drove. "You must support your mother now, Rachel Anne. Times are going to be difficult for her," he said softly as he pulled up to the front of my home.

I knew it was bad, so I ran as fast as my legs would carry me and darted up the steps. The minute I stepped into the living room, the air vanished from my lungs. Friends from church gathered around mother as she wept. Our next-door neighbor, Mrs. Howards, was dabbing an embroidered handkerchief to the corners of her eyes. She had on her church clothes, which were a solid blue dress with a hat to match.

"What is it, Mother?" Most everyone looked my way.

"Oh, Rachel Anne." She held out her arms.

"Is it awful, Mother?" I asked and swallowed the knot in my throat.

"Yes, darling. It's your father; he died today." More tears flooded down my mother's pain-ridden face.

"What?" I backed up. "But how? And why?" I didn't want to believe it.

"It was his heart. I'm sorry, dear, but that's what we didn't tell you. He went to the city to have some tests done because he hadn't been feeling well, and ..." She paused. "While he sat in the office waiting for the doctor, he collapsed."

The sobs in the room made my lip start to tremble. "No, Mother, he can't be gone. Surely, there's a mistake."

"No. There is no mistake. They are bringing him home tomorrow."

I sank down to the floor. Placing my head on my mother's lap and held her hand. I breathed in the onerous air and fought to swallow back the burning tears.

When I glanced up at my mother, her face was engraved with such a deep, unfathomable sorrow, I knew it would never be washed away. That was the moment I understood our life would never be the same. I did have to be strong, what other choice was there?

Standing up tall, I looked around at all the faces in the room. No way would I let myself cry, I couldn't. There was no doubt in my mind, that if I did, my tears would flow for all eternity.

I crossed to the center of the room and could see everyone's eyes on me. However, I needed to say what was in my heart. "From this moment on, my name is Anne. It's what Father called me." I inhaled. "So please call me Anne, for the memory of my beloved father."

The afternoon turned into darkness, and the silence of the twilight was deafening. I could hear the crickets and frogs singing, reminding me of my father, but still, I didn't let myself cry. I stayed strong, until the last soul had left.

Mother caught my eye. "Rachel ... sorry, Anne. I need to go upstairs and be alone. Can you understand that?" she said with tenderness.

I nodded and climbed the stairs to my bedroom. Once I closed the door, a knife stabbed my heart into a million pieces. I opened my bedroom window like I had done a billion times, but the fact remained, father was gone and nothing sounded the same. I'd never have a chance to see my father's smiling face again, or hold his hand when we walked through the field of daisies. Oh, how would I endure ever seeing a daisy again, or the sunrise, or hear the songs of the crickets and frogs? I could see every stage of my life with my father, his laughter, his love, and all the hugs. How would I ever be happy again? I couldn't stop myself as I fell on the bed and placed my face into the pillow. As the first sob rippled through me, there was no doubt that I would die from the pain.

* * * *

Beth Ann set the journal down and wiped away her tears. How awful for her great-grandma Anne. That couldn't be the family secret, could it? There would never be a good time to lose your father, but she was so young. Back in those days, women didn't have a lot of work options, so how did they live? She needed to take a breath and get some fresh air down by the creek. Even though she never met her great-grandma, her tragedy made Beth Ann's heart hurt. Now she understood why Grandma Anne used her middle name.

After she got back from her walk, she'd go out front and talk to Kaylob about the show. All she could do was pray that he wouldn't get upset.

Chapter Fourteen

Frankie sat in the dark, gloomy court chamber as Judge Thomas read through some paperwork. He was prematurely gray, and Frankie couldn't help but wonder if the job did that to him.

He glanced around. Man oh man, this place needed to be remodeled or gutted. Even the smell in the air was old and musky. It still had the original dark wood walls and only one small window way up high. Too depressing for his taste. It didn't seem normal to work in such darkness. Furthermore, he had thought the courtrooms were bad, but these rooms were worse. Maybe it was time for Riverside to either build a new place or remodel what they had.

He wished Brandon would hurry the hell up and get back. Not only was he famished, but he also needed to check on Ginger and Blake.

Twenty-five years had been the bargaining chip, with no possibility of parole. No doubt a good deal since he'd attempted murder, kidnapping, and domestic abuse. After today, they would also be adding resisting arrest, along with assaulting a police officer. He was going away for a long time, even longer once the other situation came forward. That would be a whole new trial.

Just as Frankie started to say something, Brandon walked in the door. "He'll take the deal." He sat down next to Frankie and waited for Judge Thomas to look up.

"Your Honor, I told him that he didn't have much of a choice, and if this trial continued, he'd more than likely end up in prison for much longer."

The judge glanced up and pushed his glasses back in place. "Okay, so we'll set the sentencing for one week." He closed his folder and frowned. "I have to say, twenty-five years is not as much time as I wanted to give Mr. Parker."

Brandon looked down at his hands. "I know, Your Honor. He is a piece of work. I might have to recuse myself from this case. After what I saw, I'm not sure I can do anything else for him."

A ton of bricks rolled off Frankie's shoulders. "Sounds good." He stood and shook hands with Brandon and the judge. "I need to go meet with Miss Roberts and Mr. Tanner at my office. She's had a hard day."

"Mr. Russo." The judge seemed serious. "You're going to make one remarkable attorney, and you did a great job today. Even more so for this being your first big case."

"I second that," Brandon agreed. "Not sure I want to be up against you any time soon."

Frankie gave them both a nod. "Thank you. I appreciate you saying that." He picked up his briefcase, feeling his confidence expand.

Once he left the courthouse, he climbed in his car and took off for the office. He sure hoped his secretary had done what he asked and got some lunch. His stomach was sounding like a lion.

Terri, the office manager, grinned and stood when Frankie walked through the doors. The next thing she did was give him a thumbs up. Terri was also a paralegal, and he was happy as hell for all her help with research. He strolled down the hallway and couldn't help but be proud of the way everything looked. Working for Rogers and Ellis was something he'd never imagined. They were one of the biggest law firms in Riverside. He stood outside the conference room with the great news and took a deep breath. Truth be told, he was excited as hell to tell them.

The minute he opened the door, he saw Blake and Ginger eating a piece of pie.

"How's the pie?" Frankie asked and tried not to appear excited.

They both nodded with their mouths full.

"Okay," Frankie said as he sat down, grabbed a plate, and took a piece of the pie. Before he spoke, he had to at least take one bite, so he made it an extra-large one.

After he swallowed, he wiped his mouth. "Well, it looks like he will get the full twenty-five with no chance of parole."

Ginger appeared nervous. "That is a long time, but I can't help thinking about when he gets out."

Frankie glanced between the two of them. "I don't think you're going to have to worry about that."

"Why?" Ginger gave him a questioning look. So did Blake.

"Well, you know, Katie Long's parents were there to testify on her behalf. What you didn't know was Arnold had found her after her parents had hidden her the first time." He glanced toward the window, and then swallowed the lump in his throat. "She was pregnant. He beat her so bad that she lost the child. There are doctor's reports, but she never turned him in. Just like you, she was terrified." He glanced at Ginger and saw unshed tears.

"How awful," she said. "That poor girl."

"They are going to be pressing charges now that he's in prison. He killed the baby. She was eight months pregnant. She doesn't live normally. Apparently, she's been living as a recluse in the woods at her parent's cabin with her grandmother. She doesn't have much of a life."

"Oh, my god." Ginger covered her mouth, tears flooding down her cheeks.

Frankie reached across the table and held her hand, while Blake wrapped his arm around her. Frankie felt horrible for everything these girls had gone through. "I know, it's awful, but at least she's coming forward now. Once she found out he was locked up, she wanted him put away for life. And this is the first time she's been out. Maybe this will be her fresh start too."

Ginger's smile was weak, but at least it was something. "That is good news. I want him gone forever."

"I agree." Blake nodded and took another bite of pie. "I hope the idiot never sees the outside of prison again."

"There is more. Another girl. If we can get her to come forward he will get life. There is no doubt about that. Although, I think he'll get life without her. But this lady has to live without a kidney because he hit her so hard that it ruptured."

"Is there a statute of limitation?" Blake asked.

"Not for this," Frankie said. "We've got this bastard. So you can relax. I wouldn't have offered him a plea deal if we didn't have this other case against him, possibly two."

"Ah. This is good news," Blake said and held Ginger's gaze.

Frankie leaned back and gave them a large smile, then took another bite of his pie. "Yes, it is. Ginger, you won't have to worry about the asshole ever again, and you don't have to be at the sentencing."

"Oh no." Her eyes got big. "I want to be there."

"I thought you might say that. Glad you'll be there to see the look on his twisted face."

"Count me in too," Blake said.

Frankie studied both their faces and said a silent prayer that he was right. He was sure the judge would throw the book at Arnold. Wouldn't he? After all, he was responsible for the murder of an unborn child.

* * * *

Beth Ann sat down by the creek on an old tree stump behind her property line. Goldie was running and splashing in the water. For May, it was warming up nicely and she could smell the fragrance of all the plants that had awakened at spring. It reminded her of what her great-grandma had said about Franklin, Tennessee. She could visualize the small town and the house that her great-grandma had lived in. What would it be like today? Would the old buildings still be part of downtown? She closed her eyes and listened to the sound of the whispering wind and the orchestra of noises all around. Even Goldie running through the water added to the symphony.

It made her think about being on stage and singing again. Would Kaylob be okay with it? Could she do it again if she didn't travel? The one thing she knew was, she missed performing.

"Hey there, baby," Kaylob said. "I hope you two aren't falling in the water again." He chuckled.

Beth Ann laughed. "Not yet. I was actually just thinking about my great-grandma Anne and an offer I just got."

"What?" Kaylob plopped down on the green grass in front of her.

"Do you want to hear about the offer first or my great-grandma?"

Kaylob glanced up at her with a questioning look. "I want to hear about the offer first."

Beth Ann's heart beat faster. "I've been asked to sing in a new show called Midnight Red, and I would be working with Mitch again."

"Ah, I see." He gave her a phony smile. "Is that what you want to do, Beth Ann?"

"Well, it sounds great, and you know why it's so wonderful?"

Kaylob shook his head and swallowed hard.

"Because I wouldn't have to travel, and it's right here in Palm Springs."

"Really?" Kaylob's smile grew wide. "I love the sound of that."

"I know." She nodded. "They would even put us in a suite if we wanted to spend the night and dogs are allowed."

"That sounds even better." He stared into her eyes. "But is this what you want? I would support whatever choice you made, rather it was here or on the road. But honestly, I'd miss you like crazy if it were the road."

She nodded. "Me too. I didn't think I'd ever be able to do this again. I can't ever leave the two loves of my life behind. It would leave me empty and sad. Mitch is stopping by tonight to talk to us about it."

"Beth Ann." He sighed. "I love you so much." He stood.

"I love you too, honey." Goldie ran up to them and frantically barked.

"What, girl?" Kaylob kissed Beth Ann's head and turned to Goldie. "What's the matter?"

"What is she doing?" Beth Ann watched her run away.

He looked in the direction of Goldie. "I better go see what she's barking at." He took off.

After a few minutes of sitting there, she heard Kaylob yell. "What the hell?"

She jumped up and headed toward his voice. "Kaylob!" All she got back was silence; even Goldie had stopped barking. Her heart jumped out of her chest, and she ran in the direction where she thought they had gone. "Kaylob!"

Once she got across the creek, she saw Kaylob on his knees, holding something that appeared to be a very large basket.

"What is it?" She ran up next to him and stopped dead in her tracks. "Oh my gosh."

Kaylob's eyes met hers. "Can you believe this?"

* * * *

Kaylob held a basket of newborn pups, along with the mother, who appeared almost starved to death. He couldn't believe someone had dumped them off. "Beth Ann, we need to get these dogs to the vet right now. The mother looks half dead. She's so weak that all she did was look up at me; she could barely hold up her head."

"Let's go." She gave the mother a soothing touch, and she licked Beth Ann's hand. "I'm so sorry someone did this to you." Her heart broke. "Kaylob, they are Dachshunds."

"I think you're right." Taking off across the creek, they headed for the house.

Beth Ann got on the phone as Kaylob gave the mother some water and fed her some soft food. Just a small amount because he wasn't sure how much she could handle.

He could hear Beth Ann calling, over and over again.

Finally, she ran in the room. "I know who we need to call." Her eyes were wide. "Wanda. She saves animals, and she'll know what we should do."

"Oh, right," he agreed.

Not only was she a wonderful, loving dog breeder, but she also rescued pets; that's where they got their dog. They had helped her out before, and he hoped she was doing great now.

"Go ahead and give her a call. Goldie and I will stay with these guys," Kaylob said.

Kaylob reached into the basket and stroked the mama's head. She was a skinny girl and was black and gray with some spots and one blue eye. "Hey girl, you're gonna be just fine." He scooped up a tiny bit more of wet food and let her lick his finger. She was so timid and almost seemed afraid, but she ate it anyway.

Goldie was watching with keen interest and almost seemed sad. "You are such a good girl." He rubbed her head.

Kaylob could hear parts of Beth Ann's conversation, but not all of it.

Beth Ann reentered the room. "She's bringing one of her helpers. They are going to come over in the van and pick up these babies. She has a vet that makes house calls."

"Great." Kaylob breathed a sigh of relief. He couldn't imagine why someone had done that. "I can't help but wonder how they got out there. What kind of person does that to any animal, much less a new mom?"

Beth Ann got down on the ground next to the dogs. "They are so precious." Kaylob could see the tears glistening in her eyes.

About forty-five minutes later, Wanda showed up with a young man. They were so gentle with the mother and pups. There was no doubt in his mind that they'd be fine.

Kaylob could tell Beth Ann was having a hard time with them leaving. "Can we come to visit?"

"Of course." Wanda paused as the guy carried them out to the car. "You two can come by as often as you want."

Kaylob grinned. "I have a feeling we will be over tomorrow morning."

Wanda hugged Beth Ann. "I'll call you right after the vet comes, if you want."

"That would be great," Beth Ann said.

They watched the van exit out of the driveway, and Goldie barked. It was as though she wanted them to stay too.

"Well ..." Kaylob looked at Beth Ann. "I need to go to the restaurant for a couple of hours. Do you want to come with me?" He wrapped his arms around her. "We will be back before Mitch gets here and we can grab some food, too."

"No." She shook her head. "I want to wait around to hear from Wanda. Plus, I think I'll read some more."

"That's what I was coming out to tell you. They called me and have some ordering issues. I need to go see what the problem is."

"Okay, honey." She gave him a kiss. "I'm so glad you found those babies."

"Me too," he said and repeated. "Me too."

* * * *

Beth Ann called about Kaylie and could hear how much Carol and Shelia were enjoying her. So with that taken care of, she settled on the couch with Goldie by her side and picked the journal back up. She had a few hours to read while Kaylob was gone and she was going to take advantage of it.

March 31, 1901
Where do I start? My sixteenth birthday is here, and I told Mother I didn't want to celebrate. I don't feel like doing anything without Father. He wasn't going to be here, but he was supposed to have been home three days after. Now, he will never be coming home again, and I am filled with grief. I feel like I'm looking through a one-way window and all I can see is my own sad eyes and weary soul.

* * * *

A knock made me jump. "Come in," I said in a voice I didn't recognize.

"Darling, I want to at least take you down to the bakery and buy you something special. They have slices of cake today. Miss Agnes brought over some pudding and a small gift for you. Also, Abraham stopped by and brought you a gift. He wanted to see you, but I thought you were sleeping. He's been by every day since the funeral."

I scooted over to make room for mother to sit down. "Mother, I'm not supposed to be happy. That would be disloyal to Father."

"Oh, Anne, it's not disloyal. Your father would want us to go on. As a matter of fact, when he started having heart issues, he wrote you a letter."

"I don't want to read it, Mother." The thought made tears build.

"Okay." She stood and stuck her hand inside her apron. "But here it is when you're ready."

I took it, but had no intention of opening it. "Mother?"

She gave me a curious look.

"How are we going to live? How will we pay our bills?"

"Your father left some money in the bank. I'm going to find out how much is there tomorrow. Whatever amount it is, things will work out. He owned this home and land and they will be able to put it in my name,

because he passed away," she swatted a tear away. "I can reopen that fruit stand, if I need to."

"But, Mother, it's old and falling apart."

"Nothing that nails, a paintbrush, and some old-fashioned hard work can't cure." She leaned down and brushed the hair out of my face. "Now, get dressed and let's go have some dessert."

Once my mother left, I wondered how she could act like everything was normal. I was quite sure my life would never be happy again. How could it be? How does one live when someone you love leaves?

* * * *

Beth Ann sat, holding the book and saw the ink was smeared. She ran her fingers across the page, thinking of the pain her great-grandma had gone through. She knew all too well how hard it was to think you'd live the rest of your life without a person you loved. There were times when Kaylob was in the POW camp that it hurt for her to breathe. After a few minutes of deep thought, coffee sounded like a plan, so she made a pot and decided to call and check on Kaylie. She glanced at the clock on the wall and realized it had been less than an hour. Okay, she was being an overprotective mom, which made her think of Cole and how he'd always been way over the top when it came to protecting her. She sure as heck didn't want to be the same way with Kaylie, so she decided not to call.

While the coffee brewed, she opened up some food for Goldie and watched as she gobbled it down. After getting everything done, she kicked back, picked up the journal, and turned the page. Wow! She had skipped time and not written anything. Darn, how would she ever find out what happened?

April 16, 1903

As I sit in my bedroom looking out at the immeasurable world, I can't help but wonder where I belong. I know it's been a long while since I wrote, but after the death of my father, it took me a dreadfully long time to find my way again, and I'm still searching. My eyes take in everything, but no matter how beautiful the scenery, I am faced with the overwhelming reality that my father is never coming home again. Even now, after two years of missing his smile, holding his hand while we strolled through each stage of my life together, the pain is fresh, tears still fill my eyes, and a blade stabs at my grief-stricken heart.

I need to move away from my depressing thoughts. There have been some good things that happened. Carlotta came back to Franklin and having her is a blessing. She's been there to hold my hand almost daily. This last year I've seen Abraham from time to time, and he has been so tender and kind. Even coming over and helping with yard work and things Father normally took care of. He has been truly wonderful.

* * * *

Today was going to be a pleasant day. My mother had gone into the city again. I was going to run the fruit stand and hopefully sell some of the leftover winter vegetables and jams. This was the time of year that everyone came out. The winter was ending and all of life was starting over again. Carlotta was going to meet me, so I needed to get going. I grabbed my apron and sweater and headed out the door.

The gravel crunched under my feet as I made my way down the driveway to the stand. The wind was slightly blowing, bringing the scent of flowers and trees blossoming through the air. I had to pause and take it all in. The fact was, I was starting to notice the beauty again, and my heart was beating in harmony with the earth.

We had already loaded the shelves with all the goodies from the pantry and had named the fruit stand "Anne's Fresh Foods." My mother wanted it to be called that. Since my father had loved that name so much.

Carlotta was already there when I arrived and had her buggy with her. "Hi Anne. I thought I'd make the deliveries for you today. I saw Mrs. Avery and she asked if you had a case of strawberry jam. I was sure you did."

I hugged Carlotta. "You are my savior. That will save me time so I can stay right here and wait for my regulars." I opened up the door and moved inside. "I'll put them on the new fruit crates. Look, we had the big printers make up our own name labels." I honestly felt proud.

"Oh, Anne." Carlotta smiled. "These are lovely."

"I'm hoping we can earn enough money to live comfortably. We need to earn at least two hundred dollars a year."

"You'll make it, Anne. I know you will." She picked up the fruit crate. "I'll get this over to Mrs. Avery, then come back and help you."

"Carlotta ..." I considered her. "Thank you for helping us. I need to repay you."

"Dare I ask for a piece of your mother's peach cobbler tonight?" She grinned affectionately. "That's all I want."

"Of course, you may have more than one piece," I offered.

"Well, my dear Anne, I can honestly say I'm deliciously excited." She giggled.

Once Carlotta was on her way, I cleaned and dusted everything. I knew that some of my regular customers would be showing up in no time.

The whole day was busy. I was happy as a bee because almost everything had been sold. That would help my mother and I could put some away.

Just as we closed the door to the stand, Abraham was walking toward us.

He had a serious walk and didn't look real happy. It made me wonder if something awful had happened. Once he was standing in front of me, his eyes grew dark. I glanced at Carlotta, who seemed bemused.

"What is it, Abraham?" I wondered if he was okay because now his entire face grew red.

Then, with a surprise move, he got down on one knee. "Anne, will you please marry me?"

Had I just heard him right? He wanted to marry me? But why?

"Abraham, we've never really courted. Unless you call fishing, meeting at the grocery store, and taking our long walks, courting?"

"I do consider it courting, and lately, we've been holding hands," he said. "I know I can take care of you and make you a good, faithful husband."

The next thing I saw he was pulling a box from his jacket. "Please accept this ring as a pledge of my love and devotion to you." He rose and handed me the box.

Carlotta came and stood next to me. "Oh, Anne. Open it."

After a few lingering moments, I opened the box. "Oh my heavens." I picked up the delicate ring and glanced at Abraham's face. The sides of the ring were engraved with flowers and the top of the ring had one small pearl.

"Will you marry me, Anne? I know you are the girl I want to spend my life with."

"Yes." I nodded. "I will be your wife."

* * * *

Beth Ann closed the book. Wow! It wasn't the kind of romance she had imagined between her great-grandpa and great-grandmother. But maybe back in those days, they just showed it differently.

Well, time to go check on Goldie and call about those pups. Beth Ann couldn't help but think about the wiener dogs.

Chapter Fifteen

Blake walked into the hotel room and glanced around. Man, he needed to get the hell out of this place. What he wanted was a home again. "Hello," he called out when he heard someone in the kitchen.

Ginger walked into the living room, drying her hands on a dish towel. Lord have mercy, her sexy gaze gave him goose bumps all over his body.

"After I called Millie, I heated up some leftovers. Is that okay?"

"Sounds good," he said. He wondered if she knew she was heating up more than food. "I had to stop by my office and get some listings ready to show Kaylob and Beth Ann this weekend."

Ginger held his gaze. "So, he's moving his restaurant then?"

"I think he's decided to open up a second one instead of closing down the other."

"That's a lot of work," she said and moved closer.

"I think he's up for it. How are you feeling?" Blake was worried about what she had been through. The whole morning had been spent in court, and then at Frankie's law firm.

"I'm feeling pretty good. Actually relieved." She grinned. "It was so nice seeing him hauled away in handcuffs. Just knowing he can never hurt anyone again makes me feel better."

"No kidding." Blake placed his hands on her hips and drew her closer. "What do you say we throw caution to the wind and find a place together?"

Her eyes widened. "You want to live with me?"

"Yes," he whispered, using his finger to lift her chin. "I want us to be together. If you're ready."

She swallowed. "I'm ready, Blake. I think I've been ready for you from the moment you walked into that bar."

Blake couldn't take his eyes off her mouth, so he inched his face closer. "I'm ready for you, too, in every way." His heart spiked when her breath tickled his lips.

He was crazy for her. Truth be told, he was not only crazy, but deeply in love. She placed her warm fingers on his chest and his legs turned to rubber. The only sound he could hear was the ticking of a clock and the pounding of his heart. Their lips touched, and she tasted like sweet honeydew. The moment she moaned, he grew with desire. Then, when she gave him better access to her mouth, their tongues slid together in the country two-step. The deeper the kiss, the more it filled him with a passion he thought he'd never have again. Only this was even more perfect because the love was mutual and he knew it.

After a few minutes, he stepped back and he held out his hand. "Can we eat later?"

Her eyes heated, then she surprised the hell out of him and led the way.

That day, Ginger undressed every inch of him and he let her. She was in charge, and he loved it. He knew one thing for darn sure, she was the woman he wanted to spend his life with. And although she might not be his first love, she would be his last.

* * * *

After a few hours of making love, she lay cuddled in his arms. It made him think of Arnold and all he'd done to this remarkable woman. He pushed the hair out of her face. The minute she opened her eyes, the love he saw reflected inside was something he'd never experienced.

"Hey …" She touched his lips. "Are you hungry yet?"

"I am. Do you want me to go get something from the kitchen?"

"Let's both go. I'm starved."

"Ginger?" He watched as she paused, giving him an outstanding view.

"Yes?"

"Do you think you'll ever want to get married again, and do you want children someday?" He let out a deep breath. "What I'm saying is … would you marry me and have children with me?"

Her eyes widened with what appeared to be complete and total astonishment. "Did I hear you right?" She held his gaze, and then glanced down. "You do realize I'm naked?" Grabbing her robe, she slipped it on.

"Yes, darlin, I'm aware you're naked, or were." He grinned. "And you heard me right." He felt his heart grow as big as a watermelon. "I want to spend the rest of my life with you."

She blew out a breath. "I want a dozen children, six boys and six girls." She laughed. "Yes! I will marry you, Blake Tanner."

He swallowed back tears and used his John Wayne voice to cover it. "Well, a dozen children is a mighty tall order, little lady." He unfolded himself off the bed and playfully swung her up in his arms. "Can we eat naked?"

* * * *

As the day faded, Beth Ann sat out back, enjoying the animals along with Frankie and Shawna, and waited for Mitch. It was a warm and toasty night, so the twins were comfortable in their playpens, making all their tiny baby noises.

Frankie stood and leaned over his girls. "Did you hear what my girls were saying?"

Shawna shook her head. "No babe, what were they saying?"

"Daddy, get over here and pick us up." He gathered them both up in his arms.

"I guess that's the daddy language." Shawna rose and took one of them.

"So Frankie …" Kaylob said as he stepped out of the house into the backyard. "How did it go today?"

Frankie explained and seemed pretty excited about a new lady that was coming forward to testify against Arnold. "Seems the guy has abused his fair share of women. This one was eight months pregnant and the baby died, another one has a ruptured kidney. He deserves life with no possibility of parole and that's what I'm shooting for."

"Oh, wow," Beth Ann said. "I'm so glad he's going to be put away for a long time. I hope he does get life."

"Me too." Kaylob's face twisted with disgust.

Frankie agreed. "I'm pretty sure he'll never make it out of prison and Ginger is going to be there to watch his sorry ass get hauled away."

"Good," they said in Unison.

The phone rang, and Beth Ann jumped up and headed for the house. But not before she called over her shoulder, "It might be about Kaylie."

Once she was in the house, she picked up the phone. "Hello."

"Hey, darlin, how's everything going?"

"Blake, I'm so happy to hear the news. I bet Ginger's relieved."

"She is and so am I." He sighed.

"Is there something wrong?" Beth Ann felt tension over the phone.

"No. I just wanted to tell you that I proposed to Ginger. We also would like to have a little gathering to celebrate our engagement. Plus, we are going to be looking for a new house."

"Oh, Blake." She swallowed hard. "I'm so happy for you both." She was extremely thrilled and pushed back the tears. Until that moment, she hadn't realized there was still lingering guilt in her heart over hurting him.

"Beth Ann, you are okay with this, right? You sound funny. You knew I couldn't pine away over you forever."

"Oh, you figured me out, and here I was, expecting that." She chuckled. "I'm so happy for you I'm trying not to cry."

"Ah ..." Blake laughed. "Thank you, Beth Ann, that means everything to me."

"When did you want to get together? Would you like to have dinner or a barbecue here tomorrow night?"

"That would be great. Are you sure?" Blake asked.

"Yes, I know Kaylob loves to barbeque, and we were going to look at places tomorrow, right?"

"We sure are, in the morning. Beth Ann ...?"

"Yes?" She could hear him start to say something, but then he stopped. "Blake?" A long silence drifted between them. "What is it?"

"Thank you for everything. You know."

"Ah, you mean the kiss," she teased.

"You will always be a brat. But forever a special one though."

For just a minor second, her heart ached. Not because he was in love—she was thrilled about that. But there was a feeling of loss that she didn't quite understand. Wow! Guilt and loss at the same time. She shook it off and knew the only thing that mattered was he was in love and happy.

She cleared the emotion from her throat. "Let me go over the details and time with Kaylob and we will call you back. I was wondering if you could come a little early tomorrow night. I want to talk to Ginger."

"Sure. Sounds good, darlin."

They said their goodbyes and hung up and Beth Ann stood staring at the phone.

"Beth Ann. Is everything okay with Kaylie?" Kaylob asked as he came bounding into the room.

"That wasn't Carol or Shelia, it was Blake." She watched him walk toward her.

"Was he setting up our time to look at possible locations or trying to get you to kiss him again?" He grinned.

"Well, yes, that's still on for the morning, but he wants to have dinner with us tomorrow evening. I volunteered you to barbecue and no he won't be asking for kisses again."

"What's the occasion?"

"Well, now, he went and got himself engaged."

"No kidding?" He picked her up and swung her around. "That's great news. Now you can stop feeling guilty."

"Aren't you going to ask to whom, and how did you know?"

"I've seen it in your eyes. And I would say it's the redhead in his life." He set her back down. "Ginger, of course."

"Well, we will have a busy day tomorrow. So, I was thinking that Carol and Shelia could go ahead and keep Kaylie in the morning, like they wanted to. I was going to pick her up early, but I guess it would be better not to drag her around to empty places. Plus, I want to talk to Ginger about meeting with Mitch. He's looking for a pianist."

"Really? Do you think she'd be interested?"

"I hope so because I love the way she plays."

Kaylob agreed. "Hey, baby." He pulled her back. "Would you be okay with Frankie and me watching Kojak tonight? If it upsets you or bothers you, we won't watch it. Shawna needed to go lay down. The nanny is staying the night in their guest room to help with the babies."

"Okay, I can read while you guys watch your show. So long as I don't see anyone get murdered, I'm usually okay."

He put his arms around her. "Beth Ann, are you going to return to see your counselor? You've been having those nightmares again."

"Not right now. I've been pretty good." She kissed his neck. "So call Blake and let him know. I'm going to go grab some casserole and come back in here to read. I'll heat the whole thing up."

"Sounds good."

An hour later, after she ate, the guys were out in the family room watching their cop show. She finally relaxed on the couch and picked up her great-grandma's journal, realizing once again that her grandmother hadn't written in a long time. There was still no clues of the secrets that her Gram had talked about. But still, she wanted to learn more about her Grandma Anne and her life.

Sept 15, 1908

Today is Abraham and my five-year anniversary. I stopped writing because my life was too dreadful and too painstakingly sad to write any words. Mother died so fast after being diagnosed with cancer, I had no strength to pick up a pen. First losing Father and then losing my mother. I almost endured death myself from heartbreak.

Now, at age twenty-three, I am days away from giving birth to my firstborn child, and should I dare say, I am married to the most wonderful man on the planet. All our plans to travel have fallen by the wayside, but we are unreservedly happy. Abraham has turned the land into profit growing. We were able to come up with enough money to buy a new gas-powered automobile plow. That helps Abraham out so much, and he's not as tired as he was at the end of the day.

I had a harder time canning today with my big belly. I have more to do, but I wanted to spend a little time writing because it had been so long. I believe someday my children or my great-grandchildren will be reading this. So I wanted to say some things from my heart.

Hello to you. If you're reading this and I'm gone, which seems odd to say since I'm only twenty-three years old. I love you and hope you enjoy hearing about my life. Rather, you are my grandchildren, or great-grandchildren, or further down the road. I'm sure you can feel my love through the years.

171

Brenda Ashworth Barry

* * * *

I crossed over to the window and opened it. Ah, the early morning calm of the sweet-scented mist across the farmland filled my heart. I took a deep, lingering breath, "I know now, I could never leave this land," I whispered.

The reason was clear as crystal. Having the farm was like having a part of my parents.

All the trees, bushes, and plants in the yard were mostly planted by Father. Although, my mother had done most of the flowers. I worked hard at keeping them all alive, so they would come back year after year.

Thinking back about my mother made me wipe my eyes with a sniff. The cancer had been found not long after my father had died from heart disease. They had first thought mother was getting so thin because of the stress of losing her husband. But all too soon, she started passing out and getting horrible headaches. I tried hard to make sense out of God's plans, but it hadn't been easy.

When I moved away from the window, my unborn child decided to cause a rumpus. "I can feel you're going to be an active one." Placing my hand on my belly, I tenderly rubbed my unborn child. The problem was I had been having a backache all morning and some lower cramping.

Even though it was still early, I needed to get things done. Fall was coming, and canned foods seemed to be a popular item. We had done splendidly last year.

"Oh, dread." I felt another sharp pain and knew I needed to fetch my midwife. But, how? Abraham was out in the barn. Should I try to make it out there? Carlotta wasn't due to come in for another hour or so. I was afraid to wait that long. Throwing on my shawl, I stepped out into the brisk, cool morning. Okay, you can do this, I was sure. I took one step at a time getting down the front porch. The last thing I needed was to fall.

Once I made it, another pain rippled through my back. "Oh Lord, help me," I cried. I crossed over the yard and was heading toward the barn when everything started to spin. "Abraham, help!" The surroundings started to fade, and everything went black.

Sometime later, I heard my husband's voice and knew I was safe.

* * * *

Beth Ann paused. How exciting—this was the birth of her gram. She sighed and continued.

Three weeks ago, on March 15, 1908, I gave birth to our beautiful daughter, Maggie Ann Williams—the most beautiful baby in the world. She came into the world kicking and screaming. Abraham says she will be a leader and strong with a golden heart. All I know is, as I sit here holding this divine child in my arms, I never knew this kind of prevailing, beyond belief love. My heart overflows with the sentiment that I can't write about or put into words.

* * * *

I started to sing a special song that my grandma had taught me. "Hush, hush, time to be sleeping." Once I finished, I glanced up in the doorway to see my smiling husband.

"You have the voice of an angel." He moved closer to her and gazed down at his sleeping child. "I never imagined such happiness." The smile on his face was priceless; he leaned down and kissed my brow.

"I have to be ever so honest and say, I never imagined this much joy," I expressed just above a whisper.

Abraham reached for my hand. "Can we put the baby down and spend a little time having a cup of tea or coffee?"

"I hope so. I just picked her up. She was fussing." I rose softly and placed our child in her small bassinet. "I love how this has wheels and I can roll it around." I covered our baby girl, and then headed toward the kitchen to make us both a cup of tea.

Once I had the tea ready, I sat down at our little table. "Is something on your mind?"

"Yes." He blew on his tea. "I've been saving every extra penny for a while now, and I think we need a telephone. It would allow us to call people and them to call us. Can you imagine that, Anne?"

"I can't imagine doing that. Why would you want that?"

"To say hello, or for people to call us and tell us what they want."

"What they want?"

"You know, if someone like Mrs. Tess wants to order another twelve jars of your preserves. You would be able to make sure you had enough.

We could take orders on the telephone and get things set up. Or if sometime in the future, you need to ring the midwife..."

"Oh, that does sound good. I could take orders and have them ready and boxed up ahead of time. That does sound exciting. What does it take to get a telephone?"

"I don't know; that's what I want to find out. I wanted to be sure you were okay with it."

"I'm enormously thrilled about the prospect of it." I moved over and sat in his lap. "Almost as delighted as I am being your wife."

"Just delighted?" he whispered in my ear.

* * * *

Beth Ann noticed that the writing came to a stop and glanced down at her watch. Where the heck was Mitch? For some reason, she thought he'd be there earlier. She thumbed through the pages. There was nothing else. What in the world? How could she just stop writing? There were more journals; maybe she'd find out in another one. It appeared that her great-grandma and grandpa did love each other, even though they never really courted for any length of time. Maybe that was how things were done back in those days. Beth Ann's heart fell, thinking about how much loss her great-grandma had experienced. Losing her father and mother so close together had to be excruciating. Still, she wanted to find out more about what happened in the future.

Beth Ann stretched, and then went into the kitchen. When she glanced into the family room, she saw Frankie on one couch and Kaylob in his recliner, with Goldie by his side. Beth Ann's heart swelled at the sight. Never in a million years did she dream of this wonderful life, not like this. Thinking back on the days of living in the car, staying in dirty old hotel rooms and being so poor, never gave her insight to this wonderful life. She was grateful beyond words.

Watching Kaylob stroke Goldie brought tears to her eyes. He was a wonderful man, and she was a blessed woman. There was no doubt that he had been the love of her life since that first night standing under the stars when he kissed her so gently. Some people might cringe to hear how deeply they felt for each other at such a young age. Nevertheless, the one thing Beth Ann knew was that love had no boundaries. Some people might have also thought it was puppy love. But there was nothing puppy about the fact that she knew by age twelve that Kaylob Shawn O'Brien was the person she wanted to spend the rest of her life with. Not only because she loved him, but also because it was written in the stars.

Frankie glanced up at her. "Hey lady, whatcha doing, standing there staring at your husband? Should I leave?" He winked.

Kaylob smiled. "Really?"

Beth Ann felt her face heat. "No, I was just thinking about when we were kids." A commercial was on, so Beth Ann asked, "Frankie, how old were you when you had the affair with Rhonda?"

The look on both their faces made Beth Ann laugh. "I'm just wondering how long after you started working for her did you have the affair."

"It was a couple of years later. I was about fourteen when she finally gave in."

"Gave in?" Beth Ann tilted her head.

"Yes, I found so many ways to beg." He laughed. "She finally took pity on me."

Kaylob stood and stretched. "Okay, why did you want to know?"

"I was just thinking of our past and how young I was when you first kissed me. Some people might think that's not a good thing."

"Those people have never fallen in love like we did. Our love was innocent and forever."

"True. I was just thinking that. We never did, well you know, anything, until I was twenty."

"Almost twenty," Kaylob corrected.

Frankie stood. "All this talk makes me want to get home to my wife and twins. I'll catch the end next week."

"Sit back down for crying out loud. It's only five more minutes," Beth Ann scolded.

"Yes, ma'am." Frankie saluted and glanced at Kaylob. "She's a bossy thing."

"Who, Beth Ann?" He chuckled. "Never."

"Hey, now." Beth Ann shook her finger at Kaylob, but smiled.

"So, Kaylob." Frankie flashed a sly grin. "When Kaylie brings a boy home at age twelve, are you going to let her go to the movies, hold hands, and kiss like you and Beth Ann did?"

"Hell no!" he said without blinking an eye. "I'm buying a shotgun." His forehead wrinkled.

Frankie's eyes rested on Beth Ann's. Within fifteen seconds, they were both laughing.

The doorbell rang, and Beth Ann ran into the living room to answer it. Once she opened it up, she smiled as Mitch stood there with flowers and his signature grin.

"Sorry I'm late. I had some tough auditions going on today."

"Come on in." They embraced, and Mitch handed her the bouquet.

Chapter Sixteen

August had swept in like the Texas floods, and things were way too hot. Blake sat at the breakfast table, looking at his gorgeous fiancée. They were getting ready to take their first vacation, and he was ecstatic. They were finally celebrating seeing her ex-husband hauled away for sixty-five years. What was even better was the way he cried like a big old baby. They'd given him the time, with no possibility of parole. Ginger's parents hadn't shown up, the cowards.

Blake was excited about them finally moving into a new home together when they got back. They couldn't stay away as long as he wanted with Ginger starting rehearsals next month and working. Beth Ann and Ginger were going to be performing together. It was an event he still couldn't believe. They were a fantastic duo.

Just then, Millie walked in the kitchen. "Well, I got all my stuff unpacked and put away. I still can't believe I'll be staying in this place while you're gone." She smiled at them.

Blake stood. "Well, you are family now, and you won't ever be without a home again." He gave her a quick hug. "I love you."

Ginger moved over to her. "I love you, too."

Her eyes got misty. "I love you both as much as I would if you were my birth children." She cleared her throat. "Now, let me go get the rest of my room together. I'll be back down to say goodbye before you leave on your trip." She blew a kiss to them both and left.

Ginger turned and sighed. "We are so blessed to have her in our life and although I'm excited about this vacation. I'm going to miss her."

Although was it was going to be a vacation, he also needed to do a personal errand for his own peace of mind. He wanted to put flowers and make a small memorial where Denny had passed away and done her last shoot. He'd gotten permission from the authorities, and he'd also

177

promised Denny's family pictures of the area where she last worked and vanished. When they did the celebration of her life, which was now planned in November, he wanted to have the photos all ready.

Everything in life was flowing smoothly now that the trial was over. Ginger could move on in her life and not live in fear, not to mention the woman who had lost her child had moved back to the real world and was starting her life over again.

Ginger also seemed more relaxed and had come to terms with her parents hurtful actions. Besides, they had Millie now; she was like a mother to both of them.

"I'm going to miss her too." Blake agreed.

"If it wasn't for you both," Ginger inhaled and said, "I would feel like an orphan."

He didn't think Ginger would ever be over what her parents did, not completely anyway. But he had something up his sleeve and was on tenterhooks hoping his surprise would fly.

"You'll never be an orphan, darlin." He reached out and took her hand.

"So how long again does it take to get there?" Ginger asked as she met his gaze.

"About five hours. We are going private, so it takes a little time off."

Once they finished breakfast, Johnny came and loaded their luggage into the limo. "So you two are going to be gone for two weeks?"

Blake nodded as they stepped outside into the already hot, sticky morning and saw Millie standing by the limo. "Yes and when we get back, we'll be moving into our new place as soon as it's finished. Did you contact the movers?"

"Done." Johnny winked at Ginger.

Blake shook Johnny's hand. "Take good care of Dana while I'm gone, and could you keep an eye on our Millie here?" He nodded toward her.

"You bet I will. She's a keeper. Also, I think we'll have a wedding date soon. I'm hoping for a December wedding if she'll say yes to that date."

"That's great." Blake placed his hand on Johnny's shoulder. "You know she will, that girl loves you and wants you to be happy."

Ginger touched Johnny's arm. "I have a feeling it will be an easy yes. December's a magical time."

Johnny's smile spread across his face. "I hope you're right."

"We are," Blake said as he took his turn hugging Millie.

"We'll call and check on you," Ginger said softly. "We left plenty of food and don't forget there is room service."

Millie shook her head. "I want you two kids to enjoy yourself." Millie smiled. "I'll be fine with this good-looking hunk here." She waved toward Johnny. "Good thing he has Dana or I might have made a pass at him."

They all laughed.

Once they climbed inside the limo, Blake was glad to be getting out of Palm Springs for the torrid summer, at least for a few weeks anyway, although he'd miss Millie a lot.

Dean, the driver, turned around. "Looks like you're ready, and I'll get the air conditioner set up high. It's already hot."

Blake nodded and pulled Ginger closer. "Are you ready, darlin?"

"Yes," she said with a nervous hitch in her voice.

"Are you okay?" Blake asked as they headed away from the hustle and bustle of summertime. It always got so crazy this time of year. Normally, Blake had gone to where the climate was a bit cooler. He was looking forward to the Little Caymen island, soft breezes, and slower living, not to mention the people were friendly and welcoming.

"I can't believe you are doing this. Have I said thank you enough?" Ginger whispered.

"You've not only said thank you." He kissed her lips lightly. "You've shown me many times." He ran his finger down her cheek and wiped away a tear.

"I love you, Blake Tanner."

"I love you too, Ginger Rogers." He laughed. "I mean Roberts."

Hours later, they were in the air, looking down at the land. He watched as Ginger took it all in. Everything appeared to be miniature. Below, the roads twisted and turned and they flew right over the majestic mountaintops.

"Wow!" Ginger's eyes got wide. "I've never seen anything so stunning."

"You must have flown over the mountains before, but they always take my breath away."

"Well, actually, I've never been in an airplane until today."

"What?" Blake had no clue. "Never?"

"Nope." She turned away from the view and looked deeply into his eyes. "This is my first."

"Why didn't you tell me?"

"I didn't want you to think I was a dork." She appeared serious.

"Dork?" Blake studied her. "Ginger, that word is not one that could ever describe you."

After a few minutes of laughter, they both got quiet as they passed over the dark turquoise waters.

"Blake."

"Yes." He felt a question coming on.

"Are you going to be okay, being at the place where your friend ..." She paused. "Vanished."

"You mean where she died?" Blake corrected.

"Yes." She nodded.

"It's something I need to do, even though I know it's going to hurt. I want to get photos for her family and friends. We at least need to know where she was when this happened and see where her last photo shoot took place. I think her parents need the closure since her body was never found."

"I understand." She took his hand. "I'll be right there with you."

Once they landed in the small and unhurried airport, it was fast. There wasn't any security fence, terminal, or baggage carousel.

Blake spotted the limousine the minute it pulled in and parked. Then he saw the driver step out and wave.

"Hey, Mr. Tanner," Ben called out. "Good to see you again."

"You too," Blake said and added, "This is my fiancée, Ginger."

Blake watched her gracefully hold out her hand. "Nice to meet you, Ben." They shook hands.

Ben opened the door and motioned for them to enter. "We'll be there in about ten minutes. As you know, it's just right off this main road." He grinned and rubbed his fingers through his wavy, chestnut hair. It was a habit Blake had noticed each time he was around him.

Ginger was taking it all in before they had scooted across the seats.

The truth was, when he was engaged to Beth Ann, he had made reservations once to take her to this place, but she told him they could never stay anywhere near water. So that killed that idea, but in a way, it was good, because Ginger would now be the first woman he had ever brought here.

Sure, he'd met women, usually the first night, and went back to their place and did all kinds of things he wouldn't mention. However, he never took them back to his room and he'd never been with any of them a second time.

"You're deep in thought." Ginger examined his face.

"I was thinking about the fact that you are the first woman I've ever brought to Coco Villa, and how excited I am about you being here."

"Wow, first, huh? What about Beth Ann when you were engaged?"

"She didn't want to go anywhere near water."

"Ah." Ginger gave him a knowing look. "Where is the place we're staying?"

"Not far down the road. We will be there soon." He gazed out at the beauty.

The view was not what some would think of on a tropical island, but it was still stunning. For Blake, it was more than the scenery—it was the whole lifestyle.

Ginger reached over and held his hand. "You know that little airport looked like a fire station or something."

"It was." Blake smiled. "It's small and quiet. That's why I love it here." He looked ahead as the sea was coming into view. "Look." He pointed.

There was no missing the surprise in her eyes. "Oh my god, Blake."

"I know. It still leaves me speechless." He pulled her closer. "But not as much as you." The white sand and turquoise sea flanked the island road as they drove along. He loved watching her eyes as much as he did the view.

Once they pulled up to the Villa, the driver said, "Starside, Mr. Tanner?"

"No, not this time. We are staying at the Royal Harbor house."

"Ah, okay, only the best," he said. He turned to the left and followed a small road that made its way by private houses with hammocks and trees all around.

After a few more minutes, he drove down another road to a private area that led right to the front door of the small house, which was a breath away from the sea. "You don't get a much better view than this." Blake grinned.

He watched as Ginger tried to collect herself. "Blake, I don't know what to say. I've never seen anything like this."

The driver got out and opened the car door. "You have arrived, Mr. Tanner. Let me get your luggage. As usual, I'm sure they left the door open with a meal waiting."

Blake nodded. "Yes. I hope so because I'm starving."

"Me too," Ginger said.

Ben set all their luggage on the porch. "Anything else I can get for you? Do you want me to take these inside?" He handed his card to Blake. "Here, just in case you need to go anywhere."

"Thanks, Ben. We can get these inside. However, we will need a ride to the big island in a few days. I'd like to take my fiancée to a few places there."

"Sounds good, just give me a ring."

He left and Blake turned to face Ginger, who was standing with her mouth open and eyes wide.

"So?" He laughed. "I take it that you like it?"

"Wow, yes. Look at the ocean right outside the door."

"Wait until you feel the water. It's warm, even at night." He took her hand. "Let's look at the house."

He opened the front door, and they stepped inside and glanced around the living room. The floors were all bamboo, and he loved the giant size fireplace on the far wall. Everything was decorated with a sky-blue theme and white cabinetry. Simple elegance and he appreciated all of it. "What do you think? The places here are not as fancy, but," he glanced around. "I like it a lot."

"I love it, and everything is absolutely perfect." She walked to the set of French doors in the dining area and opened them; it gave a full view of the sparkling turquoise water. "Listen to that sound and the aroma," She stuck her nose in the air and inhaled. "Salty, but sweet." She turned and smiled, capturing his gaze.

"Ah, darlin, you haven't seen anything yet. It's a small island with sun-drenched seclusion and the beaches are gleaming. It has miles of untouched tropical wilderness. We will spend tomorrow combing the area."

"Look, Blake." She stepped out into the sand. "A hammock for two."

With that, he picked her up and climbed into the hammock, being careful not to strain his legs. Neither said a word, just gazed out at the vast never-ending water. They drifted back and forth as the winds slightly moved through the top of the palm trees. This place was indeed paradise.

Somewhere between watching the breeze and holding Ginger closely, he drifted off to sleep.

* * * *

Ginger watched Blake sleeping and her heart skipped a hundred beats. She loved him deeper than anything. With ease, she kissed his lips and moved out of the hammock, letting him continue to doze. The first thing she did was pull off her shoes and let her feet go into the powdery sand. She stood is awe, gazing at the sun that danced across the water and marveling at all the surroundings. Never had she imagined anything so glorious. After a few minutes of taking in all the loveliness, she moved down to the edge of the water and stuck her toes in. "Wow! It's like bath water." She couldn't believe any of this and wanted to pinch herself to see if she was dead or dreaming.

Look how much her life had changed. She was with her fiancé who treated her incredible, and had a job she loved. Not to mention when she got back in a few weeks, she'd be starting rehearsals with Beth Ann and getting ready to do a show. Never in her mind had she built this kind of life for herself.

"This is unreal," she whispered as the excitement rushed through her.

She stepped into the water and let it slide across her feet. The water was warmer than anything she'd ever experienced. When the salty-sweet taste flowed over her tongue from the air, she realized her mouth was open. Something came swimming toward her, just a few steps out. "What in the world is that?"

"That's a stingray," Blake answered, and she turned to see him standing there with his bad-boy grin. "They will swim right up to you and let you touch them."

"Touch them?" She took a step back. "Do they bite?"

"Well, they can sting you, but they are gentle giants." He took her hand. "I've never been stung, and they have always been friendly. So long as you don't sneak up on them and let them come to you, they are loving creatures."

"I'll do it later." She backed up even more.

Blake cracked up. "Okay, I carried the luggage inside. How about we go see what they left us to eat? I'm starving."

"That sounds like a much better plan." There was no way she wanted to touch the creature right now. She took his arm, and they walked inside.

Once they arrived in the kitchen, Ginger opened the refrigerator. "Blake, come here." He walked up and put his arms around her from behind. She could feel what he had in mind. "I thought you were starving?"

"Um, I am." He turned her around so she could face him.

Oh, heavens, she couldn't resist him. "I guess we can eat later." She paused. "Where is the master bedroom?"

"Who needs that?" He lifted her up in his arms and put her on the kitchen table. "I think this will work fine."

"I guess since we are engaged, we better get practicing for the honeymoon." She stared into those forget-me-not blue eyes that made her tremble all over.

Blake laid her on the solid oak table. "Ginger?" He pulled her back up. "Will you marry me?"

"Of course, I already said yes." She tried to pull him back down.

"I mean now."

"What?"

"I want you as my wife now. Will you marry me?"

"But what about all your friends and well ..." She paused. "Millie, is like our family."

184

"What about them? Millie would understand, and she will be thrilled."

"Don't you want to have a big wedding? Blake, you've never been married." She couldn't believe he was asking this.

"I want you as my wife now. I want us to be the only two people."

"What about Dana and Johnny, Beth Ann, Kaylob and ...?" He held his finger to her lips, just before he melted his across hers. And oh my heavens, what he did with his lips drove her to another world.

"I want it to be just you and me," he mumbled into her mouth, using his tongue to entice her.

"Really?" She willingly gave him more access.

"Yes. That's if you're ready." His eyes clung to hers. Then he used his fingers and slid them up her thighs, making tiny circles with his hot touch.

"Blake?" She trembled and knew it wasn't going to take much to send her to the moon.

"Yes, darlin?" He ran his finger up to the edge of her panties and teased. "Do you want something?"

With that, she took his hand and lead him to touch her.

"Ah, I guess you do. You're scorching." His voice was husky.

He obliged her, showing what he could do with his fingers and lips. It didn't take long for her to come apart and the electricity between them made her want more.

The next hour was spent moving together in harmony and exploring the depths of their love. She cried in his arms as she came apart over and over again. Never had she experienced that kind of deep, enduring passion. This was the man she wanted to spend the rest of her life with.

Once they came to a slow stop, he eased her up from the table and sat her on his lap as he went down on a chair. "Ginger, is everything okay? I've never seen you cry like that before."

"Yes." She had to swallow more emotions. "I cried because I never knew what love was. I was drenched in your touch, your kiss, and everything you gave me."

She watched his eyes fill with unshed tears. "Blake, I'm sorry, did I say something wrong?" Her stomach flipped.

"No, not at all." He touched her cheek. "I just realized that never in my life, have I had someone who loves me like you do." He glanced down to the ground. "Not even my parents."

"Oh, babe, you have tons of people who do. My goodness, you were America's most eligible bachelor."

He swallowed hard. "That is meaningless. My parents never told me, and they barely showed me. Beth Ann was never in love with me. Not the right way. Sure, Dana and Johnny care about me, but they work for me. Dana has shown me the most before you. I know she looks at me like a brother. I have people who care about me—I know that. But ..." He paused again. "I've always felt I had to win love. Money, jobs, proving myself."

"Oh, my honey, you could give up all this money, and I'd still feel the same."

"I know you do and that's what touches me so deeply, and speaking of that ... are you ready to marry me?" He kissed her neck.

"Yes. How do we do this and are you sure we can?"

"Yes, I checked it out before we came. Just in case you said yes."

"You did?" She tilted her head.

"I did. We have all the documents on hand, and we can get married under the authority of the governor's special marriage license. All I have to do is make a phone call and we can be married at twilight. So long as it's before eight P.M."

Ginger was stunned as she watched Blake leave the room, and then heard him pick up the phone. She went ahead and pulled out the seafood salad and soup. She could hear part of his conversation, but not all. Once he hung up, he strolled back in the kitchen.

"It's all set for seven P.M." He grinned. "Are you ready to be my wife?"

"Yes," she said and pointed to his plate.

She watched him stuff one big bite in his mouth and try to talk. "We need to get ready soon."

Ginger glanced down at her clothes. "What do I wear? I only brought a couple of nice dresses." She stood. Why hadn't she brought something a little more special?

"That will work," he said. "I don't care what you wear. I just want you to be my wife. I don't care about anything being perfect anymore.

Mix colors, go barefoot, hell, even mix the colors of my socks. I have you and that is all the perfect I need."

With that said, Ginger went into his arms and somehow forgot all about the food. "Oh Blake, I want to be married to you, but shouldn't I sign one of those things?"

"What things?" Blake seemed perplexed.

"I don't know what they are called, but to keep all your assets safe."

"Ah …" Blake sighed. "Prenuptial agreement and no, I'm not worried about it, because we are never getting divorced." He grabbed his cane. "I better take this; I've worked out a lot today." He grinned.

"I know one thing, Mr. Tanner." She swallowed her tears. "I will never divorce you. I didn't even know this kind of love existed."

A few hours later, they were ready and Ben showed up. "Blake, we never ate the food. I only took a few nibbles."

"I know. I only took a few bites of that salad." His stomach growled right on cue, and they both laughed. "We will eat as soon as we are married. We'll go out and have a wonderful, large dinner."

* * * *

With a gentle breeze and blue skies, beneath a little wedding arch, Blake stood, glancing around at all the rose petals spread out on the ground. The ocean gave way to a stunning backdrop as Blake and Ginger stood barefoot on the sand, holding hands. He with his pants rolled up and Ginger with her long, golden red hair hanging freely, while the sun danced upon her copper strands. Jesus, she was the most radiant woman in the world, and staring at her made him know that getting married was the best thing he'd ever done in his life. He would never feel alone again; she was his everything. His family, best friend, and in a few seconds, his wife.

Pastor Dan, the officiant, was taking a moment of silence. Ben was their witness and photographer. Never had he imagined such a simple wedding would fill him with this much happiness. Ginger wore a pretty blue dress that matched the color of her eyes, and he wore a lighter shade of blue shirt with tan slacks.

Pastor Dan raised his head and turned his eyes toward Blake. "Do you, Blake, promise Ginger to be forever faithful and honest? To share with her your dreams and your fears, to cherish her for better and for worse? For richer, for poorer, in sickness and in health, and to be forever close in your souls?" He gave a gentle smile.

Blake nodded. "Yes, I do." He tried to push back the tears, but some escaped and ran down his face, hitting his shirt.

Pastor Dan turned to Ginger, Blake's beautiful fiancée, who had visible tears running down her gorgeous cheeks. He had her repeat the vow.

Once she finished, Pastor Dan glanced between the two of them. "Now you may exchange the rings, as a symbol of your love that is never ending and forever lasting."

They exchanged simple gold bands, sliding it on each other's fingers.

Pastor Dan held his hand over their connected hands.

"Ginger and Blake, live your lives with enthusiasm, compassion, and excitement. Play … dance … make footprints in the sand …" He waved toward their feet. "Sail life in the gentleness of the winds, and always give freely of your love. Climb mountains together, explore new places, and always smile together. Be sad together and laugh often. Make life delightful and extraordinary with a dash of magic. Celebrate in the beauty of life."

He paused, and they both nodded.

"From this day forward, into all of your tomorrows, you will, husband and wife, remain in love for life. Always remember one of the most important things is to be each other's best friend, lover, and family."

Blake couldn't seem to stop the emotional flow, and Ginger didn't even try. They were deeply in love, and he knew that all of Pastor Dan's words would be their life together.

Pastor Dan removed his hand. "Having witnessed the vows you have just made to each other, surrounded by your love, the sun, the tropical sea, and the loving grace of God." He held up his Bible. "By the authority vested in me, I now pronounce you husband and wife, for a forever season of love. Blake, you may kiss your bride."

So he did.

Chapter Seventeen

Two days later, after spending almost the entire time making love as husband and wife, Blake and Ginger were on their way to the spot where Denny had last worked and passed away. Which broke his heart thinking about it, but how could he stop. Even during the ceremony, it had tried to creep into his mind.

Blake still couldn't believe he was a married man. He knew when the paparazzi got the news, they'd be all over them. The ceremony had been tranquil and serene. Afterward, they'd had a romantic dinner, watching the boats all lit up on the water. It was perfect for their wedding celebration, and the music had been great.

"Here we are, Mr. Tanner," Ben said as he pulled off to the side and pointed at the area. "Do you want me to help with the flowers?"

"Sure, that would be great." They had a lot.

The minute they stepped out into the area, the slight breeze carried the scent of the ocean. The place was calm and serene with birds sailing high above. As they approached the grassy area and trails, Blake saw the water and cliffs overlooking the sea. He couldn't imagine Denny falling off. It wasn't rocky or anything, at least from what he could see. His heart sank.

Ginger pointed to the one and only lighthouse on the island. "Maybe that's why they were doing a shoot here."

Ben slowed down. "I heard about this situation, and everyone on the island was confused at why she was on the edge of the bluff. From my understanding, they weren't doing shoots out there." He shook his head.

Ginger paused, and Blake noticed her studying his face. "You okay?"

Truthfully, his chest hurt and his legs were weak, but he nodded.

Blake saw the little flag that marked the area, and tears filled his eyes. Denny would never meet Ginger, and he'd never see her again. "I guess the wind gusts get pretty heavy here."

"No, not strong enough to blow someone over the edge. There was no wind that day at all. That's why it's all so strange. I've lived on the island all my life, and I've never heard of a wind gust blowing someone off a cliff. Maybe she stumbled."

Ginger took Blake's hand. "I'm so sorry that happened to her, but what could she have stumbled on?" She waved around. "There are no rocks or anything that makes it dangerous."

A minute later, they were placing the flowers all along the area where she had died. Blake set up the easel with her picture on it. Ginger handed him the camera, and he started snapping different shots. As he glanced over the edge, he saw that it was a straight drop down into the ocean. Why hadn't they found her body?

"Ben, look at this." He pointed. "The water is so clear and calm. How could they miss her body and not find her later? And how did this fall kill her? It's straight down with no rocks or anything."

Ben stared down below. "I don't know. It's been a major mystery. People who live here have had many theories, but none of them make sense."

"What kind of theories?" Blake questioned.

"Oh, you know, the old folks think she turned into a mermaid. Some say she staged her death to escape an evil rich boyfriend, and others say she killed herself."

"Oh." Blake shook his head. "She wasn't dating anyone that I'd heard about, and Denny would never kill herself. She was just starting to make a mark in her modeling career."

Ben shook his head. "She was dating a rich man. A few people she worked with had seen her with him. He owned a large yacht, but nobody knew who he was. The thing is he never came around after this happened, so they must not have been very serious."

Ginger peered over the edge. "For some reason, I imagined it being a bigger drop."

"Me too." Blake was perplexed. "And the guy she was dating didn't even bother to come around after she vanished? What a jerk." He glanced at Ben. "I'm glad they weren't serious. I might have to try to hurt him."

Ben looked around. "She must not have been a good swimmer, because many people have jumped from these cliffs."

"Denny was a great swimmer when we were kids. She always beat me in races."

After a few more photos of the area, a long silence filled the air. Blake had to accept he might never have the answer. "Let's go. I need to think about all this," he said with a piece of his heart left behind and suspicion giving him doubt to what they had been told. Could a shark have gotten her? But wouldn't there be a trace of blood or something? Blake's legs got weak thinking about the shark theory. So he pushed the thoughts away, but with one more question.

"Ben, do you know how long it took before anyone knew she had fallen down. I need to read the report."

"They didn't know for a while. Some of the photographers thought she was in the lighthouse. So it may have been a while before they actually knew she had fallen off."

"So." Blake stopped and met his gaze. "Nobody saw her fall?"

"Not that I'm aware of," Ben said.

That was it. Blake wanted to read that report. Even if he never found out how she fell and vanished. He did want to know the details.

* * * *

The last three days of their vacation turned honeymoon, Blake wanted to take Ginger on a glass-bottom boat to see the entire ocean. The sea creatures were plentiful, and Blake couldn't help but get a kick out of watching as Ginger's gaze took everything in.

"Oh Blake, look at that." She sounded like a little girl, which gave him complete and total joy.

"I see it, darlin." He leaned down to get a closer look at a group of stingrays.

"I think I do need to touch one of those before we leave." She laughed. "I've been so afraid."

"I know you have, my little scaredy-cat." He watched and listened to everyone admiring the gorgeousness. The boat only had about twelve people on it. When they had introduced themselves and said they were newlyweds, people had hugged and congratulated them. One couple, Larry and Donna, had invited them to dinner after they got off the boat, and they had accepted. They were a nice couple who looked to be in their thirties.

Larry called out and pointed. "Look at that beauty. You have to have some serious dough to own that."

"No kidding." Blake watched a guy and girl come on deck. "What a life."

The tour guide agreed. "Some of the people stay on those yachts for months at a time."

He started the engine and was pulling away when Blake glanced up again. Why hadn't he ever bought one of those? Well, he was rich, but if he spent his dough, as Larry called it, he'd be working his ass off for a long time to try to make it up. He picked up the binoculars and was checking it out when he saw a blonde lady standing out on the deck. Her shawl blew off, and that was when he saw a familiar tattoo. One that he knew all too well. Steve had paid to have one done for Denny on her eighteenth birthday. A purple and blue star with the words '*Shine Bright.*'

"Holy shit." He stood. "Denny!" he yelled. He watched as the blonde turned around. Her eyes grew wide, and she froze for a few seconds before she darted into the cabin. "Jesus H. Christ." The boat they were on was moving away from the yacht. "What the hell?" The yacht turned and left in the other direction. It wasn't moving slowly either, as a matter of fact, his guess would be full throttle.

"What is it, Blake?" Ginger asked.

"It's Denny! It was her," he almost yelled, and everyone on the boat was staring at him.

Ginger pulled him down and leaned toward his ear. "Blake, you've more than likely had her in your mind. That lady had blonde hair, and Denny had brown."

Blake felt the air get stuck in his lungs. He knew damn well it was her. "I don't care if her hair was purple. I know what I saw." He shook his head. "She had Denny's tattoo. It was rare and it was her."

"Hun, you know it couldn't be her. There were people around when she fell."

"But it was her, and they never saw it happen …" He tried to see again, but they were too far away. "I know it was."

The big question was why was she hiding from everyone and pretending to be dead? What the hell was going on?

* * * *

Beth Ann was out on the porch with Kaylie that morning, reading and wondering how soon Gram would be arriving. She glanced at the dogs running around on the front lawn. It was fun watching Goldie play with Sadie and Mackie, their two dachshunds. Goldie was so much bigger, but she was gentle with them. Frankie and Shawna had the other two. Travis and Erica, and even though it had taken Sasha a little time to adjust to the two mischievous pups, she had. Now all of them were best friends. It was pretty wild when all the animals were together. Erica, the mama dog, tried to keep them in line. But it was an endless battle. Beth Ann chuckled.

She glanced at her watch again. Gram had said before eleven. She couldn't wait to tell her all about the journals and what she had learned about her mother and father. After a few more minutes of wondering why her great-grandma had stopped writing in the first journal, she saw Gram and Nicky turn into the driveway.

"Look Kaylie, they're here." She pointed.

Kaylob walked around from the side yard, shirtless and a little sweaty. He had been working hard on their yard, and now he was doing the sides and the back. He had lost some weight with everything he was doing, including opening up the second restaurant. He always looked good, but now he was solid as a rock and once again looked like a lumberjack. She watched as he pulled his shirt from his back pocket, wiped his face, and waved at Nicky and Gram.

Kaylie was already excited just from seeing her daddy. She was a daddy's girl, no doubt about that. Now that she was eight months old, she was starting to make sounds and say a few words.

"Dada." She kicked her legs and was repeating it over and over again. Beth Ann laughed, and Kaylob turned. "Bring my girl here," he said with a wide grin. Beth Ann stepped off the front porch, and Kaylie almost wiggled out of her arms. Gram was out of the motor home the minute Nicky came to a stop. She handed Kaylie to Kaylob and watched her little chubby hands squeeze her daddy's cheeks.

"Look at this sweet family." Gram embraced Beth Ann, and nodded towards all the animals.

"I've missed you, Gram," Beth Ann said.

"Oh, sweetness, I've missed you so much, and just look at all these pups." She kissed Beth Ann's cheek. "Now, let me have my great-granddaughter." She glanced at Kaylob who was holding her. "I also want to meet all the new members of this family that you've been telling me about."

Nicky climbed out the side door of the motor home, and Kaylob handed the baby to Gram.

Kaylie giggled and Kaylob gave Gram a kiss on the cheek. "I'm all sweaty, but it's good to have you here."

Gram replied, "It's good to be here." She held Kaylie close.

"Hey Nick, pull it up a little closer. We have the pad right over here. Got it installed for you guys. We even put up a little garden area with some built-in benches for a little private yard for the two of you."

"That's so nice," Gram said, and Nicky nodded.

Gram and Beth Ann headed towards the house while the guys got everything all set up. Beth Ann was excited because they had the pad installed and all the hookups, including the sewer. The little gate would keep the pups away from the Motorhome, and they'd have a little yard to sit out in and enjoy the mountains.

"How long can you stay?" Beth Ann asked.

"Well …" Gram paused, still holding Kaylie. "We thought if it was okay with you guys, and we promised not to intrude, we'd like to stay for a few months. I think Nicky is a little worn out from all the driving. I'd also like more time with my granddaughters, and I want to see you in your new show."

"Oh, Gram." Beth Ann stopped walking. "That would be wonderful."

Kaylie must have picked up on the excitement because she squealed. They laughed and continued inside.

The phone was ringing when they stepped indoors, so Beth Ann crossed the room to answer it. "Hello."

"Hi Beth Ann, it's me."

"Hi Blake. I hope you and Ginger are having a great time."

"We are and, well …" He took a deep breath. "We got married."

"Oh my gosh." She placed her hand across her heart. "Blake, that is wonderful. Congratulations."

"Thanks darlin, I'm very happy." His voice sounded off.

"Is everything okay? I mean, you sound funny."

"Ah, you've always been able to read my voice." He sighed again.

"What is it?"

"Beth Ann, you need to sit down." He sounded serious.

"What's the matter? You're scaring me."

"I saw Denny. I called out her name, and she ran from me. She changed her hair color to blonde, but I saw her tattoo."

"What?" Beth Ann swallowed hard. "What do you mean you saw her?"

"I saw her on a yacht, but when I yelled out, she ran away. After that, the yacht took off fast. It was her … I know it."

"But …" Her stomach flipped. "Why would she run away?"

"That's the million-dollar question. I'm going to be staying longer to see what I can find out. Something is really fishy. I will have Ginger back in time for the show and rehearsals. We already called her job and said it was a family emergency. They were okay with it."

"My grandmother and Nicky just showed up. Can I call you later?"

"I'll call you tomorrow afternoon. I'm going to do some snooping around and hire a private detective. I'm taking tonight to be with my bride, and I'll get to work on it tomorrow. I don't want Denny's family to know, not yet. It would be too hard on them."

"Sounds good." She inhaled and thought about what he had said. "You and Ginger be careful, and congratulations again … Blake …"

"Yes?"

"You really do need to be careful. If Denny is that afraid, maybe there is a reason. You know she loved her family. There might be something really dangerous going on. She did meet a guy at the restaurant once, and she mentioned he had a yacht. She also said he was from the Caribbean."

"Do you know his name?"

"No, but maybe Lisa will remember. She hung out with them for a while. It was back when I was pregnant with Kaylie and had the celebration dinner because she moved for the first time. Maybe you should call and ask Lisa. Just be careful, Blake."

"I'll call her now. We will be careful, and thank you. Something is off, and I can feel it."

"Okay, call me tomorrow. If there is anything we can do, let us know." She hung up the phone and couldn't seem to move. Why would Denny hide from Blake? Why would she pretend to be dead? It had to be something serious.

"Beth Ann." Her grandmother touched her arm. "Is everything okay?"

"I don't know, Gram. Blake is going to find out. He says he saw Denny and she ran from him." She studied Gram's face.

"Sometimes, grief can do strange things to a person's mind." Gram's eyes were warm.

Beth Ann knew that was true. But for some reason, just like when Kaylob was in Vietnam, she'd never felt Denny die. And she could have sworn she heard her call out. Could Denny be in some kind of trouble?

After dinner, Gram and Nicky went out to their motor home to get cleaned up and rest for a bit. They'd had a long trip, and Beth Ann needed a chance to tell Kaylob about everything.

Once Kaylie was down and Goldie, Sadie, and Mackie were resting, Beth Ann walked into the family room and saw her sexy husband on his back, staring at the ceiling.

"Penny for your thoughts." She crossed the room and glanced down at him.

"If you want to know the truth, I was just thinking about Walt."

"Really?" He hadn't brought up his name in a long time.

"I never saw his family. I haven't even reached out to them in a very long time. I need to call them and see how they're doing."

"I'm sorry, honey." Beth Ann knew that losing Walt in the war had been hard on Kaylob. They were like brothers. Even harder was the fact that Walt had died in Kaylob's arms. "You should do that then." She sat on the coffee table.

"I told you that Blake got married, but I did leave out something. I

196

didn't want to bring it up during dinner. Gram knows, but I haven't told Frankie yet."

"What?" Kaylob sat up.

"Blake said he saw Denny on a yacht, but that she ran and hid when he called her name."

"Seriously?"

"Yes." She nodded. "He said there was no doubt in his mind that it was her, because he saw her tattoo. He's going to investigate and see what he can find out."

"Wow! What a trip."

"I know. I can't even imagine why she would do that. Blake doesn't want me to tell anyone in her family. He wants to find out more."

"I understand," Kaylob said and took Beth Ann's hand. "Are you okay?"

"I am. I think maybe he was just in such grief that he might have imagined it."

"Maybe. But remember, nobody believed you."

"True." Beth Ann moved onto his lap. "I love you, honey."

"Aw, baby, I love you too." He pulled her close and nuzzled her neck.

* * * *

Ten days later, Blake and Ginger packed the last of their stuff. Blake was beyond disappointed. Lisa had only remembered the guy's name as Luke. She said he had a strong French accent and was hard to understand.

Blake had hired a tour guide to take them around the islands, but the yacht he had seen her on, Wind Dancer, was nowhere to be found. They had combed everywhere, but nothing and nobody had heard of this yacht, it all seemed very mysterious. Why had nobody seen what they had on that tour boat?

He zipped up his suitcase. "Well, it's all ready to go. I hate leaving this place."

"I know, babe, but I have to get back to work and start rehearsing, and you need to get back to physical therapy."

"I've had plenty of physical therapy." He chuckled. "I'll be happy to see Millie, and I know you will too."

"I will. I've missed her, but are you okay about your friend now? Do you think maybe it was just someone who looked like her?" Ginger's voice was gentle. "I did get a glance at the lady too, and I have to admit, after giving it more thought, there was quite a resemblance. I didn't see the tattoo, but I didn't have the binoculars."

"You know, darlin, I'd feel better if we had found the yacht and I could have seen who was on it. But no such luck. Hopefully, the private detective I hired will find something out."

They pulled up to the little airport and watched as Ben unloaded their luggage. The airplane was there and waiting. Blake turned around, feeling his heart tug. Denny had been on the boat, and he damn well knew it. He'd grown up with her, and he sure as hell knew what she looked like. All he could do was hope the guy found out something and she was safe.

"Come on, babe. Let's get on the plane." Ginger laced her fingers through his. "We are going home."

Blake tried to give her his best smile. "Well, back to our temporary home until ours is ready. Remember, you told me one night the things you had always dreamed about as a child."

"Yes, those were dreams I had as a child." She laughed as they boarded the plane. "I will just be happy to get into our home and start a life together."

Chapter Eighteen

Eight weeks later, Blake sat in his office. He still hadn't heard anything about Denny. The private detective had said he was hitting dead ends. Blake was beginning to wonder if he had just imagined her. But why couldn't the guy find the yacht?

He needed to stop thinking about it. There was nothing he could do. He was sure as shit glad he'd never mentioned it to her family.

The phone rang, pulling him away from his gloomy thoughts. "Blake Tanner."

"Hey babe. I'm home. I'm missing you, and I am missing Millie too. Did you know that all her stuff is gone? I went up to her room and nothing is there."

"She didn't have that much stuff and more than likely needed it all for her visit."

"I don't even know where this old friend lives. I guess she more than likely did take it with her."

He hated fibbing and needed to change the subject. "I'm missing you too, and I think I'll come on home. You're all done with rehearsals?"

"Yes, Beth Ann and I finished up early. We had such fun today." Ginger sounded happy.

A knock on the door interrupted the conversation. "Can you hold on?"

"Sure."

He pushed the hold button. "Come in."

It was his new receptionist, Terri, who was in her late forties with salt-and-pepper hair. Ginger was happy that he had hired a mature, married lady. "Mr. Tanner, excuse me, I mean, Blake." She chuckled. "Here are the keys, and everything is closed." She walked over to his

199

desk and handed him everything. "Todd said he was on his way over to turn on the lights and make sure everything is perfect and in place. He'll be out before you get there, and everything will be set for the surprise."

"Good news and thank you." He was more than a little excited. Ginger had not seen the home yet. He wanted to spring everything on her, and she had agreed to let him do it.

Terri nodded and left.

He picked back up the phone. "Ginger, guess what?"

"What?" she asked.

"We have our new home, and I'd like to take you to see it. I'll be home in twenty minutes."

"Sounds perfect. I'm so excited." She squealed.

"I know this will sound strange …" Blake paused. "Can I put a blindfold on you until we get there?"

"You want my eyes covered?" she repeated.

"If you feel uncomfortable, then never mind. I shouldn't have asked that. I'm sorry." Damn, he felt like a heel. She had been so abused. He should've known better.

"Blake, I feel safe with you. I didn't mean it that way. I wasn't expecting a blindfold." She laughed. "At least, not outside of bed."

"Ah, I see. We'll have to try that sometime. But for today, I want you to be surprised." He blew the air out of his lungs and pushed away the thought of what that might be like in bed. All he needed was his body to respond to his imagination while he was at work.

"Get your sweet ass home then." She chuckled.

"You got it." Hanging up the phone, he shook off the chills. He needed to hurry and get his sweet ass home.

Once he and Ginger pulled up to the house, he kept her blindfold on. He refused to remove it until they stepped out of the car, and then he turned her to face the house.

"Okay, we're here." He slid it off. "Our new home." He waved toward the house.

Her eyes filled with happiness as she gazed around, and then she murmured an inaudible response.

He wasn't sure what she said, but he hoped it was good. "Ginger," Blake said. "I hope you like it."

She gave him a shaky laugh. "I'm, um, oh god." Tears flowed down her cheeks.

"You like it?" Blake asked and turned her to face him.

"Like isn't a strong enough word." She looked around again. "It's spectacular and lovely, and you are the most wonderful man I've ever dreamed of." She threw her arms around his neck. "I can't believe you had a white picket fence placed around the yard with little ladybugs painted on it. That was a childhood dream, but you remembered me telling you."

"Yes, of course I did. Come on, there's more." He took her hand and opened the gate.

* * * *

Ginger stepped into the front yard of their new home and gasped. Never in a million years had she imagined anyone doing this for her. The house was exactly how she'd dreamed. A white Victorian beauty with a wraparound porch and even a deck swing. She glanced over at Blake, and there was no missing his bad boy smile with his gorgeous dimples. Did he have any idea how much she loved him? Did he understand that no matter what kind of home they lived in, she'd love him the same? It wasn't about money or being rich.

"Blake, this is stunning." Her gaze clung to his.

"Wait until you see inside." His voice was soft. "There are four upstairs bedrooms and two downstairs. Our bedroom is down on the bottom floor with a smaller bedroom right next door. You can use it as a reading room, quiet room, or a nursery." He leaned closer to her ear. "Or a sex room."

"Now, that sounds interesting." She wondered why he whispered. "You are such a bad boy."

Blake grinned and patted her bottom. "I'm *your* bad boy," he whispered again.

Once they climbed the white wooden stairs, he opened the matching front door with etched glass. The minute it swung open, the air lodged in her lungs. It was beyond beautiful. The hardwood floors, crown molding, and beautifully carved wood. Every detail looked to be a hundred years old, but well preserved.

"What age is this home?" Ginger asked. "This is like stepping back in time. I absolutely love it."

"It was built in the eighteen hundreds and completely renovated." He walked over to the banister. "This is the original." He touched the wood. "It's been restored."

"This is so amazing, Blake." She ran her fingers across the smooth banister.

He led her through almost every room, which was so much more than she'd ever dreamed of. Her dreams had not been big enough.

They stepped out onto the back deck and once again, she was overwhelmed. Everything was incredible, the swimming pool, hot tub, and even the small tennis court.

There were ten acres of manicured lawn and what appeared to be an adorable guesthouse. The charming cottage set off to the west with its own little fenced yard. It was beautifully decorated to match the main house. The little place had a big shade tree and multicolored flowers everywhere. The porch swing and the way the house was decorated made her want to go see it.

"Blake, I'm in shock. This is more than I ever dreamed. Where are we?"

"Home, darlin, home."

"But ..." She smiled. "Where is home? What town?"

"Oh, right." He laughed. "Palm Springs, Country Springs area. Only the best for my wife. That way, you won't have very far to commute to get to the hospital."

"That's wonderful." She gave him a kiss. "I want to go out back and peek at that guesthouse."

"We will later. I haven't shown you our master bedroom." He took her hand, running with her down the enormous hall until they reached a set of double doors. "Open it."

Ginger twisted the handles and opened both doors. Her feet wouldn't budge. "Blake," she whispered. "I can't believe you did this." Everything was done just as she had dreamed about as a child. The white vanity with lace hanging down the front. A beautiful floor-to-ceiling window with matching material. Everything was white and light lavender. There were French doors leading out to a sunroom that was enclosed and had a white and lavender chase. Everything was delicate and matched perfectly. The fireplace was set into the far wall, and the walls had decorated crown molding.

"Oh Blake, look at the canopy bed. This feels like a fairy tale." The bed had a dainty chandelier that hung in the center of the ceiling.

"Watch this." He switched a knob on the wall, and tiny white lights that appeared like fireflies twinkling in the canopy lace lit up.

This was just too much. She tried everything she could to hold back her emotions, but sobs echoed throughout the room.

"Oh, darlin." Blake walked up and put his arms around her. "You're breaking my heart crying like that."

"Blake." She swallowed the lump in her throat. "You didn't have to do all this. Will you even like this? It has more of what I like, than you."

"Hey, I'm cool with it. I have my own room with all my manly stuff in it."

"Blake, I just want you to know that I would love you, no matter where we live, or what we live in." She wiped the tears from her cheeks.

He turned her to face him. "I did this because I wanted to, not because I felt I had to. Not with you, Ginger. This is the first time in my life I've ever loved someone and they loved me back."

His gaze clung to hers. "All my life, I was trying to prove to myself that I was a pretty good guy. Now with you …" He swallowed hard. "You let me know every day that I'm a good man. I don't need to prove it anymore."

"No, you don't." She paused and steadied herself, or tried. "Blake, I'm pregnant."

She watched his eyes grow wide, and then he glanced down at her belly. "We're having a baby?"

"Yes." She nodded. "I didn't mean to get knocked up this soon. But it happened."

In the next instance, he picked her up and twirled her in a circle. "Hot damn! I'm going to be a dad and you're having my baby!" he said. "I can't believe it."

"So, I take it you're happy?" She laughed as he set her down on the ground.

"Oh, you bet I am. The woman I'm in love with is having my baby.

Now I understand all the tears. Lately, you've been emotional."

He was right about that. Lately, she had been more emotional and on shaky ground.

"I haven't noticed you getting sick or throwing up."

"Not once." She smiled big. "Not even a twinge."

"That's great news, but I'm afraid you're going to make some friends very jealous. How far along are we?"

"We are two months." She sat on the bed.

"Well, you still have time to get sick, right? When do we see a doctor?"

"Monday at nine," she answered. "I took the day off from rehearsal and made an appointment. Mitch was fine with it."

"That's great, darling … I have another surprise. Can you close your eyes one more time for a minute?"

"Yes, but Blake, you didn't have to do anything else. I mean, this was already too much …"

"Hi, dear."

Ginger froze. "Millie?" She opened her eyes and saw the most beautiful woman in the world with a giant smile. "I thought you were out of town. I've missed you so much." She rushed over to her, and they embraced.

"No, I'm afraid we lied to you for this surprise. I've been staying out here."

Ginger couldn't stop the tears now. "I'm so happy."

Blake cleared his throat. "Ginger, the cottage out back is for Millie. She's going to live out here with us. I deeded one acre and the house to her. She'll always have a place."

"Blake Tanner," Ginger said softly and crossed over to him. "You are the most wonderful man in the world."

"He sure is," Millie added. "He had the construction workers finish it first, so I'd have a place to stay. He's a gem, and I love him dearly. And you are looking at his new house manager."

"Oh, Blake!" She went into his arms. "That is the most wonderful gift. Our child will have a grandma, and we have a family."

Blake smiled. "Millie and I have been meeting for a while now. I wanted to get her out of the hotel and into a real home. So, we've been furniture shopping and met with some decorators. After a few days, we realized Millie had bought a home through my agency many years ago. That's why she looked so familiar."

"Wow." Ginger was truly surprised. Millie had owned a home.

Millie walked over and hugged him. "You've changed my life."

"How in the world did I ever get so lucky?" Ginger whispered.

Blake swallowed hard. "I love you, and I love Millie. You are my family."

"I feel like God gave me another son," Millie said just above a whisper as she wiped away a tear.

Ginger glanced between her and Blake. "Millie, did you lose a child?"

"Yes, I told Blake about it. I lost my husband and my son in a fire."

"Oh, Millie …" Ginger went and gave her another long hug. "I'm so sorry."

"Me too, dear. That's how I became homeless. The insurance company said my husband started the fire, and they thought I was in on it. We didn't. We were sleeping, and I had just gone down to the kitchen because I was restless and thought I'd heard a noise. So, I put on a pot of tea and closed the door, so I wouldn't wake up anyone. My husband and son were both upstairs. By the time I smelled smoke," she paused to catch her breath. "I couldn't get up to them. The fire was started in the attic. Whoever did it, put the gas can in the bedroom after I left, to make it look like my husband tried to burn our house down. It was the gas can he used for the lawn mower. But it wasn't my husband. He wouldn't have done that." She was visibly shaken talking about it.

The newspapers said it went up faster than my husband expected and things got out of hand. He was found in our son's room." Tears filled her eyes. "We were having some financial issues, but he wouldn't have done that."

Blake shook his head. "I talked to Frankie, and we are going to reopen the case. We will clear your husband's name and make that insurance company pay."

"Clearing my husband's name would be the most important thing. He was a wonderful police officer," Millie whispered. "He was a great father, and he went beyond the call of duty. He died with arson on his record. Everything he'd worked for was gone in a flash. I'm pretty sure someone my husband arrested did it, and framed him. We had been having some strange stuff going on around the house, but never took it seriously. We should have."

"We will have the whole thing investigated," Blake said. "His name will be cleared, and you'll get the money you so deserve." Blake sounded adamant.

"Oh, Millie, I'm so sorry that happened to you."

Millie waved her hand. "Now, let's talk about something fun. This is a happy day and since I'm the house manager, I'm standing firm." She grinned.

"I'm pregnant." Ginger touched her stomach. "Which means you will be the grandma."

"A child on the way. You're pregnant?" Millie repeated with joy sparkling in her eyes.

Ginger nodded. "Yes, we are pregnant."

"Oh my goodness. A grandma!" Millie's smile grew wide. "When you first said that, I was thinking you meant in the near future."

Ginger touched her stomach again. "It's not that far away."

Chapter Nineteen

Six months later, Beth Ann sat with Gram on the front porch, while Kaylie sat by Goldie, running her little train over her back. The other dogs watched and tried to take the train a couple of times.

Gram sighed. "I can't believe we've been here six months. I guess we should be heading back out again soon."

"Oh Gram, can't you stay longer? We love having you both here. Plus, it's so nice since the show got extended for so long. Kaylie loves spending time with you while I'm working, and I'd love for you to be there for the last show. I hope Ginger doesn't pop before then." She chuckled.

"Are you sure, sweetness? We don't want to wear out our welcome." Worry flashed through her eyes.

"Yes, we are both sure, and you could never do that."

"No." Kaylie shook her little head, holding her cookie. "No, tookie. Dogs can't have them."

"Cookie, sweetie," Beth Ann corrected and chuckled with Gram.

There was no doubt Goldie was in love with Kaylie and thought it was her job to take care of her. She barked each time one of the other dogs tried to take the train. Beth Ann laughed as the Doxies ran down the steps and started chasing each other.

"Gram, I was reading your mom's journal again last night. I've wanted to ask you this for a while but, well, she stopped writing right after you were born. Do you know why? The second journal is mostly pictures. The third one is large, and I haven't picked it up yet, but it seems to have been written during world war II. Is that the one with all the secrets?"

"Oh, it's a long story, but they ended up moving suddenly to care for Daddy's parents. I think she was so busy by the time Sissy was born, she stopped writing for many years."

"Really?" Beth Ann sighed. "It was like reading a good book and having a big portion missing. I think you should read it. Your dad was really a nice guy."

"I know. There were many good things about him." She got a far-off look in her eyes. "Someday, you should read the bigger journal, Beth Ann. I do know that Mother and Sissy ran an underground organization for abused women and they risked their lives to save others. That's one of the reasons they made me marry into money, they wanted me to be safe. They were busy and weren't making much money after Daddy got injured, but her and sissy went on a mission."

"Your mom, Grandma Anne, didn't seem like the kind of person who would make you stop seeing Nicky. She seemed so kind and romantic."

Gram shook her head. "She was a wonderful woman and mother. Daddy got bitter and untrusting though. He was the one who pushed the hardest because he wanted me to marry someone he trusted and knew. Mother just went along with him, she was too busy to fight with him."

"What did Grandma Anne and Auntie Maddie do?"

"Oh my, those two made a difference in the world. They saved many women from abuse and helped them to escape with the children. During World War II, it got really bad and dangerous. They weren't just helping American women—they were helping women all over. I had two cousins who got involved too. They traveled and helped women and children who were sometimes homeless and hiding."

"Wow, I do need to read that journal," Beth Ann acknowledged.

"I've never read it because I guess I was afraid. Mother was gone so much, and Sissy almost died because one of the guys beat her so bad. Information and updates would come in the form of letters. I think some of those letters are still in that chest."

"That's awful, Gram. What happened?" She gave her an expectant look.

"The rumor is that Daddy killed that guy, but before he did, he was injured badly. After that incident, Daddy was never the same."

"Oh my gosh, Gram, that is just so awful. I had no idea. You've never told me any of this before." Beth Ann saw pain flash in her eyes.

"I'd rather you read it. It's hard for me to talk about." She met Beth Ann's gaze. "I almost lost my sister, and Daddy changed so much. I was busy in school and planning life with Nickolas. I didn't want to get involved in any of that, but life changed after Sissy got out of the hospital."

"We can change the subject, and I'll read the journal someday soon. Look …" Beth Ann pointed to Kaylie, who had fallen asleep on Goldie.

"Well, now." Gram smiled. "Is that not the most precious thing you've ever seen?"

"It is, indeed." Beth Ann nodded.

Two nights later, Beth Ann stood on the stage and smiled at Ginger. She was glowing tonight, and Beth Ann could see the happiness in her eyes. Life was a funny thing. Beth Ann had never expected Blake's wife would become one of her dearest friends. She nodded for Ginger to start the last song they would perform together on this glorious stage in Palm Springs. As she glanced out at the audience, there was Millie sitting next to Blake with a big smile on her beautiful face. Kaylob grinned and mouthed, *I love you,* and there was no doubt in her mind that he was proud of her. Her family and friends were out there and she saw her brother, Cole, wink and smile. She was so happy he had been able to make it for the last performance. James had made it to the first one and now Cole was at the last.

The show had gotten rave reviews and Beth Ann had enjoyed it, but she was glad it was ending. Now she'd have more time to sing at their new restaurant and spend time with Kaylie. Just maybe she'd be able to talk Ginger into joining her a few nights a week. If she wasn't too busy being a new mom.

Ginger smiled as Beth Ann took the microphone.

"I'd like to dedicate this to my wonderful husband who is here tonight." She motioned toward Kaylob and gave him their love sign. "He is the one that talked me into sharing some of my music with others, and so I did with Mitch. Tonight, as a special departure song, I want to share it with all of you. It's called *I'll never be alone again.*"

Ginger hit the keys on the piano, and Beth Ann began.

"Dusk slides into dawn and lifts you up to find a new day, a new life, and a new beginning," she sang, putting everything she had into it.

"Dawn is my friend, who waits every day for me, always there to light the way for me. Reach out and touch my face with your light embrace, and never shall I feel alone again." Ginger's melody sailed out beautifully and gave Beth Ann goose bumps. "Never will I be lost in despair with the love of my life by my side again."

Beth Ann went on with the lyrics, while Ginger played the melody. She knew they were doing the best they'd ever done before. By the time they went into the last line of the song, the audience was up on their feet.

"The love from my heart is like the light through the fog, always guiding you home, and I'll never … be alone again."

Once it ended, they were given the biggest round of applause she'd ever heard. Beth Ann placed her hand across her heart and could feel the love bursting inside.

Now, she could honestly say her dream was complete. Her Broadway vision had always been with Kaylob by her side. Her eyes met Kaylob's and clung on with love shining through the tears.

* * * *

Summer slid into fall and fall into winter. Soon, the years traveled by. Beth Ann was sad that nothing ever came from the search for Denny. They'd never know for sure if she was alive or dead. After the sighting, neither she nor Blake brought up the celebration of Denny's life. They kept hoping and praying that she'd show up someday, but with each year that passed, hope seemed to vanish. After she finished dusting her dresser, she picked up the picture again of her childhood best friends.

"Oh, Denny, we miss you so much."

"Mama, Godee won't come inside the house. She's chasing a butterfry. She's not forbeying me." Kaylie put her tiny hands on her hips.

She glanced at her beautiful, golden-haired daughter, who was three and a half going on fifteen. "Sweetie, she loves to chase bugs, just like her great-grandpa did, and I think what you meant to say is that she's not obeying you."

"Yes, Mama, that's what I say. Godee is trying to eat a butterfry. I don't want her to eat one." Her lip trembled. "Laster day, she got one and bite it."

"Okay, let's go make her stop." Beth Ann took her daughter's hand

and led her out back.

Once she entered the backyard, she saw the twins splashing around in the pool with Shawna and Frankie.

"Goldie, get away from those butterflies, you're upsetting Kaylie," she scolded.

Goldie stopped as though she understood and ran to Kaylie.

"Good girl." Kaylie patted her head. "Mama, can I go fwiming wif Uncle Frankie and Auntie Shawna?"

Frankie must have heard because he called out. "Come on, Mama, let her come. It's hot and June, for crying out loud."

"Okay, I've just been a little nervous since her cold."

"She's fine," Frankie said with Violet on his shoulders.

"Come on, Kayfe," Violet said and giggled as her daddy bounced her up and down.

Shawna was holding Daisy. "Daisy wants a ride too, Daddy."

Kaylie took her mom's hand and spoke in a serious tone. "Let's go get my fimsuit on. Today, I'm going to teach Biolet how to say my name right."

Beth Ann did her best not to laugh. "Come on, pups. Let's get some treats for you." All of the dogs stopped what they were doing and followed.

It was fun having an entire family of dachshunds that were related. Most the time, they took turns staying at all the houses. Except Goldie, she slept in Kaylie's room and there was no way she'd take no for an answer. Goldie was more Kaylie's dog than anyone else's.

Just as they entered the mudroom, Kaylob's voice came echoing through the house. "Where are my two favorite girls in the whole world?" Goldie barked for her treat, and the other dogs followed her lead.

"Here." She threw some bones down and laughed at how they gobbled on them.

"I'm here, Daddy." Kaylie took off. "Your barry favorite girls is right here." Beth Ann heard her squeal, which meant Kaylob had picked her up.

The next thing she saw was him kissing her neck. "How's my little pumpkin today?"

"Daddy, I told you I'm not a pumpkin and you can't eat me." She giggled.

"I can't, but I'm so hungry." He nibbled Kaylie's neck again, and Beth Ann watched their sweet child hug her daddy.

"I can get you free cookies." She held up three fingers. "But only free cause Mama says more is bad for your heart, and Daddy …" She laid her little head on his heart. "I wuv your heart."

His face turned to mush as he sat her down. "I wuv you too, honey. Now, how about those cookies?" He winked at Beth Ann and crossed the room to give her a kiss. "How are you feeling today, sweetheart?"

"Better."

"Good, I was afraid you were coming down with Kaylie's cold." He tucked her hair behind her ear. "So what's up? You said you had something to tell me."

Kaylie ran in the room. "Here's your cookies, Daddy. I have to get my fwimsuit on."

Beth Ann watched him take the cookies.

"Thank you, sweetie pie." He kissed her cheek.

"You welcome." She started to run.

"Kaylie," Beth Ann called out. "No running in the house. You could get hurt."

"Okay, Mama." She took large steps out of the room.

Beth Ann and Kaylob both chuckled when she got around the corner.

"How about we let Kaylie get outside with everyone, and then I will sit down and talk to you?"

"This sounds serious." He frowned.

Beth Ann pulled him by the arm into the family room. "Just be patient."

A few minutes later, they walked Kaylie outside and Kaylob helped her into the swimming pool where she immediately swam toward her Uncle Frankie.

"There's my little niece." He picked her up and swung her around.

As they walked inside, Beth Ann could hear Kaylie laughing. "Let me make us a glass of sun tea."

"Okay, this is driving me crazy. Would you just tell me already?"

Kaylob fussed. "Forget the sun tea."

Beth Ann moved onto his lap and straddled him. "I love you, Mr. O'Brien."

"I love you, too." He adjusted her and growled. "Unless you want me to carry you in the bedroom right now, you better stop that."

"Kaylob, we are going to have another child."

"What?" His eyes filled with surprise. "Are you telling me you're pregnant again?"

"That's what I'm telling you." She placed her hand on her tummy.

"Oh, baby." His voice broke. "I can't believe it. How far along?"

"Doctor said almost three months. The baby is due in December again. Can you believe it?"

"December—another miracle child. You are making me the happiest man alive. Looks like we are going to get to use Shawn Patrick after all. Only, I was wondering because we have so many S names in the family already. Kaylob Shawn, Shawna. Can we please switch it to Patrick Shawn?"

"I think that sounds wonderful, since I know it's a boy this time."

"And since you're always right, we better get busy fixing up his room."

"We better," Beth Ann said. "And we need to let everyone know."

Chapter Twenty

Life seemed to be passing by, and it had been total bliss for Beth Ann and Kaylob. Patrick Shawn O'Brien was born on December 24, 1979. He weighed eight pounds nine ounces with curly red hair and a demanding cry. He was full of energy and let the whole world know when he wanted something. Now that he had turned two years old, Beth Ann had a feeling he was going to keep them on their toes. He was a busy child. Kaylie had been so easy and quiet. Patrick was anything but.

On Christmas Eve, Beth Ann stepped into the family room, placing down a tray of cookies. Sure enough, Patrick rushed to the tray.

"Mine." He almost pulled the tray on the ground, but thankfully, Beth Ann pulled it away. "Mine!" he yelled.

"No, honey, these are for everyone." She drew his hands away. "You still have your birthday cake and toys to open soon."

With no warning, he threw himself backward on the ground and sulked. Beth Ann had learned to walk away and let him vent, sulk, or throw tantrums. She might end up having to buy earplugs.

This was the first year she had ever had so many people to a holiday dinner and birthday parties for Patrick and Kaylie. She'd hoped their son would behave. Blake and Ginger sat next to their darling boy who was younger than Kaylie, but they were the best of friends.

"Colton." Kaylie smiled. "The miracle show is on now." She looked so cute with her red sparkly shirt and jeans.

Beth Ann would have loved for her to wear a dress and get all dolled up. But Kaylie was a bit of a tomboy and hated dresses. It was a miracle she'd been able to talk her into the shirt.

"I'm coming." He flashed his twin dimples and smiled just like his dad.

Kaylob rose. "The door stays open." His brow crinkled.

"Okay, Daddy." Kaylie laughed. "The door stays open."

"Why?" Colton turned and asked.

Blake spoke up. "Colton, just do what Uncle Kaylob says and don't ask why." He shot him a stern look.

"Okay, Dad." He turned and left with Kaylie.

Beth Ann saw Frankie and Blake both hold back a laugh.

"Well, we have a rule." Kaylob frowned. "When Kaylie has friends over, the door stays open."

Charlie nodded. "Good plan." He took Tina's hand and smiled. "If we have a daughter, I'll feel the same way."

Tina rubbed her belly. "Well, guess we'll know in two months."

Beth Ann had been surprised when Charlie and Tina got married, and even more so when she ended up pregnant. Charlie was in his late forties and Tina in her mid-thirties. But neither had ever had children, and they were both in great health. She was happy because Charlie had stayed in her life this time. After losing contact and becoming reunited, she couldn't be happier that he was a part of their family again. He would always be the Indian Chief that she grew up loving when they lived on the reservation.

Beth Ann reached down and stroked Goldie's head, just before she bounded off to go find Kaylie. She never stayed away from her for too long. The other dogs were trying to get Sasha to play, but she was having no part of it, and they were whining.

Frankie stood up. "I'm missing my girls so much that it's killing me." He got down and peeked at Patrick, who was still sulking on the floor. The minute he tickled his belly, he was up and running toward the kitchen.

Shawna glanced around. "The girls will be back from Ireland in a few days. They were totally excited about staying with Grandma and Granny, but Frankie hasn't been so thrilled. Beth Ann thinks these babies will be boys." She rubbed her pregnant stomach. "I hope she's right again."

She was twice the size of Tina, but the doctors had said she was pregnant with twins again. "Thank God they'll be home soon. Frankie hasn't been sleeping." Shawna gave him a pouty look.

After a few minutes, Gram and Nicky walked in, hand in hand. "Any coffee made?" Gram asked. "And can I get anyone a cup?" She moved closer to Beth Ann. "I called your daddy, and he wants you to call him tonight. He'll be here on Sunday."

"Wonderful." Beth Ann meant it. She was so glad she'd be spending time with so many of the people she loved this year.

Beth Ann's mom carried Patrick as she entered the room with Millie. "Let me help you get the serving tray, Gram."

"Thank you, Jean," Gram said.

"However, this little boy wants a cookie first." Jean walked over, picked up one, and handed it to him. "He's the birthday boy and needs it."

Kaylob shook his head. "A cookie machine. What do you say to Grandma Jean?"

He kissed his grandma. "Fank you, Gamma."

She sat him down and held her heart. "I love being a grandma. Now, Gram, how about we get that coffee all set up."

Millie smiled. "I can help too."

Jean threaded her arm through Millie's. "Good idea. I want to ask about those sugar cookies you made. They are the best I've ever tasted."

Gram nodded. "I want to know your secret too." All three ladies headed to the kitchen. Millie was an angel from God. Beth Ann was sure of it. She had babysat Kaylie often, and the children all called her Grandma Millie. Everyone adored her.

"How about I put on some Christmas music?" Beth Ann suggested. "Let's get in the holiday spirit." She walked over to the stereo and found a channel playing *I'll be Home for Christmas*.

Beth Ann turned around, started to sing, and motioned for everyone to stand. And as the turkey cooked and the children played together on that cool Christmas Eve, the adults joined hands. Beth Ann glanced around at all the faces she loved, and of course, the love of her life.

She loved watching him hold their son and knew just how very blessed she was. Before she could get too far into the song, the phone rang. She waved at Kaylob to stay and ran to answer it.

"Merry Christmas," she answered as the voices of all the people she loved sang in harmony. "Hello?" she said again.

"Beth Ann."

She felt the room start to spin. Was she hearing things?

"Beth Ann, it's me."

"Oh my god, Denny. Where are you and where have you been?"

"I can't say. It's too dangerous. Please don't say anything. I just wanted to say I miss and love you. Please don't tell anyone except Blake."

"But how can I not tell your family?" Beth Ann felt tears burning her eyes.

"I just wanted you to know that I'm okay. I know Blake saw me years ago. I had to say Merry Christmas and tell you I love you. Beth Ann, if you tell anyone, it could put me in danger and worse, put them in danger." The phone went dead.

Chills went down her spine, and she knew something was not right. After standing there for a few minutes, she reeled in her emotions and made her way out to the family room. Her best friend was alive. Why she was playing dead, Beth Ann hadn't a clue. But she was alive … and that knowledge filled her heart with joy.

Once she got back into the living room, she took Kaylob's hand and closed her eyes while she joined in singing.

"Who was that?" Kaylob asked.

"A lady saying Merry Christmas. I couldn't hear her well. Might have been one of our friends."

Kaylob grinned and squeezed her hand. "That was nice."

She hated to lie to him, but she couldn't put Denny in danger. Maybe she'd tell him later when they were all alone.

While they harmonized to the song, Beth Ann's heart filled with so much love, she was sure it would overflow.

The one thing Beth Ann knew for sure was that she was blessed for having each and every one of these people in her life. Even though Denny wasn't with them, she was alive and that filled her with hope, that maybe someday Denny would be home for Christmas and just maybe, she would uncover the secrets in those journals.

Yes, in all of their lives, there had been many seasons under heaven with God's love—a season of love, of war, of birth, and just maybe, a season of forever.

Kaylob met her gaze and leaned close with Patrick in his arms. "I love you, baby girl, forever and a day."

THE END

Or maybe, it's only the beginning. Stay tuned for more information on book seven....

About the Author

Brenda Ashworth Barry's first book was a memoir titled, Healing the Voices Within, which was never published, but sponsored on a local TV station and flew off the shelves at her Healing Center in Redding California.

Her most recent work is a seven-part saga of star-crossed lovers separated by the war in Vietnam, entitled Seasons of Love and War. Brenda worked for over five years to bring the six-part Saga alive.

Brenda lives in Roseburg, Oregon, by the Umpqua River, and has raised four children three birth children and one adopted, born in her heart. Her husband, who was in the military for 21 years, gave her help and encouragement while writing her novel. When she's not writing she can normally be found walking the trails with her husband and their little dachshund, or in their RV enjoying nature.

Twitter: @sunsetsky52
Website: http://www.brendaashworthbarry.com
Facebook: www.facebook.com/pages/Seasons-of-Love-and-War-Author-Page/411210412247684
Blog: brendabarry.blogspot.com
Blog: brendabarryashworth.wordpress.com

www.ingramcontent.com/pod-product-compliance
Lightning Source LLC
Chambersburg PA
CBHW030446250626
47154CB00003BA/1154